I0721347

LOVE AND LIBERTY

Love and Literature
Book 3

Aviva Orr

© Copyright 2023 by Aviva Orr
Text by Aviva Orr
Cover by Kim Killion

Dragonblade Publishing, Inc. is an imprint of Kathryn Le Veque Novels, Inc.
P.O. Box 23
Moreno Valley, CA 92556
ceo@dragonbladepublishing.com

Produced in the United States of America

First Edition August 2023
Trade Paperback Edition

Reproduction of any kind except where it pertains to short quotes in relation to advertising or promotion is strictly prohibited.

All Rights Reserved.

The characters and events portrayed in this book are fictitious. Any similarity to real persons, living or dead, is purely coincidental and not intended by the author.

ARE YOU SIGNED UP FOR DRAGONBLADE'S BLOG?

You'll get the latest news and information on exclusive giveaways, exclusive excerpts, coming releases, sales, free books, cover reveals and more.

Check out our complete list of authors, too!

No spam, no junk. That's a promise!

Sign Up Here

www.dragonbladepublishing.com

Dearest Reader;

Thank you for your support of a small press. At Dragonblade Publishing, we strive to bring you the highest quality Historical Romance from some of the best authors in the business. Without your support, there is no 'us', so we sincerely hope you adore these stories and find some new favorite authors along the way.

Happy Reading!

CEO, Dragonblade Publishing

Additional Dragonblade books by Author Aviva Orr

Love and Literature Series
Love and Literature (Book 1)
Love and Vengeance (Book 2)
Love and Liberty (Book 3)

These books, sir, thus corrupt, thus absurd, thus dangerous alike to the intellect and morals, I have read; and that I hope without injury to my judgment, or my virtue.

Charlotte Lennox, *The Female Quixote*

CHAPTER ONE

Be advis'd, fair maid.
To you your father should be as a god;
One that compos'd your beauties, yea, and one
To whom you are but as a form in wax
By him imprinted, and within his power
To leave the figure, or disfigure it.
—Shakespeare, *A Midsummer Night's Dream*

Mayfair, Late July 1869

MR. LEONARD'S HEAVY brows knitted together as he speared a slice of meat on his dinner plate and brought it to his mouth. He chewed thoughtfully, without taking his eyes off the dish before him as if measuring the beef's tenderness. Two footmen standing at the ready kept watch, awaiting his reaction. Their master had a habit of clearing the table in a rage, sending the silver and china sailing across the room when displeased with his supper. The servants' expressions relaxed as their master nodded to himself, picked up his wine glass, and saluted the dish.

Annabel Leonard smiled as she observed her papa take a long, satisfying swallow of port and then recast his focus on his supper. Papa was wholly preoccupied with his thoughts this evening, which always suited her best. The less notice he paid his eldest daughter, the better. She forked a tender morsel from her plate, turned to her stepmother, and chewed daintily so as not to attract the woman's ire. She needed Mrs. Leonard's focus to remain where it was—on twelve-year-old Florence and eight-year-old Flora—whose posture, manners, and eating habits, their mama scrutinized and periodically corrected with a stern look or wag of her finger.

Stealing another glance at Papa, she dropped her gaze to her lap and shifted the napkin concealing the open novel that rested on her legs. Sliding her finger across the page, she read silently: *I've no more business to marry Edgar Linton than I have to be in heaven, and if the wicked man in there had not brought Heathcliff so low, I shouldn't have thought of it. It would degrade me to marry Heathcliff now; so he shall never know how I—*

"Sit straight!" Mrs. Leonard barked from across the table.

Annabel jerked her head up.

"We do not stare at the floor when sitting at the table." Her stepmother glowered. "Have you forgotten all I've taught you? Where are your manners?"

Rubbing her forehead and hoping to garner sympathy, Annabel pleaded, "I'm afraid I'm rather tired and not very hungry tonight. If I may be excused, I should like to go and lie down."

"Certainly not!" Her stepmother's sharp features hardened further. "You must learn to carry yourself like a lady no matter the situation. If one is at a dinner party, one smiles and entertains one's neighbors with conversation. One does not excuse oneself and go off to bed, no matter how tired one feels. Now, straighten your back and eat supper with the rest of us."

Sighing inwardly, Annabel forked another piece of beef into her mouth with as much grace as she could muster. Seemingly satisfied, Mrs. Leonard cast her eagle eyes back to her two daughters. Papa had not even glanced up from his plate, so focused was he on evaluating each bite of meat and sip of port, which kept his footmen on high alert. But Annabel knew the food was only a distraction. Something important occupied Papa's thoughts, and whatever it was, she was pleased not to be the focus of his scrutiny.

Several tedious minutes passed before Annabel's eyes wandered back to her lap, where Emily Bronte's *Wuthering Heights* awaited. Once again, her finger found the passage, and she continued to read—*so he shall never know how I love him: and that, not because he's handsome, Nelly, but because he's more myself than I am.*

Although she'd read the words many times before, they still had the power to transport her from the stuffy dinner table in Mayfair to the wilds of Yorkshire and envelop her in a passionate love she longed to experience. Momentarily forgetting the need to conceal her crime, Annabel lifted the novel off her lap and drew it closer. *"Whatever our souls are made of, his and mine are the same"*—Annabel mouthed as she read, losing herself and becoming one with the tormented Cathy.

A loud thud set the dishes to quiver and jerked Annabel back to reality. She looked up to see Papa scowling at her—his hand curled into a fist, resting on the table where he'd brought it down.

"Didn't I tell you to stop filling your head with those foolish novels? Yet, instead of obeying me, you see fit to read one under my nose at *my* dinner table?" Papa fired out the words as if each were a bullet.

Mrs. Leonard put down her utensils and pressed her lips together. Annabel's sisters watched Papa, their eyes wide and alert to the maelstrom that was about to ensue.

Although she itched to defend her beloved books, Annabel suppressed the urge. She knew from experience that doing so would only inflame Papa's notorious temper. A man of short stature and low tolerance, Papa's bark was legendary. There was no danger of him striking anyone—certainly not a woman—but his roar was more fearful than that of the Minotaur, and like the mythical beast, he was known to throw objects and crush items with his powerful fists. Her stepmother called him "passionate" and blamed Annabel for provoking him with her headstrong nature.

"What is so important that it need interrupt my supper?" A storm brewed in Mr. Leonard's black eyes.

"Nothing, Papa. As you said, it's merely a novel." Annabel closed her book and slipped it out of sight.

"Merely a novel!" Mrs. Leonard trilled. "Don't be fooled, Mr. Leonard. Those books overexcite the senses and give young ladies foolish notions. They are downright dangerous. I certainly won't allow Florence and Flora to make such poor reading choices."

Annabel's chest burned. Her stepmother never missed an opportunity to voice her disapproval of the stepdaughter she'd failed to subdue.

Mrs. Leonard snapped her fingers at one of the footmen and barked, "Take the book and get it out of Mr. Leonard's dining room!"

Annabel handed *Wuthering Heights* to the footman and said with a smile, "Have it sent to my room. Thank you, Peters."

He hesitated and glanced at Mrs. Leonard, who nodded her consent. "No matter; she won't have need of it much longer."

Annabel's stomach knotted. *What did she mean by that?*

Peters hurried out of the room, and Mrs. Leonard redirected her attention to her daughters. "Your sister has displayed poor manners indeed. She is far too old to behave like a naughty schoolgirl." And throwing a disapproving glance at Annabel, added, "Whatever shall we do with her?"

Florence, who looked every inch like her pale, sharp-faced mama, sniggered, and Flora, whose dark ringlets matched Annabel's and Papa's coloring, giggled behind her hands.

Annabel looked poignantly at her sisters. "I should think a naughty schoolgirl is one who *refuses* to do her reading."

"Enough!" Papa pushed back his chair and stood up. "Clear the table!" He snapped his fingers at the remaining footman, who jumped forward in response. "Supper is over. There will be no pudding tonight."

"What?" Flora wailed.

"Mrs. Leonard," Papa said, ignoring his youngest, "bring Annabel to the drawing room. I want an audience with both of you immediately." He wheeled around and strode out of the dining room without waiting for a response—a signal that his orders were not negotiable.

"Mama! It's not fair that we are punished because of Annabel's silly book," Flora complained.

"I'm still hungry," Florence moaned.

"Me too," her sister echoed. "My stomach cries out for pudding."

"Hush! You are not punished. But you will be if you continue to whine in that uncomely fashion." Mrs. Leonard turned to one of the footmen. "Find Miss Allen and ask her to join the girls in the dining room, then you may serve their pudding."

"Yes, ma'am," the footman put down his pile of dirty dishes and hurried out of the room.

"Thank you, Mama." Flora bounced on her seat, and Florence stuck her tongue out at Annabel, taking advantage of her mother's turned back.

"There you are, Miss Allen." Mrs. Leonard said as the governess entered the dining room. "When the girls have finished their dessert, you may bring them to the drawing room for a special surprise."

"Hooray!" Flora clapped.

"If'—Mrs. Leonard held up a finger—"their behavior is beyond reproach."

Annabel frowned. *What surprise? Why was her stepmother acting so secretively tonight?*

"Come along, Annabel," Mrs. Leonard called as she swept out of the lavish dining room, "we mustn't keep your papa waiting."

Annabel dashed after her, stepping into the marbled hallway. "What does Papa want to talk about? And why did he end his supper over something as inconsequential as a novel?" she said, unable to resist the opportunity to strike back at her stepmother.

"Novels are not inconsequential!" Mrs. Leonard whirled around to face Annabel. "I have told you time and again, they are dangerous, especially for a young woman as headstrong as you."

Annabel opened her mouth, ready to retort, but her stepmother held up a hand to silence her. "I have allowed you leeway in the past because you lacked a proper upbringing. You were too indulged in your formative years, and it has led you to become willful. But after twelve years under my watch, you still refuse to learn. You must rid yourself of your common ways."

"My common ways? You make me sound positively vulgar. And all for the crime of reading a book."

"That is exactly the kind of behavior to which I am referring. Learn to curb your tongue, or you will find yourself an old maid."

If curbing my tongue is what I must do to gain a husband, then I shall remain single.

As if reading Annabel's thoughts, Mrs. Leonard narrowed her eyes and said, "You are soon to be one-and-twenty and will take your place in society. It's time you set a better example for your sisters."

"What do you mean, 'take my place in society'?" Annabel asked, but Mrs. Leonard was already marching up the stairs. She hastened after her stepmother, but the woman said nothing further until they reached the drawing room.

There, she clasped the doorknob and paused to address Annabel in a harsh whisper. "A word of warning. Whatever your papa says in this room is for your own good, so I advise you to listen and refrain from arguing."

Annabel opened her mouth, and, once again, her stepmother silenced her protest. "Your papa's patience has been tested enough tonight, and I think the consequences will be very harsh if you insist on continued willfulness."

Without giving Annabel a chance to respond, Mrs. Leonard thrust open the door and stepped inside.

MR. LEONARD STOOD with his hands clasped behind his back, facing a sash window that overlooked the street. He stayed in that position, without so much as a glance over his shoulder, while Annabel and her stepmother seated themselves. After a few minutes of silently staring at her papa's back, Annabel cleared her throat loudly, which earned her an angry glance from Mrs. Leonard. She toyed with the ruffles on her pale green dress and thought longingly about returning to her novel and immersing herself in a wild and passionate world so different from her own tedious existence. She wanted nothing more than a peaceful evening of uninterrupted reading.

Finally, Mr. Leonard turned from the window and paced toward his wife and daughter. He stood before them, keeping his hands behind his back as if concealing something.

"I have received an offer for your hand in marriage."

"What?" Annabel stared at her father.

"Are you not pleased, daughter?"

"I am shocked, Papa! How is it possible? I attended but a handful of balls all Season. I don't even know why we came to London. I am a merchant's daughter, not an aristocrat. No one wanted me at their balls."

Mr. Leonard puffed out his chest. "You are the daughter of the wealthiest merchant in Bristol! Leonard Confectionary is an empire. And there are always those in society who will turn a blind eye to breeding when it comes to money. It doesn't matter how many balls you attend. You came to London to be seen, and it worked. Some chose to keep you out of their homes, to be sure, but they could not keep you from the parks, the theaters, or the regattas. Those who snubbed you this Season will beg your attendance at their balls next year."

"Well then, who is this mystery gentleman? And where did he see me?"

"Who indeed!" Mr. Leonard's face beamed. "Would you believe it if I told you that he is a viscount?"

"Oh, Mr. Leonardi!" Mrs. Leonard sprang from her chair and clapped. "Bravo!"

Annabel cringed. She hated her stepmother's habit of calling her father Mr. Leonardi whenever he had done something to please her. Gwendolyn Leonard was the daughter of English landed gentry and the furthest thing from an Italian in the world. Papa was English too, but he had Italian heritage. He'd been born and raised in Bristol, as had his father. It was his grandfather who'd first come to England and changed the family name from *Leonardi* to the more English-sounding *Leonard*."

Annabel knew that Mrs. Leonard resented her mama—a beautiful, young, Italian woman who'd worked in Papa's store and then become the love of his life. And she suspected, her stepmother's penchant for speaking Italian to him in private had more to do with her mama than her papa. Ambition had led him to marry her stepmother—the daughter of a bankrupted baronet in need of financial rescuing. Now, Annabel suspected that her father was using the same tactic to climb farther up the social ladder.

"Why should a viscount want to marry me? A girl whose family is without a title?"

"For the money, my dear, why else?"

"Oh, Papa! How crass."

"It's not crass; it's business. Our family has money, but we lack the prestige of the titled nobles. And one can only obtain such prestige through birth or marriage."

"I don't know of any poor viscounts," Annabel said. "Are you certain he's not taking us for fools?"

"We are not the fools, daughter!" His father was a fool who gambled away their family fortune. While *your* papa," he pointed to himself, "was busy working hard to preserve and increase his fortune."

"Even so, there must be other ladies who are far more eligible than I—daughters of barons or baronets."

"Yes, my dear, but they ideally wish to marry title and money. And their fathers are not offering what I am."

"Offering? You are going to pay him to marry me?"

"Why not? Marriage is a business transaction—not a love story from one of your novels."

Annabel pressed her lips together. She loved her novels, but she refused to be labeled as a silly woman who confused stories with real life.

"I wasn't thinking of novels, Papa. I was thinking of you. Why did you marry my mama, a poor shopgirl, if not for love?"

Mr. Leonard's dark brows came together again, but he gave no answer. She knew she'd caught him off guard, but he'd done the same to her.

"I know you loved her," Annabel persisted. "Stella always talks of how much happier you were then." Stella was her lady's maid and childhood nanny. She'd been her mama's dearest friend and knew everything about Papa, and her mother, in the times before her mama's death.

Annabel felt her stepmother's glare before she heard her voice lash the air. "Love is for fools. Your papa is handing you the opportunity to elevate your status in society and your family's along with it. Think of your sisters. Your marriage into the peerage will make it easier for them to procure better alliances when they come of age. Don't you want to help secure their futures?"

"I'm not saying that I won't marry this viscount you've chosen; I'm only stating that I refuse to agree to marry a man I've never even met," Annabel said.

"Of course, you won't marry before you meet." Mr. Leonard slipped his hands into his pockets and grinned. "As a matter of fact, you will be introduced to him tomorrow at Lady Dawley's ball."

"Lady Dawley invited us to her ball!" Annabel raised her brows in surprise.

"Indeed. As you can see, betrothal to a viscount has its advantages. This invitation to one of the last balls of the Season is a prelude to what's in store for you next Season."

"Do you mean to say that people already know about this engagement? Even though I have not yet accepted this man?"

"People in this town know everything. They talk, and *you will* accept the man I have chosen for you."

"I will only agree to meet with him and consider the proposal. You cannot force me to marry. Once I turn one-and-twenty, I won't need your consent." She held her breath and steeled herself for his wrath.

"Have those silly novels finally muddled your brain, daughter?"

Annabel lowered her gaze. "Of course not. I merely want to assert my right to refuse should I find the gentleman in question…distasteful."

"Distasteful?" Mr. Leonard's forehead creased.

"Not to my taste, then," Annabel clarified.

"Not to your taste? What nonsense you speak. He is a viscount. You will be a viscountess. What more can a woman want?"

She opened her mouth to respond, but her father cut her off. "Do you wish to make me look the fool in a society that judges us already?"

"Of course not, Papa."

"Good. Then I shall expect no trouble from you tomorrow evening. And know this—" he lifted a finger in the air as if to mark an important point—" There won't be a long, drawn-out engagement. Plans for the wedding will commence the day after official introductions have been made."

"May I go now?" Annabel's head ached. All she wanted to do was retire to bed.

"There's one thing more." Mr. Leonard reached into his jacket pocket, a sly smile on his face, and withdrew a small gold box. "I bought you something special to wear for the occasion. You will want to make a good impression when you meet your future husband."

She stared at the box, unable to move.

"Take it." Mr. Leonard coaxed. "It's yours."

She stepped forward and accepted the box but could not find the courage to lift the lid.

"Open it, girl." Mrs. Leonard's voice teemed with irritation.

Annabel lifted the lid. An emerald nestled in an oval pendant and attached to a delicate gold chain lay on a plush green cushion.

"How beautiful." Mrs. Leonard peered at the stone.

"It complements your eyes," Mr. Leonard said. "Here, let me show you." He picked up the delicate piece and secured it around Annabel's neck.

At that moment, a knock sounded at the door, and before Mr. Leonard could respond, Flora burst into the room.

"Where's the surprise?" she squealed.

"It's here." Mrs. Leonard pointed to Annabel. "Your sister is going to be a viscountess."

Flora gasped. "Annabel's going to marry a prince?"

Mr. Leonard chuckled.

"She's not marrying a prince," Mrs. Leonard corrected, "but you might one day."

Annabel noted the wistful look that passed over her step-mother's face.

"Look at the magnificent pendant I gave Annabel to congratulate her on her fine match." Mr. Leonard puffed out his chest as he often liked to do.

"I wish I had a pendant." Florence glared at Annabel. "I have no jewelry of my own."

"You shall get a pendant when you are to be married," Mrs. Leonard said.

"Will I get a green one like Annabel's?"

"Blue, I think, to match your eyes," Mr. Leonard said.

"Then mine will be brown," Flora quipped. "I shan't like a brown one, Papa."

Mr. Leonard laughed. Annabel had never seen her father so jolly.

"You shall have a garnet." Mrs. Leonard said. "That's your birthstone."

"What color is a garnet?" Flora's forehead creased.

"Red, silly," Florence said.

"Red! I shall have a red garnet pendant." Flora twirled, and Annabel couldn't help but smile at the little girl.

"And I shall marry a duke, who is even more important than a viscount," Florence said, still eyeing the pendant. "Then you will have to address me as "'Your Grace'."

"That's what I call sensible thinking," Mrs. Leonard said, and Florence smirked as though she'd said something wonderful and clever.

Annabel sighed. It was awful to think that little Flora would likely grow up to be as mean-spirited as Florence.

"Now, Annabel, before your sister's dreams of marriage can come true, we must ensure you look your best tomorrow evening. I think we shall pair that pendant with a dark green dress." Mrs. Leonard observed Annabel and nodded to herself.

"What say you, Mr. Leonardi? Will she please our viscount?"

Annabel grimaced as her father nodded his approval. "I daresay Lord Craventhorp will not be disappointed in my beautiful daughter."

Craventhorp. So that's his name. I am to be Lady Craventhorp. Annabel shuddered. She hated the name already.

CHAPTER TWO

'Loved!' I cried;
'Who tells you that he wants a wife to love?
He gets a horse to use, not love, I think:
—Elizabeth Barrett Browning, *Aurora Leigh*

SOMEWHERE IN THE recesses of his mind, Lord Henry Hudsyn knew he should be dancing the waltz at Lady Dawley's ball, yet he could not make himself get up from the table where he sat playing poker and drinking brandy at Madame Katrina's infamous brothel house.

"Scoundrel! You win again!" Burdington exclaimed as Henry scooped his winnings toward him. "How do you do it?"

"Who knows? Just luck, I suppose." Henry picked up his brandy glass and drained it.

"It's because he doesn't give a fig whether he wins or loses," Hobsworth said. "He's already come into his inheritance and doesn't have a master lording over him and making him pinch pennies."

"Who's making you pinch pennies?" Henry asked.

"Your stepfather—as you bloody well know. The Earl of bloody Stokeford. He's going to live forever, and he intends to drain the life out of me before he's dead." Hobsworth collected the cards.

"Well, at least you'll have it all one day," Burdington said. "As a second son, I will have to grovel for pennies the rest of my life."

"Shall we play again?" Hobsworth glanced at Hudsyn. "Give Burdington a chance to win back his losses, hey?"

"As you wish." Henry shrugged.

"Cheer up, Hudsyn; you're on a winning streak. Why do you always look as though someone strangled your dog?" Lord Craventhorp pushed back strands of dark hair from his face.

"What's it to you, Craventhorp?" Henry snarled.

Craventhorp narrowed his steel gray eyes, brought his cigar to his lips, and inhaled deeply, sucking in his already-hollow cheeks. Seconds later, he exhaled a cloud of smoke in Henry's face. "Someone ought to remind you of your place in the hierarchy, *Baron* Hudsyn."

Henry sprang up. "Remind me? You are a bankrupted viscount who believes himself a duke."

Craventhorp stood up and removed his jacket. "And you are in need of a good thrashing."

"Come now, sit down. You're causing a scene." Burdington tugged at Henry's sleeve.

Henry ignored his friend, pulled off his jacket, threw it on his chair, and began to roll up his sleeves.

"Now, gentlemen, calm down! You know the rules. No fighting in this here fine establishment." Madame Katrina's lithe form stepped between them, silencing both men. She possessed a regal air about her, more becoming to a lady than a madame. She snapped her fingers, and two buxom girls—one blond and one ginger—appeared on either side of her. "Something to cool your tempers, sirs?"

Henry glanced at the big-breasted blond and shook his head.

"Hudsyn's afraid of whores," Craventhorp sneered. "Never used to be, did you, Hudsyn?"

Henry moved aggressively forward, but Madame Katrina's hand stayed him. "My girls are certified clean; you know that."

"Of course." Henry inclined his head. "But Hobsworth is

about to deal a new hand. Perhaps I will indulge later."

Madame Katrina smiled and waved away the blond courtesan. "How about you, Lord Craventhorp?"

"Certainly, madame. I've played enough cards for tonight." Craventhorp eyed the ginger-haired harlot. "I haven't seen her before. Is she new?"

"Her name is Ivy," Madame Katrina said pointedly. "She's only been with me two weeks. You be gentle with her," she warned.

"Naturally." He grinned as he clutched the girl by the elbow and steered her away like a prized mare.

Henry took his seat. Madame Katrina smiled at the three remaining men. "It seems all is settled, then. I'll leave you to your game, gentlemen," she said before sashaying across the room.

"Craventhorp is right, you know." Hobsworth glanced at Hudsyn. "You've changed."

Henry swallowed the sting of his friend's comment. A little over two years ago, he'd learned a dark secret about his past—one that ended his carefree existence. His ever-righteous mama had put a question mark over his legitimacy when he discovered that she'd committed adultery with a degenerate poet, who'd bedded both courtesans and ladies alike and spent his final days in an asylum riddled with syphilis. Although his father died never having discovered the secret, ever since Henry had learned the truth, anger gnawed at him daily. His mother had not only betrayed his father, but she'd also turned Henry into a fraud.

Henry glanced at Hobsworth, who still shuffled the cards. "Do you intend to deal those cards or use them to keep your hands warm?" he snapped.

Hobsworth shook his head and dealt.

FORTY-FIVE MINUTES AND several rounds later, Hobsworth threw down his hand of cards. "There's no winning against you tonight, Hudsyn."

"Agreed." Burdington held up both hands.

"Fine by me." Henry swallowed his brandy and pocketed his winnings.

"Don't pack it all away yet, lads. I'm ready for another round." Craventhorp swaggered toward the table.

"What? Are you back already?" Henry snorted. "That was fast."

Craventhorp plunked onto his chair and cracked his knuckles. "Deal the cards, Hudsyn, and make it quick. I promised the father of my bride that I'd make an appearance at Lady Dawley's tonight."

"Your *what?*" Hobsworth leaned forward in his chair.

"I'm getting married to save my estate. Her father is a rich man seeking a way into the peerage. And I am a peer in need of money. Simple as that."

"Who is she?" Burdington asked.

"A merchant's daughter from Bristol. Miss Annabel Leonard. Her father owns—"

"Leonard Confectionary," Burdington said. "He must have hundreds of thousands of pounds at his disposal."

"I suppose he does. Although, he is only paying me eighty thousand to take his daughter off his hands and give her a title. Perhaps I should ask for more."

"Eighty thousand pounds! And you think it a good idea to meet your prospective wife smelling like a bawdy house?" Hobsworth said.

"Yes, that way, she'll think it's my natural scent and won't question where I've been when I come home smelling of whores."

"Have you no sense of decency?" Henry snapped.

Hobsworth glanced up at him and gave a slight shake of his head.

"At least I care about my estate. You're the one that's a disgrace. I can't think when I last saw you sober."

Henry started to get up but was distracted by the sight of Madam Katrina dragging the ginger-haired harlot toward their table.

"What have you done now, Craventhorp?" Burdington asked in a low voice.

"This is going to cost you extra!" Madame Katrina stopped in front of Craventhorp and pointed to a red welt on the woman's pale cheek. "Tomorrow, her whole face will be swollen purple."

"Fine." Craventhorp reached into his pocket and slammed a handful of silver coins onto the table.

"I warned you to stay away from my girls' faces." Madame Katrina put her hand over the coins and closed her fist around them. "These girls are my product, and you are damaging the goods."

"She deserved it," Craventhorp sneered. "You should teach your whores that when their betters give them a command, they should follow it." He snatched the harlot's wrist, and she cried out in obvious pain as he pulled her forward.

Henry leapt to his feet. "Let her go!"

Craventhorp gave the woman's wrist a sharp twist, and Henry heard a sickening crack.

She shrieked, and Craventhorp released her, laughing.

Several card players turned to see what the commotion was all about.

Anger swelled in Henry's chest. He reached across the table and grabbed Craventhorp by the cravat.

"Get off me, you bastard!"

Hobsworth and Burdington leapt out of their seats and pulled Henry back.

"Hold him, lads," Craventhorp said, lunging forward and striking out with his fist. Henry moved his head to the side, and the punch clipped him on the jaw. His two friends immediately released him.

"Bloody hell, we were holding him back from striking you,

not so you could thrash him," Hobsworth said.

"Get out!" Madame Katrina's voice silenced them. "All of you, get out now and never come back."

She put her hands to her fingers and whistled. Seconds later, a bald giant emerged from the shadows and came to stand by her side.

"Well," Craventhorp said, pulling on his jacket and positioning his hat on his head, "I do believe it's time to leave." He doffed his hat at Madame Katrina and sauntered away with Hobsworth and Burdington in tow. Henry reached into his pocket, pulled out his winnings for the evening, and handed the money to Madame Katrina.

"I am truly sorry," he said, glancing at the sobbing woman, who crouched on the floor at the madam's feet.

"Use this for the doctor's bill and give her whatever is left. She should rest for a while."

Madame Katrina snatched the money. "Take her upstairs," she ordered the bald giant, and he scooped the woman off the floor and carried her away.

"You're better than your friends," Madame Katrina said, turning back to Henry. "You should get yourself a wife and settle down to a nice life. These places," she gestured to her surroundings, "are not for the likes of you."

HE APPRAISED HER with his steel-gray eyes, combing the length of her body, as though she were an expensive piece of furniture that needed a thorough evaluation before purchase.

Annabel wasn't going to stand for it. She lifted her chin and stared icily at Lord Craventhorp. She recognized him the moment she saw him—or his type, anyway. He was the sort of man who treated people with sneering disrespect. He was strikingly handsome, to be sure, but there was no warmth or kindness in his chiseled face. He looked as if he'd been carved from marble and had a demeanor to match.

"Miss Leonard," he said, "We meet again."

"Have we met before, Lord Craventhorp? I do not recall."

He stiffened and narrowed his eyes slightly. "We've never been formally introduced before today, but I have had the pleasure of seeing you from afar."

"You had the pleasure of seeing me, Lord Craventhorp, or simply hearing about me?" She knew very well it was the latter. Her papa had used his resources to ferret out a bankrupted noble and let it be known that he was looking for a title for his daughter, for which he would pay a handsome price. Lord Craventhorp had seized the opportunity. She doubted the viscount cared what she looked like or how she behaved. And who could blame him? He could marry her and continue living life exactly as he pleased, while she would have to do exactly what he wanted. As her husband, he would have the power to lock her away in an asylum if he wished to rid himself of her. She'd heard more than one such story about husbands who did that very thing from her lady's maid, Stella.

Mrs. Leonard cleared her throat loudly, indicating her displeasure at Annabel's behavior and, no doubt, hoping to elicit a reaction from her husband.

"Lord Craventhorp." Mr. Leonard, duly alerted, fired a warning look at his daughter, "why don't you and Annabel take a turn in the garden and get acquainted? You desire a short courtship, as I understand it, so now is as good a time as any to begin, is it not?"

"Papa, I don't even know this gentleman, and you suggest I take a stroll alone with him?"

Mrs. Leonard's face reddened. She flung her fan open and fanned herself vigorously.

"He's to be your betrothed. It's perfectly acceptable." Her father's eyebrows knitted together. No doubt, he thought the viscount a perfect gentleman and wondered why his daughter seemed intent on embarrassing him.

"She's quite right, Mr. Leonard. Although we have agreed to the marriage, every young lady wants and deserves a formal proposal."

Mr. Leonard grinned and nodded in agreement. "Yes, yes. I am a married man myself and the father of three daughters. If a man wants peace, he must indulge his lady's whims."

Annabel's stomach churned. Could her papa not see through Lord Craventhorp's pretenses? Had he not looked into the man's eyes and seen his icy interior? Didn't he care about her welfare at all?

"Don't fret, Annabel dear. Lord Craventhorp will not deprive you of being properly wooed and proposed to. But, as I said, he desires a short courting, so we shall not prolong these niceties, although I agree, they are necessary."

Annabel set her jaw and glared at her papa. She hadn't agreed to marry Lord Craventhorp, nor would she ever. But if Papa wanted her to walk out alone with him, then so be it. She hoped it ruined her reputation so no other mercenary lord would ask for her hand in marriage. Then she'd be free to meet her true love.

"Shall we, Miss Leonard?" Lord Craventhorp asked.

Annabel forced a smile and allowed him to escort her to the terrace. "My dowry must be extensive indeed to attract a viscount."

"It is." Lord Craventhorp appeared unperturbed by her insolence.

"Well, I am sorry to disappoint you, my lord, but I won't be marrying you, so you'll just have to find an alternative way of saving yourself from your financial difficulties," she said as they stepped from the terrace into the garden.

Lord Craventhorp smiled tightly but said nothing until they'd ventured farther into the garden. He stopped near a dimly lit area populated with sculpted shrubs, took hold of her upper arm, and leaned forward to whisper in her ear. "Don't think I shall let you get away with talking to me like that once we are husband and wife." He tightened his grip on her arm, squeezing the delicate flesh until her eyes watered from the radiating pressure. She winced, refusing to give him the satisfaction of hearing her cry out in pain. "That's right. Now, keep smiling as though I have just whispered something sweet in your ear. If you make a scene, you will only serve to embarrass yourself and your dear papa by behaving like the shopkeeper's daughter you are."

Annabel attempted to step out of his grasp, but he only tightened his grip.

She bit back a whimper, not wanting to give him the satisfaction of knowing how much he was hurting her. "Go ahead and make a scene if you wish but remember one thing—society has a long memory, and people will not forget your common behavior when your papa wants to make a good match for your sisters."

"Let go," Annabel hissed, "or I shall scream as loudly as possible."

He laughed. "Feel free. I should be most entertained to watch you shrieking like a madwoman who needs to be locked away." He drew back and released his grip.

Annabel's upper arm throbbed, but she resisted the urge to caress her tender flesh and instead squared her shoulders.

He sneered in response to her bravado, pulled a handkerchief from his pocket, and held it out to her. "Now, be a good girl and dry your eyes. And when we go back inside, you will tell your papa how much you enjoyed our walk."

She stared at the handkerchief, breathing shakily.

"Take it!" Lord Craventhorp said, more as a warning than a command.

She shook her head.

He stuffed the handkerchief back into his pocket and grinned. "I'm going to enjoy marriage to you."

The fine hairs on Annabel's neck and arms stood at attention. She saw nothing but enmity in the viscount's cold eyes. Her body sensed danger and urged her to flee, yet she did not move. A lady would bury her fears and smile, keeping her decorum. Lord

Craventhorp knew as much, and his eyes sparkled with malice, daring her to break society's rules.

"Go on," he said in a low voice, "run." His lips curved into a smile. "I dare you."

Annabel's body trembled. Once, in Bristol, she'd seen a group of boys corner an alley cat. The creature was so frightened its hair stood on end. She'd felt such sympathy for the poor thing that she'd thought nothing of stepping forward to intervene. The boys had paid no heed to her. They only laughed, and one dirty-faced urchin even took a stone out of his pocket and threw it at the cat right in front of her. But his laughter quickly turned to a wail when Stella grabbed him by the collar and boxed his ears, shouting, *"mascalzone,"* which sounded far more intimidating than yelling *rotter* or *scoundrel* in English.

How she wished Stella was here now.

Out of the corner of her eye, she spotted two women exit the house through the French doors leading to the garden and step onto the terrace. Thinking of that cat again, she remembered how it took the chance at escape while Stella had the boy by the ear. It had scurried past his distracted friends and disappeared into the night. Now, it was her turn. This was her chance.

She dashed forward, brushing past Lord Craventhorp in her haste to get away. Panic blurred her vision as she hurried across the lawn, weaving between the tall shrubs. She glanced back, envisioning Lord Craventhorp closing in behind her, but forced her legs not to break into a run.

Hands clutched her shoulders. She gasped and struggled like a trapped animal. He wasn't behind her. Somehow, he'd gotten in front of her.

"Are you in need of help, miss?"

The strong smell of spirits infiltrated her nostrils and fear commanded her thoughts.

"Please, allow me to help you."

The only voice Annabel could hear and the only face she could see belonged to Lord Craventhorp. He was everywhere.

She had to get away. Twisting out of her captor's grip, Annabel raced toward the terrace, where she narrowly missed colliding with the two ladies in her haste to reach safety indoors.

CHAPTER THREE

And—would it were not so!—you are my mother

—Shakespeare, *Hamlet*

HENRY HAD SPENT the last two years trying to avoid his mother, but he should have known better. Lady Stokeford, previously Lady Hudsyn, would not be ignored.

Instead of displaying remorse and shame after Henry confronted her with the dark secrets of her past, she dismissed the fact that she'd cuckolded his papa precisely nine months before his birth and continued to portray herself as the queen of morality. Safe in the knowledge that Henry would protect her secret, just as her sister and his father had done, she made a habit of judging and scorning others while refusing to be judged. And she'd become even more insufferable in her criticisms since elevating her status in society by marrying William Ryde, 5th Earl of Stokeford, one year ago.

After losing no less than three young wives and a total of seven babes, Lord Stokeford, having reached his seventieth year, stopped trying to sire an heir and decided to settle down with a woman past her child-birthing years. Henry imagined it hadn't been difficult for his mother to worm her way into Lord Stokeford's broken heart. After all, she possessed an extraordinary ability to connive and manipulate others.

Henry looked at his mother, who sat like a queen on her throne next to her husband with her lips pursed in disapproval as she eyed her wayward son. When he was a little boy, he'd thought his mother the most beautiful woman in the world, but now all he could see was her black heart.

"Henry," Lord Stokeford clasped his hands together, "you are neither my son nor my heir, but out of respect for your mama and the good name of this family, I must speak out against your behavior. You dishonor your father's memory and embarrass your mother, behaving like a common drunk, frequenting houses of ill repute, and neglecting your duties. I have remained silent for too long, but last night, you went too far. I must speak, and you must listen. A drunken, unprovoked attack on one of Lady Dawley's guests—it's unacceptable."

Henry glared at his mother. How dare she preach to him through her husband—who knew nothing of her own revolting behavior—committing an act of infidelity so vile that he felt shame at being her son and perhaps the result of her crimes.

"Do you have anything to say for yourself?" the earl asked.

Henry shrugged. "I dislike the man."

"It will behoove you to remember that you are no longer a boy in the schoolyard. I cannot fathom why you attacked Lord Craventhorp in such a brutal manner."

Henry touched his bruised jaw and recalled the feel of the young lady's lithe, trembling body. She'd flown into his path like a confused bird whilst Craventhorp watched her from afar with the same expression of pleasure he'd worn after hurting the harlot at Madam Katrina's bawdy house. Henry recalled the burning rage Craventhorp's smugness had ignited in him but had no memory of what followed. According to Hobsworth, he'd tackled Craventhorp to the ground and attempted to choke the life out of him, yet he had no recollection of the incident.

"It wasn't unprovoked, I assure you. Earlier that evening, I watched him break a young woman's wrist right in front of my eyes. The man is a bully, and he deserves a good thrashing. I'm only sorry I wasn't able to give it to him." He glared at Hobsworth, who sat beside him on the couch.

"He what?" Lord Stokeford turned to Hobsworth. "Is this true? What young lady are we talking about?"

Hobsworth shook his head at Henry and groaned. "She was a—one of Madame Katrina's girls."

Lady Stokeford whimpered, loud enough to garner a sympathetic look from her husband, who then turned back to Henry stony-faced.

Henry smirked. *You gave birth to a rotten egg, mother. There's no escaping the consequences of your actions.*

"So, this was the continuation of an earlier disagreement over a courtesan?" Lord Stokeford said.

Henry shrugged. He wasn't going to explain about the young woman in the garden. He preferred the narrative as it stood. Let people talk about how Lady Stokeford's son defended a harlot.

A gentleman does not strike a fellow peer in defense of—" Lord Stokeford glanced at his wife—"such a person," he said through gritted teeth.

"Then you ought to be having this conversation with Craventhorp. I did not strike him. Yet he saw fit to strike at me with his closed fist while Hobsworth and Burdington held me back, I might add."

"Viscount Craventhorp is not my stepson, nor my heir." He turned to Hobsworth, who sat mutely on the couch like a schoolboy waiting in line for a thrashing.

"Tell him, Hobsworth," Henry said.

"What he says is true. Craventhorp behaved like a brute, and now we are all barred from Madame Katrina's—" Hobsworth stopped, obviously realizing his error at revealing too much information.

"How dare you speak of your whoring ways in the presence of my wife?" the earl snapped, and Lady Stokeford sniffed at the air as if she'd suffered an unmeasurable injury.

Henry clenched his jaw. He'd had enough of this hypocrisy.

"Lord Stokeford, I came here out of respect for you, but I owe you little allegiance, and I do not intend to sit here while you berate me like a child. I took action because I saw a man brutalizing a woman, and I would do the same again." Henry stood up.

"You were drunk and defended a peer against a harlot in a bawdy house." Lord Stokeford stepped forward. "And then you carried your sordid disagreement into Lady Dawley's home. I may hold no sway over you, but I hoped you would listen to reason. My heir, on the other hand—" he turned to Hobsworth— "will cease your company until you grow up and stop these antics, or he will find himself with a severely restricted allowance."

Hobsworth groaned.

Henry's body went rigid. "Very well. So be it," he said, keeping his eyes fixed on the earl.

Lady Stokeford stood up from her chair like a queen ascending her throne. "May I have a few moments alone with my son, my lord?"

"Are you certain that is wise, my dear?" The earl's demeanor softened as he turned to his wife.

Henry sighed. "Perhaps, you'd best call the armed guards. You never know when my madness will take over." He glared at his mother and felt a twinge of satisfaction to see her flinch.

"Stop your silly talk, Henry, and give your mama a few minutes of your time."

"You, come with me," Stokeford snapped at Hobsworth, who leapt up and followed the earl.

Then the door closed, and Henry stood alone in the room with his mother. "When will you stop this demoralizing behavior? Your father would be ashamed—"

"Don't you speak a word to me about my father—the man you cuckolded with your own sister's husband!"

Lady Stokeford strode toward her son and slapped him across the face. "How dare you repeat such filthy lies to me? You believe a vindictive man over your own mother—a man who is himself guilty of cuckolding my dear sister?"

Henry smiled. "On the contrary, Mama, it is you who convinced me of the truth. You knew that my cousin Ottilie might well be my sister and so kept us apart for most of our lives, and when that was no longer possible, you grew so fearful of our close bond that you attempted to marry her to a man twice her age."

"I did what I thought best for Ottilie. Lord Towns may be old, but he is a respectable peer with a fortune. She would have been a lady. But she refused my help. And where is she now? Stuck in Canterbury with that—that—"

"Do you mean to say that successful writer who worships her and dotes on their child?" Henry intercepted. "I have never known anyone happier than Ottilie. And your interference almost ruined her life, as you ruined mine."

"How is your life ruined? You have a title, an estate, and a fortune."

"But who am I? You took my identity as a peer and as a poet. I cannot serve in the House of Lords, knowing I might not belong there, and I cannot write or publish my poetry with pride because it will remind me, every day, of what you did to Papa."

"Stop this at once, Henry! You are not and have never been a poet! But you are the 8th Baron Hudsyn. Yet, you spend your days drinking and visiting brothels instead of serving in Parliament and looking for a wife so that you can carry the Hudsyn name forward."

"How can I marry and pass on this burden of fake peerage to my child?" Henry scoffed. "No! This farce will end with me."

His mother's lips trembled, and she pressed them tightly together.

Henry sneered. "Is that all you have to say, Mother?"

Lady Stokeford straightened her shoulders. "If you cannot curb your bad behavior, then you must keep your distance from Hobsworth, or you will drag Lord Stokeford's heir down with you. Moreover, if you care for your friend at all, then you will—"

"Say no more, Mother." Henry stepped back. "You can assure the earl that your bastard son will no longer taint the Stokeford earldom by consorting with its heir."

"I hope you take some time to reflect on your actions and how badly they injure your mother who loves you."

Lady Stokeford lifted her chin and turned her face from her son with the martyred air she had perfected over the years, once again transforming herself from villain to victim.

⇛⇜

ANNABEL WINCED AS she lowered her nightgown to inspect the tender bruise on her upper arm. The size of a thumbprint and a horrible purplish black color, it paled in comparison to the welt Lord Craventhorp's cruel fingers had left on the sensitive skin of her underarm. It was a good thing that summer was coming to an end, as she wouldn't be able to wear short sleeves for quite some time.

"*Cara mia!*" Stella caught sight of the bruise and bustled over to Annabel. "What happened? Did you hurt yourself?"

Annabel shook her head and blinked back her tears of shame.

"No?" Stella raised her hands as if the answer to her question hovered above in an invisible cloud. "Then why is your beautiful skin bruised purple?"

Annabel bit her lip and sank onto the tufted green ottoman in front of her dressing table.

"He...he kept pressing his fingers, and I couldn't make a sound because I didn't dare cause a commotion."

"He? Pressing fingers? Who? Did someone hurt you *on purpose?*" Stella's voice grew high-pitched and frantic. "Was it your papa?" Her hand flew to her mouth. "He has been so cross lately. But I never thought he'd—"

"Not Papa," Annabel interjected. "The man he says must be

my husband, Lord Craventhorp."

Stella drew back, fear and surprise etched into the creases of her matronly face. "Then we must show him this at once, so he can release you from the monstrous agreement!"

"He'll never believe me. I objected to the union before I met Lord Craventhorp, and Papa thinks me willful. He is furious that I questioned his judgment. You know, Papa. He doesn't like to be corrected, and he'll think I'm making up tales to prove him wrong." Annabel shifted her body and caught sight of herself in the looking glass. The bruise sat on her arm like a stamp, marking her as the property of Lord Craventhorp. "I have been too strong-headed and stubborn in the past. Papa believes I'm a foolish girl who reads too many novels and will do anything to avoid a good match."

"Don't worry, *cara*. You have proof of your words. You will show him the bruise, and he will see you are not lying." Stella smoothed Annabel's dark hair. "I know your papa. I know how much he loved your mama. He won't let that brute hurt his *bambina* again. I am certain. Trust me."

Annabel shook her head. "You are determined to remember Papa as he was, even though you've witnessed the change in him over the years. He won't believe me. He will say it is my fault. That I did it to myself or caused it to happen." She looked up at Stella. "Perhaps I did. I feel so ashamed." She buried her face in her hands.

"Your fault! *Impossibile!*"

Annabel repositioned her nightgown and stood up. "I should have screamed and not worried about causing a disturbance." She twisted her hands. "Why did I keep quiet and let him hurt me?"

"Maybe there is a witness?" Stella's voice raised, sounding hopeful.

"That wouldn't help at all. If anything, it will hurt me. Lord Craventhorp was clever. He made it seem—romantic—hurting me while making it appear as though he was whispering sweet nothings in my ear. If someone happened upon us, they wouldn't have suspected anything was amiss." Annabel scoffed. "And who would believe me, over a viscount?"

"You don't know that to be true. Try to remember if you saw anyone else in the garden. There must be someone—"

Annabel forced her mind back as she tried to recreate the scene. "All I see are tall hedges. The lighting is dim. Except for the terrace. That's flooded with gaslight, and—yes—there are two women!"

"Where?" Stella's face brightened.

"On the terrace. I ran past them, but I don't think they saw Lord Craventhorp," Annabel stopped as her memory flooded back. "Unless…"

"What?"

"I thought Lord Craventhorp was following behind me, and when I turned to look over my shoulder, someone grabbed me— or maybe, I collided with the person. I don't know. I was so frightened I couldn't think. It was a man. He said something to me, but I don't remember what. All I could see was Lord Craventhorp's face, so I freed myself and ran from him."

"Was it that devil, Craventhorp?"

"I still don't know. I thought so at the time, but how could he have gotten in front of me when I was running away from him?" Her heart thumped as she tried to recall the details, and the panic from the night before returned. She rubbed her forehead and squeezed her eyes shut. "I can't make sense of anything."

Stella rested her fingertips against her temples. "Did you tell your papa what happened when you went back inside? Surely, he noticed your distress."

"I couldn't face him. I felt so confused and ashamed after Lord Craventhorp laughed in my face and dared me to make a fuss. He said people would say I was hysterical."

"You poor child." Stella's brow creased. "What did you do?"

"I went directly to the ladies' room. I remember feeling cold. My body trembled so badly that a kind lady—I forget her name— sent for Mrs. Leonard. When she arrived, I pretended that my monthly courses had come early and so had to excuse myself from Lord Craventhorp's company in a hurry. I could tell Mrs. Leonard was furious, but I reassured her that all went well with Lord Craventhorp and said he'd promised to call on me, which seemed to appease her. It was a lie, but I didn't care. All I wanted to do was escape that horrid house and go home."

Stella balled her hands into one fist and rested them on her chin—a sign she was not about to give up thinking of a plan. "You must appeal to Mrs. Leonard." Stella moved her hands on her chest as if wanting to soothe her heart. "When she sees that bruise, she will believe you."

"What makes you say that? She's the one behind this arranged marriage. You know what airs she has, and she is desperate to wipe away the shame of her past. She only married my papa because her father lost all his money. Now, she wants better for her daughters and intends for them to marry titles. She's forcing me into this marriage for the sake of my sisters. In her eyes, I must marry a viscount so that when Florence comes of age, she can marry an earl or, perhaps even, a duke."

"That may be true, but she is a woman, and she will see her error in judgment when she learns the truth about Lord Craventhorp." Stella reached for Annabel's hands and clasped them tightly in hers. "I think she will listen to reason. She *must*."

"I don't know," Annabel said.

"If you don't want to tell her, let me do it for you."

Annabel freed her hands from Stella's grasp and massaged her forehead. She wasn't as certain as Stella that Mrs. Leonard would listen to reason. Annabel had long suspected her stepmother disliked her because Papa had married her mama for love. But surely, she would not want Annabel to suffer marriage to a cruel man. It was true that she and her stepmother sometimes clashed, but Annabel had to admit she wasn't blameless in that respect. She'd been eight and already well accustomed to her freedoms when Papa remarried, so she'd rebelled against her new mama's strict rules. Mrs. Leonard wasn't warm and affectionate like Stella, who'd overseen her care since birth, but she wasn't malicious either. She had raised her two daughters with the same restrained affection and strict rules she'd imposed on Annabel. It was the way she'd been raised and what she deemed proper. Unpleasant as her rules sometimes were, Annabel didn't believe her stepmother was without heart.

"Please, *mia cara*! Let me speak to Mrs. Leonard. I will tell her that I saw the bruise on your arm while helping you dress and say that I begged the information from you. She is a woman and mother. She will not want this for you."

Annabel sighed. Perhaps Stella was right? Papa's pride would never allow him to admit that he'd made a mistake. Her stepmother was her only hope.

"Very well," she relented, "if that's what you think is best." But the nagging feeling in the pit of her stomach suggested otherwise.

CHAPTER FOUR

*A fine bundle of trash you study in your leisure hours, to
be sure:*

why, it's good enough to be printed!
*And what do you suppose the master will think when I display
it before him?
I hav'n't shown it yet, but you needn't imagine I shall keep your
ridiculous secrets.
For shame!*

—Emily Brontë, *Wuthering Heights*

ANNABEL LOVED LONDON'S royal parks and enjoyed them best outside of promenade hours. She relished her morning walks in Hyde Park with Stella where they could meander amongst the greenery and talk freely without restriction or intervention from her stepmother, sisters, or Papa.

On this morning, however, she found it difficult to relax.

"I spoke with Mrs. Leonard first thing, and I think all will be well," Stella reassured Annabel as they strolled alongside the Serpentine. "I explained how that scoundrel hurt you and advised her to take the matter up with your papa because he'd be furious to discover the truth from someone else."

"Was that a wise thing to say?"

"To be sure, she did not appreciate such boldness coming

from a servant, but I risked it all the same because I hoped it would make her think twice about not bringing such an important matter before your papa. If I'm right, she will speak with him today."

"How can you be sure?" Annabel linked her arm with Stella's. "What did she say? Tell me her exact words."

"Not much of anything. She kept a straight face while I talked and clasped her hands together as she likes to do. Then she thanked me for the information in that cold manner of hers and dismissed me."

"That doesn't sound promising. She wasn't alarmed or upset?"

"She may have been, but I'm a servant, and she would never display her emotions in front of me."

"You are not just a servant! You were my mama's dearest friend and are a part of my family."

"To your mama, I was family. But to Mrs. Leonard, I belong in the basement and have no business upstairs unless it involves service."

Annabel sighed. "I do believe she's spiteful toward you because you were so dear to my mama. She's jealous of the love my parents shared because her marriage is one of convenience."

Stella patted Annabel's arm, still linked with her own. "Mrs. Leonard comes from a different world than me and your mama. I doubt she sees anything wrong with a marriage of convenience. She likes everything in its proper place; messy doesn't suit her. And love is sometimes messy. I am messy in her eyes because I love you and because you love me. I do not fit neatly into her servant box, and that is unacceptable in her world. So, she sets more and more rules for me to follow each year. I believe she'd like to be rid of me altogether, but your papa won't allow it."

"Don't say such a thing, Stella! Don't even think it. You shall always be with me, even after I marry. I shall insist upon it."

"I would not leave you of my own free will, but a man like Lord Craventhorp surely will not allow me to stay with you. He will want his wife friendless and fully under his cruel thumb. That is why we must do all we can to make sure you get free of him."

Annabel shivered. "I suspect he took pleasure in brutalizing small animals when he was a boy."

"It breaks my heart to think your papa has been so careless with your safety and your future. Offering your hand in marriage to a brute like Lord Craventhorp!." Stella gazed at Annabel. "I remember his joy when your mama told him she was with child. He cherished you before you were born. How times have changed."

"Those days you speak of were long ago—before Mama died birthing me. I am almost one-and-twenty, and I've never seen Papa overjoyed—not even when Florence and Flora were born. The only Papa I know is the one who is either distant or thunderous, and neither of those is welcoming. This doting and joyful Papa you speak of is foreign to me."

They turned and made their way back through the park toward Mayfair. "I only wish he would remember what it feels like to be in love. Perhaps then he'd give me the same chance for happiness."

"You will find love and be happy," Stella said vehemently. "It was your mama's dying wish, and she is protecting you from above, steering your life right when it goes in the wrong direction." A breeze stirred the trees. "There she is now," Stella said, "making her presence known."

"I like to think she is still with me." Annabel gazed up at the rustling leaves.

She is. All you have to do is pay attention to her whispers," Stella said as they exited the park, and made their way to the magnificent, red-bricked mansion Papa had rented on Park Lane for the London Season.

"I'm not ready to go inside. Shall we have a cup of hot chocolate in the kitchen, like we used to do when I was a little girl?"

Annabel pushed open the iron gate at the top of the stairs to the servants' entrance and held it open for Stella.

"Are you trying to provoke Mrs. Leonard at a time when you need her help the most?" Stella took hold of the gate and shut it. "You know how she hates it when you fraternize with the servants."

Annabel groaned. "You're right, as always." She linked her arm with Stella's and together they ascended the stairs that led to the front door. "I am growing so tired of Mrs. Leonard's silly rules. She's become tyrannical in her quest to marry me to the right person. All she thinks about is reentering high society and readying my sisters to become future duchesses. If she only knew what little minxes they are when her back is turned—"

The words sat on Annabel's lips as she stepped indoors. A heavy weight tugged at the atmosphere in the house. The footman paled visibly upon greeting her at the door, and two housemaids arranging flowers in the hallway glanced up and then at each other before lowering their gazes and continuing their work in hushed silence. Annabel exchanged a worried look with Stella, who moved to help her out of her coat.

Just as Stella handed Annabel's coat, hat, and gloves to the footman, the butler entered the hallway, looking somber. "You are wanted upstairs in the drawing room, Miss Annabel," he said before clearing his throat and turning to Stella. "And you are to come with me, Mrs. Bruno."

"Has something happened?" Annabel asked.

"I'm not at liberty to say, miss."

"Has one of my sisters fallen ill? Or Papa?"

"Not to my knowledge," the butler said. "All I know is that your parents have requested your presence in the drawing room."

Annabel bit her lip. The awkward atmosphere could only mean one thing. Mrs. Leonard must have spoken to Papa, and he must have thrown enough vases to alert the household of an impending storm. As long as he kept his anger directed at Lord Craventhorp, Annabel would welcome it. But what if he didn't believe her story? She swallowed.

"Go on." Stella gave Annabel an encouraging prod. "All will

be well. You'll see."

Annabel forced a smile and breathed shakily as she headed for the stairs.

All will be well. She told herself as she climbed the stairs to the first floor. *All will be well. It simply must be.*

ANNABEL WAS SO deep in thought as she stepped onto the first-floor landing that she almost collided with a footman, carrying a heavy load.

"I'm sorry," Annabel said.

The footman paled, and he glanced at the bundle in his arms. Annabel's gaze followed his. Then her body stiffened. He was carrying an armful of her books.

"Those are my books! How dare you take them from my room!"

"I'm sorry, miss," he stammered. "I was ordered to deliver them to the drawing room."

Ordered? Why? What is he talking about?

"I don't understand."

Another footman carrying a load of books descended from the second floor. He'd come from her bedchamber! Annabel marched forward. "Who told you to take those books from my chamber?"

The footman froze midway on the stairs and gaped at her, but he gave no response.

Mrs. Leonard appeared on the top of the stairs and eyed her with a look of stern disapproval. Annabel felt herself shrink under her stepmother's gaze.

"I ordered the removal of your books." She nodded curtly at the two footmen, who'd both turned to face her, and barked, "Carry on."

Like automatons reanimated on command, they continued with their tasks.

"Why?" Annabel struggled to keep the anger out of her voice. Her stepmother had never invaded her privacy thus, and she was both hurt and fearful of this new distrust.

"I have asked your father to meet us in the drawing room. You shall have a chance to explain yourself to him."

"Now?" Annabel asked.

"Yes." Her stepmother continued her descent. "I shouldn't keep him waiting if I were you."

Annabel bristled at the implication that she'd done something wrong when she was the one who'd been hurt.

"Very well." She strode across the landing to the dining room without waiting for her stepmother.

"Papa!" she said, entering the room in a whirlpool of indignation.

Then she froze.

Her father stood frowning at a pile of books on the table before him.

"Papa?" she ventured forward.

He looked up but did not smile.

Her stepmother swept into the room and positioned herself next to her husband.

Annabel shivered. Despite the blaze in the hearth, a chilly atmosphere engulfed the drawing room.

Mrs. Leonard picked up a book and handed it to her husband. He opened it without a word and studied the pages in silence.

Annabel's stomach seized into a knot. What book had she given him to scrutinize? His hand covered the title, and all she could see were the edges of a green leather cover.

No one spoke as Mr. Leonard flipped to a new page. Annabel's limbs weakened when his hand shifted, and she saw that he held *Wuthering Heights*.

At that moment, he glanced up at his daughter, his face thunderous. "What is the meaning of this—this filth?" He snapped the book shut, and the image of dungeon doors clamping flashed in Annabel's mind.

"Nothing, Papa," Annabel struggled to keep her voice steady. "It's only a story. It's perfectly harmless."

"Harmless?" His voice teetered on the edge of a roar. "You believe this—" he lifted the novel—"to be harmless? Is it, to your mind, appropriate reading for a respectable young lady?"

"I—I don't know what you mean."

"The people in this book are coarse, and they curse each other like dogs."

"It's only a story," Annabel repeated in a whisper.

"In this *story*, the heroine stamps her foot, shouts orders, and slaps the face of her gentleman caller. Do you still say it's appropriate?" Papa's voice rose in warning like the rumblings of a volcano before an eruption. "Is this what you deem harmless?" He roared. "Is it the example you wish to set for your impression-able sisters?" He smashed the book onto the table, making Annabel jump.

"Of course not. They are mere children, but I am a few months shy of one-and-twenty and old enough to know the difference between real life and a book."

Papa bristled like an enraged bear. "Mrs. Leonard is right. These novels aren't simply foolish, they are dangerous. They've put ideas in your head that have turned you willful and made you disobedient."

"I'm sorry, Papa." Annabel attempted to placate her father. "I did not mean to—"

"Who gave you this filth?" His voice cut into her apology like an executioner's blade.

"I purchased it with my pin money. The same way I did all of those." She gestured to the pile of books.

"From where? Who sells filth like this to young women?"

Annabel hesitated. She could not tell her papa that Stella had purchased most of the books on her behalf. Her lady's maid was in enough trouble already.

"I believe Annabel knows as much," Mrs. Leonard interject-ed, "and that is why she has been sending Stella out to purchase these books for her."

No! She couldn't allow her stepmother to implicate Stella. Fear gripped Annabel's throat. If her papa believed that, he'd send Stella away. Her stepmother's mouth continued to move rapidly, and her Papa's frown deepened. But all Annabel could hear was the pounding of her own heart. *What is she saying? Someone stop her! She wants Stella gone.*

"That's not true!" Her voice rang out, surprising everyone.

But it *was* true. And Annabel knew this was how her stepmother would punish Stella for speaking against Lord Craventhorp.

"I have been too lenient with you, Annabel. Mrs. Leonard has been warning me for years that Stella indulges you far too much, and I neglected to act, but I cannot do so any longer."

Annabel's legs grew weak. "What are you saying?"

"I'm saying that you are to be the wife of a viscount, and you need to learn how to behave like a lady. A new lady's maid accustomed to the ways of high society will be engaged to prepare you accordingly."

"Replace Stella?" Panic clawed at Annabel's throat, choking her.

"Stella will be allowed to stay on as a housemaid—*if* you cooperate and refrain from making a fuss," Mr. Leonard said.

"A housemaid? Stella is no housemaid. She is my lady's maid, and I trust her unequivocally. Did she not tell you about Lord Craventhorp—what he did to my arm?" She looked from her stepmother to her father. "He hurt me. I can show you his fingermarks—"

"Silence!" Mrs. Leonard's command bit into Annabel's words. "Enough of your lies. Do you expect us to believe that Lord Craventhorp mishandled you during a ten-minute walk in the garden while Mrs. Dawley's guests milled about? And while your Papa awaited your return inside the house? Preposterous! Those fingermarks belong to your dear Stella, who will do anything to give you whatever it is you demand."

"No, I swear to you. Lord Craventhorp is malicious. He knew I would not be believed, precisely for the reasons you just stated."

Mrs. Leonard put a hand to her forehead and turned to her husband. "Make her stop, please. It's all too much. I just received word that my dear Papa is ill, and I'm so worried about him. How can I cope with her theatrics as well?"

"I'm speaking the truth. Please, you must listen!"

"Enough lies!" Papa bellowed. "Your stepmother's father is ill. You are upsetting her with this rebellious behavior! It ends now, daughter. You *will* marry Lord Craventhorp, and you *will* have a new lady's maid. Mrs. Leonard is taking your sisters to her father's estate in Yorkshire tomorrow. And when she returns, she will bring with her your new lady's maid."

"The very woman who served me when I resided in Yorkshire," Mrs. Leonard said smugly.

"You can't! Please, Papa." Annabel wanted to fall to her knees or cry. Anything to get him to listen to her. "How can you not believe me? Your own daughter?"

"How?" He picked up Annabel's worn copy of *Wuthering Heights*. "Because, like the heroines in your novels, you've become willful and dishonest," he barked. "And your behavior shames me!" He flung the book into the hearth.

"No!" Annabel sprang forward, but it was too late. She watched with helpless fury as the rapacious flames devoured *Wuthering Heights*, gilding the edges of its pages bright and orange, before singeing them so that blackness swept over the words, charring them. The fire popped and crackled as it danced, growing higher; darkened bits of burned paper flew up the chimney and away. The rest turned to ash in the grate.

It was as if pieces of her were flying away with them. Annabel stood, hands clenched, as tears began to course down her cheeks.

"Immorality has no place in books!" Mr. Leonard flung *Jane Eyre* into the fire.

Another piece of her burst into flames. "Blasphemy has no place in books!" He picked up *Frankenstein* and tossed it into the flames. She began to shake.

"No, Papa! Please! Stop!"

"Vulgarity!" He roared, feeding *The Tenant of Wildfell Hall* to the flaming beast.

"And debauchery!" He picked up *Moll Flanders* in one hand, *Madame Bovary* in the other, and flung both into the fire.

Annabel sank to her knees, watching her beloved books burn.

"Burn them all!" he ordered the footmen before striding past Annabel and out of the room. She knew then, without a doubt, that her Papa didn't care what happened to her. After all, he'd willingly destroyed her heart.

CHAPTER FIVE

*Either, said she, the Lady must be thought to have very
violent inclinations
(and what nice young creature would have that supposed?)
which she could not give up; or a very stubborn will, which she
would not;
or, thirdly, have parents she was indifferent about obliging.*

—Samuel Richardson, *Clarissa*

ANNABEL SAT AT her dressing table and pulled the pins from her hair. With each tug, her locks uncoiled until finally, waves of dark tresses tumbled down her back. Wasting no time, she picked up the scissors from her dresser and grabbed a fistful of hair. Then, taking a deep breath, she squeezed her eyes shut and snipped.

The blades were sharp and efficient. With each cut, the strands separated, and soon Annabel clutched a sizable chunk in her fist. She opened her eyes and stared at her reflection in the oval mirror that sat above her dressing table. For a moment, the world felt surreal. The chopped hair, hanging above her shoulder, looked like a wound.

The sight immobilized her, but only for a second. Then she blinked and told her mirrored self, "Get the ribbon, Annabel. We must tie this up prettily, so it can fetch a good amount." Having given herself this task, she came to life again, and taking one of the precut velvet ribbons from her dresser, secured the hair and placed it into a cloth sack. "Now," Annabel faced the mirror again, "you must be more efficient." She got to work dividing her hair into sections and securing each piece with a ribbon. Then she picked up the scissors again. Minutes later, bundles of thick, glossy locks lay securely tied in the cloth sack, ready for the wig makers. *These will fetch a tidy sum.*

Turning back to the mirror, she inspected her image. Her hair hung in choppy strands above her shoulders. She'd left it long enough to secure it back with pins so no one would notice the difference. And if they did, she didn't care. It didn't matter. They'd already done the worst to her that they could; anything else would be superfluous.

Her bedroom door creaked open, and Stella slipped inside, carrying a black cape. "*Il mia cara!*" She dropped the cape and covered her mouth with her hand, staring wide-eyed at Annabel.

"Don't be sentimental, Stella. I need the money. It's only hair, and it will grow back."

Stella picked up the cape and set it down on Annabel's bed. Then she ran a hand over Annabel's chopped hair. "Let me pin it up for you. I'll arrange it so you'll hardly know the difference."

"No, I'll do it. If I am to be my own woman, I must learn to take care of myself."

"You will never be alone. I promised your mama that I would watch over you until the day I die, and that is what I will do. You might be in Canterbury and I, far away in Italy, but we will never truly be apart—" Stella choked back her words.

Annabel's stomach lurched. She clasped Stella's hand, suddenly losing courage. "Must you go to Italy?"

"Only until the storm passes. Your papa will never leave me in peace if he thinks I know your whereabouts."

Annabel nodded and took a few calming breaths. Tomorrow, after discovering she was gone, Papa would gather an army to search for her, but what would he do when he found no trace of her? He'd search for Stella. "Are you certain you'll be safe in Italy?"

"You needn't worry about me." Stella planted a kiss on Annabel's head. "And you will be quite safe too. Tomorrow, you will have a new name and a new home. Nate, my dear departed Alfonso's nephew, has arranged for you to lodge with a kind and decent family in Canterbury. The wife is a seamstress, and the husband a sailor, away at sea. They have one child—a little boy, I think. Nate will introduce you as Mrs. Anne Crawford, the widow of his dear friend. You'll use the money from your dresses to pay the first three months' rent, which includes two daily meals. They are not rich, mind you, so I'm afraid the food will be quite different from what you are used to, but you won't go hungry. And Nate has promised to deliver fresh fish from his catches at Whitstable whenever he can. He will get a good price for your hair too—" She broke off speaking and let out a muffled sob.

"Dear Stella," Annabel squeezed her hand. "Don't be sad. I'm not afraid of hard work or plain food. I'd rather be a free bird, weathering storms and dodging danger than locked in a gilded cage with clipped wings at the mercy of a cruel master."

Stella picked up the cloth sack containing Annabel's hair. "So beautiful." She took out a ribboned lock and kissed it. "It breaks my heart that your papa has put you in such a desperate situation. If he only knew that you'd rather sell your hair and live like a peasant than marry that monster, then I am sure he would change his mind."

"He wouldn't, and you mustn't think of reasoning with him. Mrs. Leonard has hardened his heart against me, and there is nothing you or I can do to change that."

Stella shook her head and closed her fist around the hair. "If only your mother were alive…"

Annabel gestured to the beribboned locks in Stella's fist. "Why don't you keep that one? I want a little piece of me to go with you to Italy."

"I'll treasure it."

"Here, let me wrap it for you." Annabel took a piece of velvet cloth from her drawer and Stella kissed the lock again before wrapping it up and slipping it into the pocket of her skirt from whence she retrieved her kerchief and pressed it to her eyes.

"What time will Nate come for us?" Annabel said, wanting to change the subject. Stella's emotions would only serve to make her fearful and hesitant.

"In the early morning hours, well before sunrise." Stella sniffed.

"And Papa, is he still—"

"In his study nursing his back pain, yes." Stella nodded. "His valet informed the staff earlier that the master will sup from a tray in his study. In truth, I think he's taking advantage of his freedom while Mrs. Leonard and your sisters are in Yorkshire."

"Yes, we all feel relief from her presence." Annabel put down her hairbrush. "It's a strike of luck that her papa fell ill."

"Hush!" Stella crossed herself. "You mustn't say such things."

"I don't wish him sick, you know that. But it would have been near impossible for me to escape with her in the house." Annabel sighed.

"How can we be sure Papa won't wake?"

"You have nothing to fear in that regard." Stella grinned. "He always enjoys a few extra glasses of brandy when Mrs. Leonard is away, so he is sure to sleep like the dead tonight."

"Good," Annabel said, and the storm in her stomach quieted a bit. "And what of the servants? Do we need to worry?"

"They're a weary bunch in need of their rest. With Mrs. Leonard gone, they are finally able to relax. Believe me, none of them have the energy to wake up in the middle of the night if they don't have to." Stella tenderly drew her hand across Annabel's shorn hair, a gesture she'd used since Annabel had been a child. It was meant to soothe her, but right now it only strengthened her resolve to leave. She met Stella's eyes in the mirror with her own.

Stella gave her a small, fond smile. "Now, I'm going to fetch your supper. You can eat in your room since your papa won't be dining downstairs."

"No, Stella. I couldn't eat a thing."

"But you've got a long journey ahead of you, and you'll need a good meal in your stomach."

"I can't."

"Then I'll bring us some bread and cheese for the journey." Stella left the room, shaking her head, and Annabel got to work pinning her hair into a chignon. Ten minutes later, she admired her handiwork—not as good as Stella's, but she'd get better with practice. Moving to her writing desk, she extracted a crisp white paper from her drawer and picked up her quill pen. She dipped it into the ink and began to write:

Dear Papa,

By the time you read this, I will be a married woman, and quite out of your reach. I am sorry it came to this, but I must do as my heart tells me and marry for love.

The man I am marrying is kind, loving, and industrious.

You needn't worry about me; I will have a good life with him.

Your loving daughter,
Annabel

She put down her quill and read the letter, imagining her father's rage, reading how she'd run off and married her true love, seeking happiness and shirking her duty as a daughter and sister.

She sighed. *If only it were true.*

HOURS LATER, WHEN the house stood dark and silent, Annabel slipped into the black hooded cloak secured for her by Stella and tiptoed downstairs. As she stepped into the hallway, Stella slipped from the shadows to meet her. Together, they exited the house and crossed the street where a black carriage, complete with two black horses and a driver who also wore dark clothing, waited in a darkened corner under a thicket of trees. Anyone watching the two cloaked figures shuffling toward it would have thought they'd vanished into the night when they slipped into the carriage—at least, that is what Annabel imagined as she and Stella ensconced themselves in the waiting vehicle.

Stella pulled the door gently to a close, and as soon as it clicked, the horses stirred, and the carriage inched forward onto the road.

Only then did Annabel shiver and acknowledge the terror that gnawed at her insides.

IN PICCADILLY, A mile and a half from Park Lane, Lord Henry Hudsyn crawled into his black brougham with a brandy bottle in hand and instructed his coachman to head for his estate in Kent.

CHAPTER SIX

Good my lord, what is your cause of distemper?
You do surely bar the door upon your own liberty
if you deny your griefs to your friend.

—Shakespeare, *Hamlet*

Hudsyn Estate, Sevenoaks, Kent
Six weeks later...

HENRY LAY IN his darkened drawing room, nursing another bottle of brandy when his butler entered and announced, "Mr. Bastin is here to see you, my lord."

"What?" Henry lifted his aching head off the settee and peered at his butler through blurred eyes.

"Mr. Bastin. He's waiting in the parlor, my lord."

"No, I'm not!" Jack Bastin strode past the butler into Henry's study.

Henry groaned and laid his head back onto the settee pillows.

"Bring up a strong pot of tea, Bales," Bastin said.

"Yes, sir."

"Why are you here, Bastin?"

"You know bloody well why." Bastin snatched away the half-empty brandy bottle tucked in the crook of Henry's arm.

Damn. He hadn't finished that. Henry frowned. "How did

you know I'd arrived in Kent? Do you have spies following me?"

"Something like that. Sit up!"

Henry forced his aching body to move. His head throbbed. "Let me guess. My cousin sent you."

"She's *worried* about you. First, you turn down a publication offer for your work of poetry, then you abandon your home in Berkley Square for Albany and let your country estate go to ruin. It's been two years of self-destruction." Bastin strode to the window and pulled open the dark green drapes.

"My head! Stop that!"

"This house is a bloody mausoleum."

Bales reentered and set down the tea tray. "Will there be anything else, my lord?"

"Laudanum," Henry mumbled.

"Very good, sir."

"No!" Bastin held up his hand to stop the butler. "No laudanum, thank you, Bales."

The butler hesitated.

"Bring it!" Henry barked, and Bales hurried out of the room.

"I need you focused and present, not asleep or with your mind in Kubla Khan."

"It's for the throbbing in my head. I won't be much use to you without it."

Bastin poured a cup of tea and handed it to Henry. "Drink up. *This* will make you feel better."

In Henry's unsteady hand, the cup rattled in the saucer. But he managed to get it to his lips and took a sip to satisfy Bastin, who loomed over him.

"Look, Hudsyn," Bastin said, turning away to pour himself his own cup of tea, "we both know I'm here for Ottilie's sake. I don't care if you want to waste your talent and drink yourself to death, but my wife does, and if you care for her at all, you will pull yourself together." He sat down opposite Henry and sipped his tea.

Henry said nothing as his friend eyed him over the rim of his teacup.

"Are you in love with her?" Bastin finally said.

"Who?" Henry frowned, genuinely puzzled by Bastin's question.

"Ottilie," Bastin said bluntly.

"Ottilie?" Henry plunked his teacup onto the table, spilling half the contents into the saucer. He stood up and ran his hand over his chin. "*Your* wife? My *cousin*? Ottilie?"

"Do you know of another?"

Henry shook his head. "Are you mad?"

Bastin stood and placed his teacup down. "Look, Hudsyn, I won't fault you if that's what's been troubling you. Ottilie's a beautiful woman and—"

"Stop!" Henry lunged forward and grabbed Bastin's shirt.

Bastin pushed him off. "Get a hold of yourself and sit down! I have something to say to you."

"I'm not going to sit here and listen to your mad theories!" He strode to the door and opened it. "Get out of my house, or I'll have you thrown out."

Just then, Bales appeared in the doorway, carrying a tray with the bottle of laudanum. Henry snatched it and said, "Go now!" He'd directed the words at Bastin, but the frightened butler scurried away.

"What do you expect me to think? Your melancholy began when I asked Ottilie to marry me two years ago in Margate. From that time on, you seemed determined to drink yourself to death and let your inheritance and reputation fall to ruin."

Henry blinked. Bastin didn't know. Ottilie had never divulged his secret. She'd kept the truth from her husband out of loyalty to him.

"She's with child again," Bastin said, "and healthy as she is, I fear the stress of worrying about you might be too much for her."

Henry dropped his hand from the doorknob.

"It's early, but the doctor has confirmed she is with child." Bastin clutched the back of his neck. "And she insists on teaching until the pregnancy becomes visible. She says it is bad to teach the girls that a woman becomes useless the minute she's with child. You know her; she's stubborn and independent and being married hasn't changed that about her."

A wave of shame washed over Henry. He'd put his cousin in an unimaginably cruel position; by forcing her to keep this secret from Bastin—in effect—she was made to lie to her husband. He closed the study door. *It's time Bastin knew the truth.*

"Sit, and I'll explain everything." He slipped the laudanum bottle into his pocket, stumbled to the settee, and sat down, but Bastin remained standing.

"Well," he said, crossing his arms.

"First, you must promise to forgive Ottilie for not telling you herself."

"Not telling me herself?" Bastin sunk onto his chair like a ship slowly going down with the storm, then. "Are you saying my wife is hiding something from me?"

Henry pressed his palms together. "Yes, but it's not her secret; it's mine."

Jack narrowed his eyes and frowned before saying, "Go on."

Henry closed his eyes and took a deep breath before speaking. "Two years ago, Ottilie and I went to Oxfordshire to see her stepfather."

"I remember. That is when Ottilie discovered the truth about her real father."

"Exactly. Her stepfather confirmed what my mother had told Ottilie. Her father had not died when she was three but was confined to a madhouse after contracting syphilis. He was a heavy drinker and a philanderer with little discretion as to whom he—."

"Yes, I'm aware of all that," Bastin interjected.

"Well, in 1844, Ottilie's mama fell deathly ill, and my mother traveled from London to be near her sister."

"I thought they were estranged because she disapproved of her sister's marriage." Bastin frowned.

"Our grandfather did, and that is when Ottilie's parents were relegated to Oxfordshire, but they weren't wholly estranged. My grandfather supported them financially, and my mama still corresponded regularly with her sister. And, at least on that one occasion, she traveled to Oxfordshire for an extended stay. The estrangement came after that visit…" Henry closed his eyes.

"Are you going to continue?" Bastin's voice revealed his impatience.

"While my aunt lay in her sickbed, her husband engaged in a liaison with her sister—my mother."

"Good God!" Bastin stood up and ran a hand through his thick, black curls. "The prim and proper Lady Stokeford? Hater of poets—" He laughed out loud.

"I'm glad you think it funny," Henry said.

"I'm sorry," Bastin stifled his laugh. "It's so incredibly ironic."

"I'm aware." Nausea crept into Henry's throat.

"Well, now it's making more sense. No wonder she hated me. Ottilie said it was because of her father, which seemed a bit extreme even for your mama. But now, her virulent hatred for creatives makes sense. In her eyes, they are all depraved and guilty of debauchery." He paced the room. "The hypocrite! Does she take no responsibility for her actions? A liaison with her brother-in-law while her sister lay deathly ill?"

Henry watched him, vaguely aware that he should defend his mother but unable to justify doing so. Everything Bastin said was correct.

"And she escaped without consequence and then proceeded to spend the rest of her life judging and condemning others?" He laughed. "The Earl of Stokeford is a bigger fool than I thought. If it weren't for you and the damage it would do to your reputation, I'd not hesitate to inform the earl that the picture of manners he married is no more than a harpy!"

"It wasn't without consequence," Henry said quietly.

"What?" Bastin turned to Henry, his face blank as if his brain refused to comprehend what Henry's words implied. "What do you mean?"

"Three weeks after my mother returned to London—and her husband—she discovered that she was with child."

Bastin's eyes widened. "You?"

Henry nodded. "So, you see Bastin, your wife might not be my cousin at all. In fact, she might be—in fact, she probably *is*—my sister."

"Ottilie never said anything." Bastin dropped back into his chair as if he was too shaken to remain standing.

"I made her promise. I know a husband and wife should have no secrets, but this is a very serious matter involving my title, as you know, and if it ever gets out—"

"Ottilie knows I would never tell anyone! Are you saying my wife doesn't trust me?"

"No! I'm saying it wasn't her secret to tell. And I think she didn't want my destruction on her conscience."

"What do you mean?" He stared at Henry, still flummoxed.

"Don't you see? My whole life has been a lie, and Ottilie wanted me to have at least one person who was true—one person in the world I could trust. So don't blame her for keeping this secret. It's my fault. I know it must have killed her to keep this from you, and that's why I'm telling you myself." Henry ran a hand through his hair. "I honestly thought she'd told you. When you said—when I realized that you didn't know—I knew I owed it to her to tell you and take that burden away from her."

"I agree it's a horror story, but you can't be sure that the late Lord Hudsyn isn't your father. Your mother was home three weeks before discovering she was with child, so it isn't certain."

"That is why I live in limbo, unable to give up my title, which might rightly belong to me, and unable to embrace it in the likely event it does not."

"Can you not see how self-destructive that is?" He shook his head. "Of course, you can't. Of all people, I should understand. I know what it is like to be caught in a downward spiral of injustice."

"The difference is that you could put things right. You

avenged yourself and got your inheritance returned to you. I never can."

"I got my inheritance and life returned to me, but I also lost years that I can never reclaim. I had to accept that there was nothing I could do about that, and you must accept that you can do nothing about events that occurred before you were born. You are Lord Hudsyn, so you may as well honor your father's legacy by honoring his title."

"Do you think I don't know as much!" Henry clutched his forehead. "I've tried, but it only works for a short time, and then the thoughts creep back in my head—the ones that tell me I am a fraud, a usurper, the child of a degenerate who cuckolded my papa?"

"So, what if you are?"

Henry jerked upright.

"That degenerate you speak of is Ottilie's papa, and it hasn't diminished her in your eyes. She is the most honorable, gifted woman I have ever encountered, and I dare say you will agree."

"It's not the same." Henry averted his gaze. Bastin didn't understand. He'd lived many different lives, but Henry only knew one. And he'd lost his identity.

"But it is the same." Bastin strode forward and sat next to Henry. "You simply can't see it from where you're standing. What you need is a change."

Henry turned to face his cousin's husband. "What are you talking about? Are you saying I should run away to the continent like my mother did for twenty years?"

"No, that's too self-indulgent. You need to do something for someone else and take the focus off yourself."

"Like what?"

"Come and live with us for a while. Spend some time with little Alice, and Violet will put you to work giving lessons at the college. She runs charity lessons twice a week in the evenings. It's basic reading and writing for girls who've had very poor or very little schooling. It's rewarding work, and these women are grateful to be given a chance. Why they haven't yet made school mandatory in this country, I'll never understand."

"I'm not fit company; it won't work."

"What you mean is you'd rather lie around, filling your throat with brandy and feeling sorry for yourself while my pregnant wife frets for your safety."

Henry sighed. How could he argue when Ottilie's health and happiness depended on him?

"Very well," he conceded. "I'll come. My valet will need a day to ready my things. I'll ride in my own carriage, so you can head back home to Ottilie."

"No, you'll come back on the train with me. Your valet and coachman can bring your luggage and carriage separately if you like, but I'm not leaving here without you. I promised Ottilie I'd bring you back with me, and so I shall."

Henry opened his mouth to protest, but Bastin cut him off.

"You don't wish to disappoint her, do you?"

Henry slumped into his chair. Ottilie was the only person he wished never to disappoint, but he was afraid it was too late for that.

CHAPTER SEVEN

And out of the cups of the heavy flowers
She emptied the rain of the thunder-showers.

—Percy Bysshe Shelley, *The Sensitive Plant*

Greyson Manor, Kent

Bankrupt Viscount Scorned by Merchant's Daughter

The bold letters in the *Kentish Times* caught Henry's eye as he entered the dining room where Bastin and Ottilie breakfasted.

"You're up bright and early this morning," Ottilie said.

"That's because I haven't slept yet." Henry ran a hand through his hair. "It seems sobriety is killing my sleep patterns."

"It's what happens when you've overindulged for months on end. But it will get better." Bastin kept his tone light, but Henry did not miss the warning behind his voice.

On their way to Greyson Manor, Bastin had laid down his "rules of conduct" for Henry.

"Under no circumstances are you to become inebriated while in my home. I don't expect you to give up drinking but brooding about something beyond your control and drowning yourself in brandy has to end. I know what it's like to be eaten up by resentment and anger, but you need a plan, or you will remain stuck."

"Well, I can hardly use your methods of revenge. One cannot cuckold and duel one's mother like you did to avenge yourself against your uncle." Henry referred purposely to this dark time in his friend's history by reminding Bastin that his life had once revolved around wreaking havoc on the man who'd stripped him of his identity, indentured him to an American slave owner, and usurped his inheritance.

"No, you certainly cannot, nor would you, were you given the chance. You and I are different creatures, Hudsyn. I know you. Angry though you are, you don't want to inflict pain on your mother or anyone else. Yet, you punish yourself. You couldn't live with yourself if you destroyed someone else's life, yet you are quite content to destroy your own. And that perplexes me. It goes against human nature."

"It feels as though I'm living someone else's life. As though I were an imposter."

"I know what it feels like to be furious at the world, to rage at the unfairness of it all, but you've got to fight. I've seen men claw their way out of the worst situations. You need a plan that doesn't involve self-flagellation. Use the next week to sober up and think about it. If you don't have a solution after that, I'm putting you to work."

Now, Bastin glanced at Ottilie as if reminding Henry of his earlier warning.

Henry responded with a slight nod. Bastin had used the only person in the world who Henry cared about to bring him to his senses. He would not intentionally cause his cousin stress and compromise her health—especially now that she was with child—so he had no choice but to do as Bastin asked.

"You are missing the London gossip, I see," Ottilie said, bringing him back to the present.

Henry looked down; he was still clutching the newspaper. He picked it up. *The Canterbury Journal* lay underneath.

Daughter of Confectionary Giant, Bernard Leonard, Shuns Viscount for Mysterious Lover

Henry read the headline and smiled to himself as he poured tea into his cup.

"What are you smiling about?" Ottilie asked.

"I know the betrothed of the young lady who is the subject of those headlines. Lord Craventhorp. He's a cruel, arrogant man. It looks like he finally got what he deserved." Henry seated himself next to his cousin.

"Craventhorp? Isn't he the one you engaged in fisticuffs with?" Ottilie picked up *The Canterbury Journal* and frowned as she scanned the article.

"How do you know about that?"

"We had a letter from Hobsworth," Bastin said. "He was worried about you."

Damn him! So that's what had prompted Ottilie's concern.

"He shouldn't have done that," Henry said, making a mental note to tell Hobsworth off the next time he saw him. "It was a minor scuffle. I've known Craventhorp since Eton, and he's always been a bad sort. I tend to steer clear of him, but Hobsworth tolerates him, so I've found myself forced into his company on more than one occasion this year."

"What was the skirmish about?" Ottilie continued to press Henry for information. "Did it have anything to do with this young lady?" She gestured to the newspaper.

Henry massaged his jaw, thinking how best to answer his cousin. Engaging in fisticuffs at a bawdy house wasn't something that needed mentioning, and his memory of what had happened in Lady Dawley's Garden was fuzzy at best. So, he said, "Craventhorp treats women poorly. It's no wonder the young lady ran off with someone else. I pity the woman who eventually marries him."

"If he's so terrible, why does Hobsworth tolerate him?" Ottilie asked.

"To keep the peace. I think he's afraid of crossing Craventhorp and causing trouble. Lord Stokeford restricts his funds anytime he dares step out of line."

"And how is Lady Stokeford?" Ottilie asked, changing the subject.

"She's Lady Hudsyn with power," Henry said dryly.

Ottilie laughed and rose from the table. "Oh, Henry, I've missed you. But I'm afraid we'll have to continue our conversation later. Jack and I must get Alice and make haste if we're to make it to the college on time."

Bastin patted his mouth with a napkin and pushed back his chair. "I'll get her, and we'll meet you outside." He kissed Ottilie's cheek, patted Henry on the back, and left the room.

"Alice too? Isn't she a bit young to be teaching?" he teased.

"I'm pleased you're getting your sense of humor back." Ottilie smiled and opened one of the silver serving dishes to scoop scrambled eggs onto Henry's plate. "Alice stays in the nursery with Violet's little ones while I teach, and Jack writes in his office. It's the only way to see Alice and each other throughout the day."

"That sounds too good to be true."

"It's ideal." Ottilie opened the second serving dish. "We're lucky. Since our family operates and funds the school, we make our own rules."

"Don't do that," Henry said as Ottilie heaped bacon on his plate. "I am quite capable of dishing my own food. You need to hurry."

"I know you are, but I like to do it." Ottilie put the plate in front of him. "And I worry about you. You've grown too thin."

"And you've turned into a proper mama," Henry said affectionately.

Ottilie smiled and planted a kiss on his cheek. "You should take a walk today. The weather looks lovely, and the fresh air and exercise will do you good."

"That sounds rather nice. I think I shall—now off with you!"

Ottilie kissed Henry again before leaving the dining room.

Once alone, Henry turned his full attention to the newspaper. No likeness of Leonard's daughter accompanied the article, which made perfect sense to Henry. No doubt, Mr. Leonard wanted to avoid a public manhunt, which would lead to his being besieged by people, claiming they'd found his daughter and demanding a reward.

He sipped his tea. Had it been Annabel Leonard who'd collided with him in the garden that night? He supposed it must have been, since Craventhorp had said he was going to Lady Dawley's expressly to meet his fiancée. Henry tried to remember the young lady's face, but his mind had been blurry with drink that night, and his memory remained the same. All he could recall was the tension he'd felt in her petite frame, and Craventhorp's shadowy figure watching her from a distance.

Yet the article alleged that Miss Leonard had eloped with her lover. Could it be true? Could that young, terrified woman have taken such a bold and defiant step? Or was the truth more nefarious? He certainly hoped not, but the thought of a young woman humiliating Craventhorp and getting away with it seemed unlikely. He'd bruised the harlot's cheek and probably other parts of her body not visible as well, and he'd claimed she deserved it. Of course, he could not strike Miss Leonard in public; hence he'd let her run off that night. But things may have gone too far if he'd caught her alone in private.

When they'd been together at Eton, Craventhorp used to torture insects and small animals. He'd enjoyed watching them writhe in pain. And he had done the same to the junior boys once he got older. Not everyone realized his propensity for cruelty, however, for he also could be deceptively charming. And that, together with his status in society and striking features, had been enough to make most people dismiss his unsavory behavior. But these articles suggested that the viscount's charm hadn't wormed its way into the hearts and minds of reporters, who harped on Craventhorp's financial problems and suggested that the young lady felt she deserved a better match. Henry chuckled. *Craventhorp must be fuming.*

A maid entered the dining room, and Henry saw her hovering about the table. Bastin and Ottilie kept servants out of necessity but did not follow society's rules for their management. There weren't any ranks amongst their servants. Aside from the nanny, coachmen, and cook, the housekeepers shared all duties, from answering the door to serving meals and cleaning. Ottilie had a lady's maid, mostly because she was often in a rush, but Bastin continued to dress by himself as he always had.

Henry folded the paper and smiled at the maid.

"Can I get you anything else, sir? Some fresh eggs, perhaps?"

"No, these are delicious." Henry picked up his fork and scooped up a mouthful of eggs to prove his point.

The maid curtseyed and disappeared. Henry forced himself to eat the rest of his now-cold breakfast, knowing his cousin would likely receive a report from her servants regarding his activities that day. He washed down his last bite with a swallow of tea and pushed back his chair. Tucking the newspaper under his arm, he retrieved his coat, hat, and umbrella before exiting the house.

Ottilie wanted him to get fresh air, so that is what he would do. Seeing his cousin happy was the one positive thing in Henry's life, and he'd do all he could to ensure her continued contentment.

THE LADIES' COLLEGE sat nestled on acres of private green land about a mile from the bustling market town of Canterbury. The area was quiet, undeveloped, and unaffected by the noise of steam engines since it was built far enough from the Crab and Winkle rail route which carried passengers between Whitstable and Canterbury daily. Annabel had made a point of rising an hour early each day since the start of the new term, so she could walk the mile from her home in Orange Street in time to watch the young ladies leave the residence halls and flood the green yard as they made their way to their morning lectures.

On this particular morning, she settled in her usual spot on the grassy hillside opposite the college and watched the day students arrive and converge with the boarders as they filtered from the left wing of the stone building onto the surrounding lawn. As happened every day she watched, some walked in groups and kept their books tucked under their arms, while others read as they walked. She'd never get tired of seeing them. In fact, she'd never seen anything quite like it before, and it energized her. These women were free and happy. They did not need to hide their books, hold conversations in secret, or fret about concealing their thirst for knowledge.

Quite the opposite.

A woman clad in black exited the right wing of the building and crossed the lawn, her black robe flying behind her like the feathers of a magnificent bird. She nodded at the girls as she passed them, and they waved in response.

The headmistress!

To think that a *woman* could don an academic robe and command respect like the headmasters' of boys' schools made Annabel want to weep with joy. It gave her hope. Who knew such a life existed for women? How had they managed it? Perhaps, all papas weren't like hers—demanding their daughters marry titles. Perhaps their papas wanted them to *learn*—even encouraged it.

She watched until the building had admitted the last of the students, shutting them inside its walls of knowledge, leaving the green lawn empty and silent. A yearning rose inside her. She envisioned herself racing across the grass to the heavy wooden door, which remained firmly shut despite her pounding. Such a school surely cost money she did not possess. Annabel opened the new copy of *Wuthering Heights* she'd recently managed to obtain and settled into reading, a ritual she followed every morning, weather permitting.

APPROXIMATELY AN HOUR and thirty minutes later, Annabel closed her book, marking her place with a scrap of silk that the seamstress with whom she lodged had given her. Then she stood and started down the slope to make her way back to Canterbury. From the hill, she could see the spires of Canterbury's famous cathedral peeping through the clouds.

Annabel smiled. Although lacking the luxuries she'd been accustomed to all her life, she would not swap her new existence for her old. Life as a young widow in Canterbury had afforded her the freedom she'd craved, and that was worth more to her than a thousand luxuries.

Starting down the country path home, a route she preferred to the main road down which both pedestrians and carts trundled, Annabel thought about the possibilities that lay before her. She'd been in Canterbury a little over six weeks and had already started looking to her future. Although she'd paid three month's rent in advance and had an additional month's rent saved from the sale of her hair, she understood that she'd need a skill of some sort if she hoped to survive on her own indefinitely, so she'd offered herself up as an apprentice to Mrs. Taylor, who'd readily accepted the help. But her sewing proved so hopeless that she settled on assisting her by serving the customers, taking their sewing orders, tending to any complaints, and collecting the money due to Mrs. Taylor. Annabel hoped it would provide her with the experience she needed to get a paying job in a proper shop one day. She liked the idea of working in a shop like her mama had done before she'd met her papa. She'd also decided to attend the free evening classes offered to working women by the ladies' college, which were to begin next week. Those were her plans for the near coming future, but she believed there was more to come—she didn't know what exactly, but surely, there had to be something or someone special out there—just for her.

Annabel was so deep in thought that she didn't see the gentleman coming up the path in the opposite direction until she collided with him, causing him to drop his newspaper in the mud.

"Heavens! I'm so terribly sorry!" Annabel bent to retrieve the paper and then froze. The headline glared at her from the mud-splattered page. *Bankrupt Viscount Scorned by Merchant's Daughter*

She jerked her hand back as if the paper had suddenly grown teeth.

"Don't touch it." The gentleman, a smartly dressed, well-spoken young man, picked up the newspaper using two fingers and eyed Annabel. "It's ruined, I'm afraid."

"No, it is still decipherable." She snatched the newspaper from the man's fingers and shook it. Splatters of mud flew in the air, and the gentleman leapt back to escape them.

"Don't worry about trying to clean it, truly. I've finished reading it."

"I don't mind a little dirt." Annabel clutched the page and attempted to read between the mud splatters. *A source close to Mr. Leonard...will spare no cost...searching for his daughter...*

"May I at least help you with that?" The gentleman eyed her with a puzzled expression.

"No, thank you. It's perfectly fine now." She attempted to keep the panic from her voice. It had been weeks since she'd run away from home. Why was her story suddenly a headline? Papa had kept silent for so long. She'd been confident he would suppress the story. He wasn't the type of man who could tolerate gossip in the papers about his private matters. He'd want to take control of the situation himself. She was certain he had private inspectors searching for her at this very moment. Perhaps, then, one of the servants told someone, or went to the newspapers—

"If you would be so kind as to point me in the direction of the main road," the gentleman's voice interrupted her thoughts, "I'll leave you to your reading."

She eyed him. He was too proper and too upper-class to be wandering about in the muddy fields of Kent. He looked as if he should have a fancy carriage or at least a fine horse to take him wherever he wanted to go. He was handsome too. She was especially drawn to his clear blue eyes and the dimple that marked his square jaw. She would have asked him where he'd come from and where he was going, but she was too anxious to get back to the newspaper article.

"I'm not from Canterbury, you see," he explained. "I'm visiting my cousin and decided to take a walk after a quick visit to the cathedral. But I veered off the main road, and now I can't seem to get my bearings."

"It's that way." She stuck out her left arm to indicate the direction without looking up from the newspaper. *Mr. Leonard...will spare no expense in searching...daughter, nor...limit his search—*

"Thank you," he said.

"Good day, sir," Annabel replied, giving the newspaper another shake before attempting to reread the sentence.

...will spare no expense in searching...daughter, nor...limit the search to Scotland.

Annabel's heart quickened. *Papa does not like to lose or be outwitted. He'd no doubt already scoured all of Scotland for her, and now he would search every corner of England.*

She squinted to make sense of another smudged sentence when a great rumble sounded overhead, and a raindrop splattered onto the page. She lowered her newspaper and looked up to see a black cloud frowning over the horizon.

The weather was so beautiful earlier—ideal for a walk—where had this ominous cloud come from?

As if in response to her thought, a great deluge suddenly began to pour from the sky. Raindrops assaulted her body, falling so hard and fast that she had no time to run or seek shelter. The newspaper began to disintegrate into a soggy mess in her hand as she looked about, wondering if she should risk running through the mud to take shelter under a tree or find some other place. She looked wildly about for something—anything—nearby. But the downpour was so heavy, she could barely see. She dropped the newspaper and crouched, buried her head in her arms, and prayed for the lashing to end.

Seconds later, it did.

Annabel straightened and as she rose she found herself stand-ing beside the flaxen-haired gentleman and under the shelter of his wide umbrella. He stood so close to her that their arms almost touched, but he had little choice. The rain came down in a torrent around them and stepping out from under the brolly even an inch in any direction would soak him—or her—through.

"I gather you forgot your umbrella," he said, pleasantly, as if talking over a cup of tea.

Annabel laughed. "Whatever gave you that idea?"

CHAPTER EIGHT

From rainbow clouds there flow not
Drops so bright to see
As from thy presence showers a rain of melody.

—Percy Bysshe Shelley, *To a Skylark*

EVEN HALF-SOAKED WITH her hair falling out of its pins, she was beautiful, Henry thought, admiring the young lady's piercing green eyes and olive complexion.

She must have caught him looking at her because she touched a dripping strand of her hair and said, "I'm certain I look like a drowned cat at present."

"You don't," Henry said, though he hadn't meant to say it out loud.

She smiled and started to remove the pins from her hair. "I'm sorry, but I cannot abide this dripping about my face a minute longer." There must have been hundreds of pins in her hair, and she used both hands to get each one out, which left her reticule dangling from the crook of her arm. Henry wondered if he should offer to hold it for her but decided against it, choosing instead to avert his gaze, and feeling as though he had wandered into the lady's intimate space.

"That's better," she said, and he looked to see her squeezing the moisture from her locks—her short locks. Henry could not help but stare at the way her dark hair hovered awkwardly above her shoulders in a rude cut. All the women he had ever known, even servant girls, wore their hair long. This was different, and unique, and didn't detract from her beauty in any way.

In fact, he realized, it only made her more alluring.

Unaware of his perusal, she continued to fuss with her hair, deftly twisting the now-drained locks behind her head and started reinserting the hairpins, fishing them from her pocket where she'd stored them, and working to re-secure her hair.

"That feels better," she said when she'd finished. Even without the aid of a mirror, she had done an excellent job securing her hair so that its choppy length was no longer detectable.

"Now, if you can just escort me to the nearest tree, you can be on your way."

"A tree?" He said, perplexed.

"For shelter."

"Mightn't I escort you home? It won't be any trouble."

"But you were walking in the opposite direction," she said. "I don't want to make you walk back to Canterbury for no reason. I'm sure the storm will end soon."

"I'm farther from my lodgings than I thought, so it's best if I return to Canterbury and get the train or hail a cab to take me home."

Henry was lying. He'd been on his way to surprise Ottilie at the college, having asked directions in the village. But that plan didn't seem as appealing anymore; instead walking back to Canterbury sounded excellent. Hell, he'd walk to *London* if he could do so huddled under an umbrella with this delightful young woman.

"I suppose you may accompany me as long as the rain lasts," she said hesitantly.

"That's very kind of you," Henry said, and he meant it.

She gave him a shrug. "Sorry, I don't mean to sound ungrateful. It's very chivalrous of you to share your umbrella with me."

"I think the chivalrous thing to do would be to let the lady have the umbrella all to herself, but I'm afraid I am not quite that knightly."

"I wouldn't hear of it," she said. "That is taking chivalry a step too far, in my opinion." She laughed then, a delightful, sweet laugh. "But I'm afraid I must insist on knowing your name if you are to escort me home," she said.

"Henry Hudsyn," he said, and then after a slight pause added, "*Mr.* Henry Hudsyn," deciding that for now, he just wanted to forget his title and become just a plain *Mister.*

"Mrs. Crawford," she said.

"Mrs. Crawford?" The words escaped Henry's throat like a cry of disappointment.

"You sound surprised," she said.

He was—surprised *and* disappointed. "Not at all," he said. "I'm pleased to meet you, Mrs. Crawford. I hope Mr. Crawford will not object to a stranger escorting you home."

"He would not,' she said, and Henry could not help but notice the bemused look on her face. "I'm a widow." *How deplorable of me to feel such relief at hearing these words.* "I'm sorry to hear that." He creased his brow in a genuine effort to feel grieved.

"You're wondering how such a young woman ended up a widow."

"Not at all—I mean, it's none of my business."

"I was married young, at eighteen, and six months later, my husband drowned," she said as if reciting a practiced speech. "That was two years ago, and I don't like to dwell too much on sad memories, so that is all I am going to say on the subject."

"Of course. You needn't have said anything at all." Henry dropped his gaze, somewhat uncomfortable talking about this woman's husband, though he couldn't think why. "I'm afraid it looks as though the newspaper is now truly unsalvageable."

"Oh, no!" Mrs. Crawford sounded genuinely irritated as she looked at the soaked newspaper, now integrated into the mud. "I did so want to read that interesting story about the viscount and his runaway bride."

"I could always tell you the details of the article while we make our way to Canterbury."

"Would you?" Her face brightened as though she were a child promised a bedtime story.

"It would be my pleasure," Henry said. "Shall we go?"

The torrent had subsided, but the rain had not stopped. And the threat of new clouds on the horizon promised another deluge.

"We best start for Canterbury."

"Yes," Mrs. Crawford nodded and shivered at the same time.

"May I offer you my overcoat?" Henry asked, handing her the umbrella before she could decline.

"Thank you," she said after he'd shrugged out of his overcoat and draped it over her shoulders.

"Shall we?" His gloved hand briefly closed around hers as he reached for the umbrella handle, and he felt a definite thrill race up his arm.

⇶⟩⟩⟩⟨⟨⟨⇷

THE PATH HAD become sodden and difficult to maneuver, so they made their way to Whitstable Road, which provided them with a dryer path home. Mud clogged Henry's boots and clung to his trousers. The walk was cold and uncomfortable, but Henry could think of no other place he'd rather be.

"The whole affair is quite scandalous," he said, delivering on his promise to tell Mrs. Crawford the story of the runaway bride that had appeared in the newspaper. "You've heard of Leonard Confectionery, I assume?"

"Of course, who hasn't? Was Mr. Leonard's daughter the one set to marry a viscount?"

"Indeed, a rather mercenary viscount. Not a pleasant man, as I understand it."

"Did the article say as much?" she asked.

"Not in so many words, but I think I read something to that

effect in the gossip columns," Henry lied. He had a strong desire to distance himself from the whole sordid affair, and so decided not to reveal his connection to Craventhorp.

"Perhaps that is why she eloped with her true love to Scotland—I managed to read that part," Mrs. Crawford clarified. "Have they named her lover?"

"Not to my knowledge, but they'll be scouring the country for both of them. If she got married in Scotland, her father can do little about it. Scottish law does not require parental consent for a girl over the age of twelve."

"How scandalous. I'm surprised an important man like Mr. Leonard made this information public."

"I doubt he did so willingly," Henry said. "It was most likely a servant or another insider who gossiped or sold the information. Of course, it could be that Mr. Leonard has grown desperate. He claims his daughter was kidnapped and the letter forged. They didn't mention when she disappeared; it could have been weeks ago. Who knows how long he has been searching while keeping the story quiet."

"Perhaps she is dead," Mrs. Crawford suggested.

The comment struck Henry like an unexpected blow as the image of a frightened young woman, trembling in his arms came to mind. *What if he killed her, and I did nothing to help her? I saw the malice on Craventhorp's face that night, and I knew what he was capable of, yet all I could do in my drunken state was make a fool of myself.*

"Do you think she might be dead?" Mrs. Crawford asked.

Her tone sounded hopeful, as though Miss Leonard's death would be an exciting turn of events. "That's a rather morbid thing to say," he snapped.

"Do you mean for a young lady?"

"For anyone. Why would you say such a thing?"

"I didn't say that I hoped she was dead; I said she *might* be dead. If she was kidnapped, that is."

Henry frowned, trying to shake off the memory.

"I am sorry if I shocked you, but the reality is that life can be difficult for women, even inside the sheltered walls of Mayfair and Belgravia."

He swallowed rising nausea in his throat and endeavored to change the subject. "Have you been to London? You sound as though—"

"No," she interjected. "I like to read, that is all. "Brontë, Collins, Dickens."

"Novels!" His sense of relief escaped in the form of a laugh. *She's got fiction in mind, but stories are purposely sensationalized, and quite different from real life. There is no reason to think that Miss Leonard isn't somewhere safe, living happily with the love of her life.* He swallowed the discomfort rising in his throat, unable to suppress the knowledge that this scenario was more fanciful than the notion that a young female runaway lay dead and discarded.

"Do you dislike novels, Mr. Hudsyn?"

"I have no objection to them."

"Perhaps you object to women reading novels because they encourage morbid thoughts?" She eyed him, and Henry knew she was testing him.

He laughed. "I'd be in serious trouble with the women in my life if I disapproved of their reading."

"The women in your life?"

"By that, I mean my cousin. She's the only woman..." He found himself fixated on the freckles that sprinkled her pert nose and left his sentence dangling mid-air. "What I mean to say is that she's very independent, and I respect her for that."

"That's rather enlightened of you. Most men—I mean—*some* men think women incapable of controlling their emotions and making decisions for themselves."

"I'm not one of those men." Henry smiled. "My cousin has proven herself far more capable and resilient than me." He cleared his throat and rubbed the back of his neck with his free hand. He'd let his mask slip and revealed a sliver of the shame that lived permanently inside him. He laughed with a forced attempt to regain the safety of his mask. "I hope you intend to apologize," he teased. "We still have a good way to go, and I've got a mind to keep this umbrella all to myself."

The corners of her lips curved into a smile. "You have my sincerest apolo—oh, look, I do believe the rain is stopping." She stepped out from under the umbrella. "It appears Zeus doesn't think you warrant an apology."

Henry tilted his umbrella back and peeked at the sky. The rain had indeed stopped, and the sun began to emerge from behind clouds.

"That's English weather for you." He turned his umbrella upside down and shook the wet drops from its silk exterior.

They neared Westgate, and the road previously devoid of people suddenly turned busy. Men and women came bustling out of the shops and buildings that lined the street, rushing to make up for the precious minutes the downpour had stolen from them.

"I should hurry back. Mrs. Taylor, my landlady, is a seamstress, and she has a small shop. I help her, so she'll be waiting for me."

"Allow me to escort you." He didn't want to let go of her—not yet.

"That's not necessary but thank you. It isn't far, and the station is just behind you. Don't you need to catch the train home?"

Henry didn't want to go home. He wanted to keep talking to Mrs. Crawford, and he was about to say that he desired to explore Canterbury farther before catching the train when an open wagon rolled to a stop beside them.

"Mrs. Crawford," the driver, a broad-shouldered, man who looked to be about thirty, called out to her.

"Mr. Trawler," she said. "What a pleasant surprise."

"I'm on my way to the market." He eyed Henry. "May I save you the trouble of walking?"

"Yes," she answered without hesitation, and Henry felt an absurd stab of jealousy. Moments ago, she'd refused his offer to walk her home, yet she eagerly accepted this man's offer to escort her.

Mr. Trawler hopped down to help Mrs. Crawford ascend. He was a tall man with the rugged look of one who worked outdoors. Brown curls, lightened by the sun, peeked out from under his head cap, and his muscular build indicated that he spent much of his time doing manual labor. His wagon smelled strongly of fish, so Henry fathomed that the man was a fishmonger.

"This gentleman is Mr. Henry Hudsyn," Mrs. Crawford said as Mr. Trawler approached. "I was out for a walk, and he kindly offered me shelter under his umbrella."

"Pleased to make your acquaintance, Mr. Trawler." Henry doffed his top hat in greeting.

Mr. Trawler reciprocated by doffing his tweed cap while eyeing Henry with the suspicion of a jealous lover, and Henry wondered how the man fit into Mrs. Crawford's life. Mr. Trawler turned to help Mrs. Crawford before climbing in and settling beside her. She waved as the cart horse pulled them away. A strange hollowness settled in Henry's stomach as he watched the wagon trundle through Westgate's stone archway.

I'm not ready to go back to Greyson Manor. Henry's fingers closed around one of the buttons on his waistcoat and twisted hard. The button popped off into his hand, and Henry smiled.

I'm in dire need of a seamstress. He tossed the button up in the air and caught it again. *I wonder if someone in the village can direct me to the home of Mrs. Taylor.*

"WHO IS THAT man?" Nate asked as soon as they passed through Westgate.

"What do you mean? Annabel said with a laugh. "I just introduced you to him. His name is Mr. Hudsyn, and he sheltered me under his umbrella."

"What I mean to say is—*who* is Mr. Hudsyn? How do you

know that he doesn't work for your papa?"

"What?" Annabel's body tensed. "How could that be? I just met him by accident on my walk home. He wasn't even walking in the same direction as me."

"Don't find that a bit strange? A gentleman of that sort walking on a country road by himself? Surely, a man dressed in a fine suit like the one he wore owns a carriage to go with his grand estate and title."

"He doesn't have a title. He introduced himself as Mr. Hudsyn, remember."

"Exactly. Perhaps you are used to seeing gentlemen dressed as finely as he was, so you've become numb to it, but I haven't. And I'm telling you, he is no ordinary gentleman."

"Perhaps he needed fresh air and wanted to take a walk."

Nate sighed. "You're too trusting, lass. Did you forget that you're the daughter of one of the richest men in England?"

"What are you saying?"

"How do you know that gentleman wasn't following you?"

"Because he was coming from the opposite direction. He couldn't have been following me."

Nate grunted. "Was this the first time you walked that road?"

"No, I do it every day. I like to watch the students at the ladies' college. I like it when the bell rings, and they all cross the yard and make their way to their morning classes. It's exciting."

Nate frowned at her. "You wouldn't find school exciting if you'd been bitten by the master's cane as many times as I have."

Annabel laughed. "It's not that sort of school. It's a sort of university for young ladies. They award certificates of knowledge in all kinds of subjects like mathematics, science, and classical literature. They even offer free classes to working women twice a week."

Nate snorted. "Sounds like a waste of time. I don't know any working man or woman who needs university. It's a place for bored rich folk to while away the hours." He eyed her. "So, you walk the same way every morning, do you?"

"Yes, I suppose I've established a bit of a routine," Annabel said. "It's helped me settle in here."

"It also explains why your Mr. Fancy Suit knew you'd be coming down that very road." Nate turned off the High Street.

She hadn't thought about that. Annabel pressed her lips together. What if Nate was correct? She had to be more careful.

"Did you say anything that could give you away?"

"Of course not!" Annabel remained silent about the discussion she and Henry had about the newspaper article. *Was it merely a coincidence that he carried a newspaper that headlined my story?*

She swallowed the fear that formed in her throat. "How could my father or Lord Craventhorp possibly know I'm in Canterbury? They think I've eloped to Scotland!"

"Rich men have eyes everywhere." Nate turned onto Orange Street and pulled the reins, signaling his cart horse to stop outside the half-timber building that served as both shop and lodging for the Taylor family.

Annabel remained in the carriage, her mind fraught. Would she never be free? Was she going to have to hide for the rest of her life?

"I don't mean to scare you," Nate said gruffly. "But you must be careful. Your father won't give up that easily. They'll still be searching. Remember. if you're caught, my life and Stella's, for that matter, will be—"

"Never. I'll never betray you or Stella."

"You might not have to. Like I said, eyes everywhere."

"Have you had a letter from Stella? Is she safe?" Annabel pressed her palms together.

"It's too early. She'll need to wait until the story dies down before it's safe to write."

Annabel sighed. "I miss her. Are you certain she's safe?"

"She's safe. They'll go looking for her, but they won't find anything. There's only contempt for Mr. Leonard where they'll search. He denies his heritage and looks down on his people. They won't take his money to betray their own."

Annabel sighed. It was the truth. When her mama died, her papa turned against everything and everyone who reminded him of her—including his own daughter.

"Give this to Mrs. Taylor." Nate reached behind and produced a parcel of wrapped fish that he handed to Annabel. "You ladies deserve some fresh oysters after a long day's work."

"Thank you." Annabel took the parcel and climbed down from the wagon. She waved to Nate before pushing open the wooden door to the seamstress shop and stepping inside. A small bell fixed to the top of the door chimed as she entered, and Mrs. Taylor looked up from her sewing and smiled.

"There you are. I was worried about you being out in that rainstorm."

"I'm fine. Just a little wet, that's all." She smiled at baby Rupert, who sat on a small blanket next to his mother's chair and chewed on a doll made from brightly colored fabric. He gurgled and kicked his chubby legs when he saw Annabel coming toward him.

"Mr. Trawler gave us some oysters for supper."

"How wonderful," Mrs. Taylor took the parcel and pressed her nose to it. "Freshly caught. What a treat!"

Annabel bent down and scooped Rupert up in her arms. Still clutching his rag doll, Rupert squealed and kicked his chubby legs as she lifted him from the blanket. She settled next to the fire and bounced the little boy on her knee. "Would you care to come with me to the ladies' college tomorrow morning for the free lesson?"

"That sounds wonderful, but I cannot. With Rupert's papa out at sea, I must work every day except Sundays when we go to church. He's a growing boy, after all." She smiled at her son.

Guilt pricked Annabel's conscience. "Perhaps I should stay too," she offered.

"No, go and enjoy yourself." Mrs. Taylor pulled a thread of green through the garment on her lap. "I can manage. Rupert's a good boy, and you have helped me so much already. All that, and your sweetheart brings us fresh fish for our supper." She smiled.

"He's not my sweetheart."

"Maybe not. But a man doesn't bring fresh fish for a lady unless he's fixin' to marry her."

"He's simply helping the widow of his friend." Annabel averted her gaze. She hated having to lie to Mrs. Taylor.

Rupert squirmed, dropped his doll, and clawed at Annabel's chest. "I think he's hungry," she said, kissing the child's rosy cheek.

"Again? Never stops eating this one." Mrs. Taylor took the baby from Annabel and kissed his forehead. Rupert arched his back and shrieked "Okay, I hear you." She smiled and shook her head at Annabel. "This little boy knows what he wants."

"Go on and feed him. I'll be here if Mrs. Moffat comes to collect her dress."

"Thank you, Luv." Mrs. Taylor carried Rupert up the stairs to the rooms above where the family lodged.

Annabel hummed as she walked around the little shop, picking up bits of fabric and thread and putting them in a pile for Mrs. Taylor to sort through. Passing the mullioned window, she peered out to see if she could spot Mrs. Moffat coming down the street.

Annabel gasped and drew back from the window. Mr. Hudsyn stood across the street, watching the shop.

What is he doing here?

Nate's words echoed in her mind. *Rich men have eyes everywhere.* Her heart began to pound and her mouth dried as she realized that his suit *did* look finely made. And worse, he and that suit were supposed to be on a train home!

CHAPTER NINE

The accurate habits of thought and the intellectual polish by which the scholar is distinguished ought to be no less carefully sought in the training of women than in that of men.

—Emily Davies, *The Higher Education of Women,* (1866)

VIOLET THOMAS'S PETITE stature, plain features, and alabaster skin gave her a deceptively demure appearance. But as the headmistress of Canterbury Ladies' College, she'd proven otherwise. Improving the future for women in England through higher education was her life's passion, and she worked tirelessly to encourage her students to pursue their academic interests and to elevate her school.

Like her counterparts, many of whom had founded and funded ladies' colleges of their own, she would not rest until all the universities in England opened their doors to women and allowed them to earn degrees.

"My little Frances is the brightest child," she told Henry as they distributed ink pots and quill pens on the desks, "and when the time comes, she must have the right to earn a degree alongside her brother at any university of her choosing. My heart breaks when I think about how generations of great-minded women have been stilted and denied an education simply because of their gender. It must not continue."

"But you are making progress, are you not? Ottilie tells me women are now permitted to study at the University of London, and there is a great deal in the papers about a new women's college at Cambridge."

"Oh, yes." Violet's blue eyes sparkled. "These are promising steps in the right direction, but it's simply not enough. Women may study at the University of London and are subject to the same rigorous examinations as male students, yet still, they are not permitted to earn degrees. They must make do with a certificate. It's the same situation at Cambridge. My colleague Miss Davies, a tireless advocate for women's education, will open the college at Hitchin this month. However, her students aren't guaranteed admission to lectures. They must beg permission from the professors, who have no obligation to them." She shook her head. "I am certain they will face an uphill battle. One cannot believe the fuss made over the presence of a mere five women attending lectures at Cambridge."

"Only five!" Henry said.

"Only five." She laughed. "Still, it is Cambridge! What a miracle. There is no educator more diligent and strategic than Emily Davies."

"I'm an Oxford man," Henry said, "and I happen to know that some men are terrified women will make them look stupid if they let them into their universities."

Violet laughed. "I think you may have a point. But I remain convinced that they only agreed to let our students sit for their local examinations in the hope we would fail miserably. Fortunately, that didn't happen. Our movement has made great strides, to be sure. And each victory is a crucial step forward." Her eyes scanned the room, and her lips curved into a smile. "If someone had told me, when I first arrived in London eight years ago clutching my carpetbag, that I'd be the proud owner and headmistress of one of the finest ladies' colleges in England, I would have thought them mad."

"Yet, here you stand," Henry said.

"Correction, Lord Hudsyn, here we stand." She placed the last inkwell in her hand on the desk before her. "I was so pleased when my brother told me you'd volunteered your services today."

Henry forced a smile. He hadn't so much as volunteered to help as he had been pushed to do so by Bastin, who'd surprised him with the news that he'd offered Henry's services for the twice-weekly, free women's classes.

"It will make Ottilie happy,"' Bastin had reminded him, which was enough to convince Henry. He owed his cousin his support and wanted her and her unborn babe to remain happy and healthy. Still, the prospect of spending the next two hours in a room with a group of female students unnerved him. He didn't know the first thing about teaching, nor did he wish to spend his morning within the confines of a lecture hall when the ancient, cobbled streets of Canterbury beckoned. He'd happily spend all day perusing its gardens and shops if it meant another chance encounter with the delightful Mrs. Crawford.

"I'm afraid I may be more of a hindrance than a help. I don't have any experience with adult students—particularly ladies."

"You know more than you realize. After all, you've had plenty of experience in the classroom, as a student, that is, and our free classes aren't geared toward higher learners like the rest of our classes. They are merely a service offered to working women who hope to improve their reading and writing skills—whatever those may be. All the students have different skill levels. So, the first thing I like to do is assign them the task of writing something about themselves—there are no rules. Each student writes whatever she wishes to share and however much she can manage. Some may not even know their letters yet."

"Is it that bad?" Henry said more out of fear than ignorance.

"Unfortunately, school is not compulsory in this country. So many children, particularly girls, are kept at home to learn housework or to care for their younger siblings. And if their mamas cannot read, how can they prepare their daughters for a better future? Too many women and children are left vulnerable from a lack of education and opportunity. Thankfully there are those in power who understand the gravity of the situation and are working toward change. The National Education League wants Parliament to pass legislation to make education compulsory for all children."

"You're right." Henry ran a hand through his hair. "I'm ashamed to say I've taken my education for granted."

"No doubt. But now, you can use that education to do something meaningful for these women."

Henry thought back to his school days. His Masters had always delivered corrections with the sting of their canes. He gripped his neck. The task of teaching an adult to read seemed utterly daunting. He doubted even his degree from Oxford would be of help.

"Don't look so worried, Lord Hudsyn. As I said, the students vary in their abilities, and I will assign you to work with those who have the strongest skills. All you need to do is remember not to judge or make the students feel ashamed, lest they turn from education forever."

"In that case, I must insist you refrain from using my title in front of the students. I don't want my presence to intimidate them."

"That's a wise idea and very gracious of you." She smiled. "I think my brother was right, you will make a fine teacher."

Henry grimaced. He wasn't so sure.

Footsteps sounded in the hallway, and Violet moved toward the door. "Here they come," she said. "I typically stand by the door and greet them as they enter the classroom. As I said, it's most important that these vulnerable women feel this is a safe and comfortable learning environment."

"What will you have me do?" Henry looked around the room, suddenly seized by an urge to busy himself.

"If you'd be so kind as to collect the composition books on my podium and distribute them to the ladies as they take their seats, that would be most helpful."

"Certainly." He turned and went to the podium, half grateful for the distraction and half feeling like he'd gone from Lord of the Manor to butler or valet and recalling Bastin's words that he needed to humble himself if he hoped to change his mind set and improve his life.

That was all very well for Bastin to say now, but Henry remembered a time when their situations had been reversed, and his friend had almost let his anger and desire for revenge destroy him.

It fascinated him that the somber-minded Violet Thomas was Bastin's elder sister. The dark-eyed Byronic novelist and the once-notorious rake was the opposite of the studious and diminutive headmistress who now greeted students in her black academic robe.

He took longer than necessary to gather the composition books, shuffling them needlessly while throwing furtive glances at the room. Three or four ladies were already seated at their desks and more filtered inside, but he didn't want to step forward until Violet had returned to the front of the room and was ready to introduce him to the students. So, he pretended to busy himself with counting the composition books until he heard the door close and glanced up to see Violet making her way to the front of the room. Only then did he step forward with the composition books tucked under his arm. At that same moment, the classroom door opened again, and another young lady stepped inside.

His breath caught in his throat.

It was Mrs. Crawford.

Is my imagination playing tricks on me? He fixed his eyes on her, faintly aware that his lips had spread into a smile. The heaviness in his chest dissipated. As if awakening from a deep sleep, his nerves tingled to life.

Then he realized she wasn't smiling. She glanced at him, and her face clouded. A look of—was it fear, or disgust—came into her eyes? And it made his heart still.

She turned and placed her hand on the doorknob as if hoping to make a quick escape.

"Welcome," Violet said. "Please do take a seat." She gestured to an empty desk in the front row.

Mrs. Crawford hesitated. It appears she could not make up her mind about what to do.

"Don't fret; the class has not yet begun.," Violet assured her. "You are most welcome to join us."

It seemed that politeness won whatever mental war Mrs. Crawford had engaged in, and she walked to the front of the class, taking care to avert her gaze from Henry.

His stomach sank. What had he done to make her despise him?

Nate was right. Henry is a spy.

The shock that skittered through Annabel's veins upon seeing Mr. Hudsyn had momentarily paralyzed her. It was plain he was working for Papa or Lord Craventhorp. What other explanation could there be for his presence at the ladies' college?

Her mind had screamed at her to run, but the headmistress's welcoming words and invitation to sit down had given her pause. Annabel couldn't bring herself to disrespect a woman she so admired. Seeing no alternative, she made her way to an open seat at the front of the room and sat down.

The headmistress addressed the class, introducing first herself and then Mr. Hudsyn. Annabel purposefully kept her eyes on her desk, but her mind whirled with unanswered questions.

How did he know she'd be attending the ladies' college? Were there others watching her? Or had she mentioned her plans to him during their walk? She could not remember.

As the headmistress gave instructions to the students, Mr. Hudsyn moved toward the front of the class. Annabel shrunk back, certain he was about to grab her by the arm and haul her out of the building into Lord Craventhorp's carriage. She shuddered at the thought of the viscount's fury and how he would punish her for embarrassing him by running away.

But he only smiled at her and started distributing composition books to the students. As he approached her desk, she grabbed the cloth bag made for her by Mrs. Taylor and pulled out her notebook. Henry paused and then veered away.

"I see you brought your own composition book." Annabel jumped at the sound of the headmistress's voice. The woman leaned over Annabel's shoulder and peered at the blank pages of her open book.

"I'm sorry," Annabel said, her heart still racing. "I didn't know it wasn't permitted."

The headmistress laid a gentle hand on her shoulder. "Don't be sorry; it's wonderful! I encourage all my students to keep their own composition books in which to practice their letters daily."

"My letters, ma'am?" Annabel frowned up at the headmistress. She'd learned the alphabet and to write her name before turning five. Why should she need to practice her letters?

The headmistress leaned a little closer to Annabel and lowered her voice. "How many letters of the alphabet do you know? Don't be shy. There are no judgments here."

"I know all of them." Annabel glanced at the women around her, wondering if she'd come to the correct classroom. A few stared blankly at their open composition books, but most held their quill pens and were busy writing.

A young lady raised her hand, and Annabel saw Mr. Hudsyn walk over and talk to her.

"We are all at different stages in our learning journey," the headmistress said, and Annabel turned to see that a warm smile accompanied this comment. "But I am glad to hear you know all your letters. Are you able to do a little writing today? Introduce yourself on the page, perhaps?"

Annabel froze. "What do you mean? What is it you want to know?"

"Anything you wish to tell us. As I mentioned to the class, there are no rules. You may write whatever you want to share about yourself. The exercise will help me better understand your needs. You will not be judged, only helped."

Annabel heard the low scratch of quills as the other students got on with their assigned tasks. She'd been so distracted and deep in thought that she hadn't been listening when the headmistress had given her instructions to the class. No wonder the woman thought she didn't know her letters. What else could she think upon seeing Annabel staring blankly at her composition book?

"You don't have to fill the entire page. Write as much or as little as you feel comfortable with."

"I will. Thank you, ma'am."

"If you need help, do not hesitate to raise your hand. Mr. Hudsyn and I are here to assist you."

Annabel stiffened. The last thing she wanted was for her father's spy to ask her more questions, but she nodded and thanked the headmistress again.

Out of the corner of her eye, she saw Mr. Hudsyn move to another student's desk. He nodded and smiled kindly in response to the young lady's question. Then he inscribed some letters in her notebook. After which, he gave her the quill and watched as she copied the letters. Annabel frowned. *Was this show of kindness and patience an act? What man goes to such lengths to trick a woman like herself? A handsomely paid man might do anything*, papa had often said.

At that moment, Mr. Hudsyn glanced at her and smiled. Annabel thought she saw a glint in his eye. *Is that a gleam of victory I detect?*

She dropped her gaze, picked up her quill, and focused on her composition book, determined not to look at Mr. Hudsyn again or give him cause to think she was frightened of him.

The writing flowed easily from her mind onto the page. Grateful to be someone other than Annabel Leonard, she'd memorized the details of her new history and tried to internalize her new identity as Mrs. Crawford.

Now, she hoped to legitimize it by putting everything down

on paper. If she brought her story to life, describing the sights, sounds, and smells of her invented past, perhaps it would erase Mr. Hudsyn's suspicions, and maybe she could convince him to look elsewhere. The widowed Mrs. Anne Crawford, he would tell her papa, was the daughter of a humble and now-deceased merchant and not Mr. Leonard's wayward daughter.

Annabel became lost in her invented world until the sound of the headmistress's voice pulled her back to the present.

"Thank you, ladies. It's been a joy working with all of you today. Please leave your composition books on your desks, so you can use them when you return to class next week."

The students around Annabel stood and started to exit the room. *How had time passed so quickly?* As if in protest, her hand cramped, and she dropped her ink pen. She'd filled page upon page in her notebook with neatly scripted words. Pride swelled in her chest as she admired her work. At least Papa's money had not been wasted on her tutors. Surely, her detailed account of her life would be sufficient to convince everyone, including Mr. Hudsyn, that she was who she claimed—an orphaned and widowed young woman, who hailed from Whitby.

"I must say, I admire your focus and diligence," the headmistress said, approaching Annabel again and glancing at her filled composition book. "I was hesitant to disrupt you, but I am eager to read your work. You look to be a most promising student."

Annabel picked up her notebook, intent on giving it to the headmistress. Then a notion struck her. She hadn't altered her handwriting. If Mr. Hudsyn got hold of her composition book, papa would recognize her writing immediately. She'd be handing him concrete evidence of her identity.

Annabel pulled the book to her chest. "I'm afraid I can't leave it with you," she said.

"Don't worry; Mr. Hudsyn will give you a new composition book to take home so you can continue to practice your writing."

"That's not necessary." Annabel sealed her ink pot and stood up, now in a hurry to escape with her composition book. "I'm afraid—" she lowered her voice and threw a fearful glance in Mr. Hudsyn's direction; certain he was eavesdropping—"I'm afraid, I won't be returning."

The headmistress turned to look over her shoulder at Mr. Hudsyn before saying, "May I walk outside with you?"

Annabel hesitated, stunned by the headmistress's offer. "Thank you," she said, not wanting to be impolite.

"Excuse us, Mr. Hudsyn?" the headmistress called to him. "I won't be a moment."

"Certainly," he said, glancing at Annabel.

Annabel saw the confusion on his face, but she avoided looking back at him as she exited the classroom with Headmistress Thomas.

The headmistress didn't speak until they'd exited the building and stepped outside. "Now, tell me what's truly bothering you," she asked.

"Nothing at all," Annabel protested. "I like your class very much, and I wish I could return, but—"

The headmistress linked her arm to Annabel's, cutting off her words, and led her across the lawn. "I've been doing this for many years, Mrs. Crawford, and you didn't come here today out of curiosity. You came here because you enjoy learning and crave a safe space to do so without judgment. You want to give voice to your thoughts and surround yourself with people who'll listen and take you seriously. Isn't that right?"

Annabel's heart sank. Everything the headmistress said rang true. It was as if she'd read Annabel's heart. She'd finally held freedom in the palm of her hand, only to have her papa snatch it away again.

"Is it Mr. Hudsyn?" the headmistress asked pointedly. "Does the prospect of a gentleman reading and assessing what you wrote today make you uncomfortable?"

Annabel nodded.

"While I want to assure you that I know all my teachers personally and that Mr. Hudsyn is a trusted member of this establishment, I also understand your concerns. And the solution is quite simple. "You needn't worry because I'll be assessing all the writing from today's class myself. Rest assured, Mrs. Crawford, all your work will be safe with me."

Annabel worried her bottom lip. She wanted more than anything to show her work to Headmistress Thomas, but how could she return to the college with her father's spy lurking? How, in fact, could she remain in Canterbury?

"Tears stung Annabel's eyes. "I'm sorry," she said, "but I shan't be coming back." Then she turned and fled from the future she'd coveted for so long.

CHAPTER TEN

*Let this evermore be my caution to individuals of my sex—
Guard your eye: 'twill ever be in a combination against your
judgment. If there are two parts to be taken, it will be forever,
traitor as it is, taking the wrong one.*

—Samuel Richardson, *Clarissa*

IT MUST BE *that fishmonger's doing. He wore his jealousy plainly on
his face when he carted Mrs. Crawford away from me yesterday. I'm
certain he wasted no time turning her mind against me once he had her
alone. What other explanation can there be for her sudden change in
demeanor?*

"Such an interesting young woman!" Violet swept back into
the room, her words breaking into Henry's thoughts. "She's
exactly the type of bright young lady who needs this college to
provide her with a little encouragement and validation. It seems
she's already had a solid education and would blossom with
higher learning." Violet sighed. "She filled half the pages of her
composition book. Alas, she is not ready." Violet shook her head.
"Such potential and so much promise. I can only hope she
changes her mind and decides to return."

"She won't be coming back?" Henry couldn't believe it. What
had he done?

"I'm afraid she's not ready to share her experiences. She

seemed perturbed by your presence in the classroom. Don't take it to heart. Some women are uncomfortable with a gentleman reading and perhaps judging their thoughts and ideas."

"But I would never—"

"Of course not, but she doesn't know that. She doesn't know you. And we don't know her situation. I find her behavior more typical of women who have controlling fathers or husbands."

"Right." Henry forced a smile, knowing full well it was personal. Mrs. Crawford had looked at him with such distrust—as though she was afraid of him. But that was absurd. He'd never do anything untoward. Unless it was Mr. Trawler she feared.

I must talk to her. I must find out if she needs help. If she'll only just explain what happened yesterday to change everything today.

Are you coming back to the house for some well-earned tea? Your cousin and my brother will be waiting for us, and I am sure they are excited to hear about your first experience with teaching." Violet picked the composition books Henry had collected and placed on her podium while she was outside.

"Oh dear, I'm afraid I forgot all about tea, and I have a few errands to run in Canterbury. Will you let Ottilie know that I'll be back in time to dine with them tonight? I'll tell them all about my day then."

"Mr. Thomas and the twins will be disappointed not to see you. Perhaps next Saturday?"

"I'll look forward to it," Henry said.

They exited the classroom and made their way down the stone hallway. When they reached the exit, Henry stepped ahead of Violet and pushed open the arched wooden door, holding it open as she stepped outside. "How do your students manage this thing?" Henry asked, looking at the heavy door. "It's positively medieval."

"Well, it does date from the Middle Ages," Violet said with a laugh. "We thought about replacing it when we first opened the school, but I changed my mind when I started to think of it in symbolic terms—as the barrier women must overcome to access higher education and the strength they need against that barrier. Every day, the students wrestle with this door as a reminder of the daily struggle women in higher education face."

Henry stood back and observed the wooden door above which the Latin phrase: *Luctor et Emergo was engraved.*

"I struggle and overcome," he translated aloud, then turned to the headmistress. "I never noticed that before."

She smiled in response and said, "You did an outstanding job today. The other students seemed very comfortable with you."

"I enjoyed the experience very much."

"I'm so glad. Does that mean we will see again on Wednesday evening?" she asked.

"Yes, I'd like that very much."

She bid him goodbye and turned in the direction of the east wing. Because Byron Thomas had converted the rambling stone mansion of his childhood home into a ladies' college, the Thomas family lived on the premises, unlike Jack and Ottilie whose residence was at least a half-hour carriage drive away.

Henry turned and hurried to the stables where Bastin's coachman awaited him. His own man was back at Greyson Manor tending to a broken wheel on his brougham, so Henry had borrowed one of his cousin's carriages, and he was glad he'd opted to do so instead of taking a cab. He had to set things right with Mrs. Crawford, especially if he was going to continue helping at the ladies' college, but more so because he couldn't bear the thought that she'd turned her mind against him.

"Where to, my Lord?" The coachman sprang to attention as soon as he caught sight of Henry.

"Canterbury," Henry instructed, his nerves already singing in anticipation of his next encounter with Mrs. Crawford.

Henry fixed his eyes on the window as the carriage rolled down the rural road toward Canterbury, his heart lifting each time he spotted a female pedestrian and then falling upon seeing it was not Mrs. Crawford.

Perhaps Mr. Trawler had been waiting outside for her to take her home in his cart. He may have grown possessive after seeing her with Henry. In that case, he'd have to seek her out at the seamstress's shop. But how would she react? He didn't want to frighten her with his unwanted attention. He thought of the curiosity and ease with which she'd chatted to him the previous afternoon—and the way her green eyes sparkled with life and of the freckles that spread across the bridge of her nose each time she'd wrinkled it in laughter. She'd been perfectly comfortable in his company. And he in hers. What had changed? He had to find out.

ANNABEL SLAMMED HER book shut, wondering why she'd doggedly persisted in finishing this novel that upset her so much. It was an awful story, *Clarissa*, that both scared and angered her. But she suspected the author had striven to do just that.

At first, she'd liked the fact that the author had taken the time to write a story about an independent-minded young lady, like herself. But it was obvious—at least to her—that the terrible consequences his heroine was made to suffer had been contrived to scare young women into compliance.

Why else would Mr. Richardson create a heroine bold enough to defy her parents and refuse a marriage of convenience, yet weak enough to be duped by a rake like Lovelace? Mr. Richardson punished his heroine for this disobedience in the worst possible way. A punishment so foul—Annabel shuddered— that he was left with no choice but to murder her by her own hand!

She stood up and smoothed her skirt. After leaving the college, deflated, she'd stopped to sit on a grassy knoll and read the final chapters of her novel, hoping it would distract her thoughts. But she'd picked the wrong book for that purpose.

"Mrs. Crawford!"

Annabel turned to see Mr. Hudsyn striding toward her, and she drew back.

He stopped. "I'm sorry; I didn't mean to scare you."

"What are you doing here?" She clutched *Clarissa* to her chest. The book was thick enough to be used as a weapon if necessary.

"I was on my way to Canterbury"—he pointed to a black carriage waiting by the side of the road—"and when I saw you walking, I thought to offer you a lift."

She eyed the carriage and took another cautious step backward. "No. Thank you. I'm quite enjoying my walk."

"Well then, perhaps you'll allow me to join you?"

The image of him lurking across from Mrs. Taylor's shop resurfaced in her mind as his black carriage loomed behind him like a waiting cage. She lifted her chin, refusing to show fear.

"Why don't you tell me what you really want from me?"

He blinked, looking genuinely perplexed. "Have I done something to upset you?"

She eyed his tailored suit. "You are no schoolmaster, are you?"

"You're right. I'm not. That said, I hope I did not make my teaching inadequacies too obvious. Although, I promise to do better next time." He smiled, as though desperate to lighten the mood.

"Except, you weren't there to teach, were you, Mr. Hudsyn, if that is indeed your name? Because why would a finely-dressed gentleman like yourself volunteer to teach a charity class for hard-working women?"

He opened his mouth to speak, but she hadn't finished yet, and she needed to do so before her courage evaporated. "I don't believe you're here to offer me a lift to Canterbury but rather to lure me into your expensive carriage, so you may take me where you will. Isn't that right?"

"What?" He frowned. Then his gaze fell on *Clarissa*, and he let out a short laugh. "It's true; I am no teacher. But I am no

Lovelace either. I have not come to abduct you."

Her face grew hot with anger. "You—how dare you accuse me of being some type of—of female Quixote?"

"I hadn't thought of it that way, but it fits. After all, you're fighting an imaginary battle with an imaginary enemy."

"You dare to assume that novel reading is making me act irrationally? And therefore, I acquaint you with Lovelace?"

"You accused me of plotting to lure you into my carriage and kidnap you, did you not?"

"And you admitted to not being a teacher, yet you are teaching at the ladies' college. Is that a coincidence? The same type of coincidence that led you to wander onto my path yesterday. These chance meetings with you seem rather odd. Perhaps they're not chance encounters after all."

He placed his fingers on his temples as if their conversation had exhausted his brain. "I agreed to volunteer at the college to help my cousin. She's a teacher there." He extended his open palms toward her. "I told you I am visiting my cousin, did I not?"

"You did, but why should she need your help when you are not a teacher?"

"It's not so much that she needs my help as—" he ran a hand over the cleft in his chin—"the thing is—her husband, my friend—volunteered my services."

Annabel frowned, trying to decide what to make of his oddly concocted explanation.

"My cousin is married to the brother of Headmistress Thomas. You can verify as much with her if you like."

She captured her bottom lip as she thought about the headmistress's words. *Mr. Hudsyn is a trusted member of this establishment.* She'd been so intent on escaping with her notebook that she hadn't stopped to consider this. Surely, Headmistress Thomas wouldn't hire a strange man, who was not even a teacher, to instruct young ladies. Perhaps Mr. Hudsyn spoke the truth. But how did that explain his presence outside Mrs. Taylor's shop the previous day? Why had he been watching her?

Looking up at him, she sought the truth in his countenance. "I saw you outside Mr. Taylor's shop yesterday. You said you intended to take the train back home. Instead, you followed me. Why?"

Henry stepped forward, closing the gap between them. "Because—" his soft blue eyes searched her face—"you're the most interesting woman I have met in a very long time, and—well, the most beautiful too."

Her cheeks warmed, but she wouldn't be won over by sweet words alone.

"After our walk yesterday, I didn't want to leave thinking I might never see you again, so I came to your shop to ask if you'd care to attend the theater with me one day."

"But you did not ask."

"I'm afraid my courage failed me. And to be frank, I didn't want to intrude on another gentleman's involvement."

"Do you mean Mr. Trawler?" she said, with a slight laugh. The idea struck her as absurd—why, exactly, she didn't know.

Henry nodded.

"Mr. Trawler was a dear friend of my husband's," Annabel recited the explanation that Stella had helped her rehearse. "When my husband fell ill, he made Nate promise to watch over me. He feared for my well-being—as a young woman alone in the world. So, you see, he only seeks to fulfill a dying man's wishes."

As she spoke, she thought about Nate's warning. Had he purposely made her fearful of Mr. Hudsyn because he'd wanted her for himself? No. Impossible. He'd never expressed any such sentiment toward her. His only motivation was loyalty to Stella.

"And Mr. Trawler has no other hold over you? Because he seemed—"

"I believe he would consider that dishonoring my husband's memory. Mr. Trawler believes himself bound to me because of his promise, and that is all." She straightened, confident her answer was correct—after all, Nate had made a similar promise to Stella.

Henry's demeanor relaxed. He inched closer to her. "I can't tell you how pleased I am to hear you say that Mrs. Crawford."

"Anne," she said. "Mrs. Crawford doesn't seem right if we are to be friends."

"Anne," he repeated.

She liked the sound of her new name on his lips. For the first time, it felt right—like the name truly belonged to her.

"Will you allow me to accompany you into town, Anne?"

Annabel thought for a minute. Assuming the identity of a widow afforded her privileges not available to unmarried women. She felt a sense of power and control for the first time, and it thrilled her. "I don't see why not. I'm a widow, and it's not as though I need a chaperone. Nonetheless, I'm not in the habit of getting into closed carriages with men I barely know."

"Wait here." He grinned and sprinted down the grassy hill to his carriage.

Annabel watched him and suppressed a smile. Life had been so dull for so long, and now, it seemed alive with possibilities. Someone had been telling her what to do all her life, and she was tired of it. If she decided to spend time with Mr. Hudsyn, the choice would be hers, and no one else's.

Nate had been wrong to scare her—putting ideas in her mind that Mr. Hudsyn was a spy for Papa. She understood that Nate was only doing what Stella had asked of him, but even dearest Stella couldn't watch over her forever. She was a woman now. A smile tugged at the corners of her lips. Mr. Hudsyn had only lingered by the shop because he admired her and wanted to ask her to the theater.

Mr. Hudsyn conversed briefly with the coachman before waving the carriage away. Then he turned and sprinted back up the hill toward her, sending her stomach aflutter.

CHAPTER ELEVEN

She listened with a flitting blush,
With downcast eyes and modest grace;
For well she knew, I could not choose
But gaze upon her face.

—Samuel Taylor Coleridge, *Love*

"H ave you spent much time in Canterbury?" Anne asked as they stepped onto the rough path next to the River Stour. The shrubs and grass along the bank were nourished and green after the rainstorm, attracting an array of birds who chirped merrily as they foraged.

"I vaguely remember my grandfather bringing me to see the cathedral once. My mother moved to Germany when I was a babe, so I spent my school holidays there."

"Your mother is German?"

"She's English, but we have German ancestors, and she decided to move there shortly after my father died."

"His death must have been very painful for her."

Henry shrugged. Not wanting his mood to turn, he made no answer.

"I'm sorry," she said. "I always ask too many questions."

He forced a smile, refusing to let his mother stain the moment. "It was a long time ago. I was so young that I don't remember him." He gazed at the peaceful river, wanting to absorb its tranquility.

"In some ways, not remembering can be more painful. I lost my mama the day I was born, and sometimes the loss feels almost too much to bear. It seems unjust that I didn't know her and that she didn't even get a chance to hold me."

"If I've learned anything, it's that life isn't fair," Henry felt the bitterness return. "And oftentimes there's nothing we can do to change that."

"I disagree," she said. "I think one ought to take control of one's life. Even when it seems impossible, there's always a way."

"What about situations that occurred before you were born? How is one to do anything about those?"

"You can't do anything about past situations, but you can take charge of the future. I can't change losing my mama at birth, but I can try to live a good life. That's what she would have wanted."

Henry frowned into the distance. He wished it were that simple.

"Listen to us!"—Annabel laughed as if sensing Henry's mood had darkened—"It's such a lovely day, and here we are dwelling on unpleasant memories."

"You're right," he said, relieved to leave the past behind. "Here I am in an oasis with a charming lady, and all I can do is brood. Forgive me."

They walked in comfortable silence along the riverbank, listening to the rippling water and chirping birds, until they arrived at a small bridge where bent willows lined the bank and kissed the water as if in reverence to the Great Stour.

"This is my favorite place," Annabel said.

They mounted the bridge and watched a family of ducks dive for food.

"Oh, look at that one." She pointed to one of the ducklings, struggling to get out of the water and onto the bank.

Henry shared her laughter but could not keep his eyes on the ducks. While she watched them, he watched her, mesmerized by her long, dark lashes and perfectly arched brows, and captivated by the sensual curve of her lips.

"What is it?" She glanced up at him, her cheeks a lovely shade of pink. "Is something out of place?" She touched her awkwardly-pinned chignon, hidden under a blue satin tail that extended from the dainty bonnet perched on her forehead.

"Nothing's wrong," he said. "Nothing at all."

"But you've been staring at me. There must be something."

"I didn't realize," he said. "I couldn't help myself."

The color in her cheeks deepened. She averted her gaze to the water. Pressing her lips together, she suppressed the smile that tugged at the corners of her mouth.

The moment brought a passage from one of Coleridge's poems to his mind: *She listened with a flitting blush, / With downcast eyes, and modest grace; / And she forgave me, that I gazed / Too fondly on her face!*

It saddened him to think he'd lost the inclination to write his own lines about such an experience. And for the first time in two years, he felt the tug of creativity—the force deep inside him that compelled him to write. Then just as swiftly, he pushed it aside. Acknowledging that desire—worse, claiming it—meant owning the imposter and giving up his father.

"Something's upset you," she said.

"Not at all; I'm fine."

But it hadn't been a question, and she continued to watch him, her brows slightly furrowed.

"I was thinking about a poem. By Coleridge, that's all. It popped into my mind."

"Do you read a lot of poetry?" She inclined her head in question.

"I dabbled in writing it for a while—" he forced a smile—"but that was a long time ago."

"Do you have any? Poems, I mean. I should like to read your work."

"Not anymore," he said, wondering what her reaction would be if she knew that two years ago, he'd been offered publication and refused, choosing to slip safely into obscurity instead.

He ran a hand over his face and looked down at her. He should apologize for his forwardness and offer to see her home, but he could not take back his words. It was the most honest he'd been in a long time. He didn't want to part from her—not yet.

"Do you know, all this fresh air has made me hungry," he said. "Is there a place in town for tea?"

"More than one."

"Would you like to accompany me?"

"Oh, I should love to," she said with a smile. "It's been some time since I've had a proper tea."

"Well," he said, "then we shall have a tea that outshines all others—a tea to remember."

They crossed the bridge into the village and made their way through Canterbury's narrow streets, eventually coming to the canopied Butter Market, where a plump, middle-aged woman beckoned them with tiny wedges of cheese on a platter. A little boy raced forward and stretched a hand toward the tray, but the woman moved it out of his reach.

"Buyers only!" she barked, and the child scampered away.

"Poor thing," Anne said.

"He ain't poor; he's a butcher's son an' has plenty sausages to fill his belly. Now, go ahead and give my cheese a taste. All lovingly made by yours truly."

Anne accepted a tiny wedge and chewed thoughtfully. "That is delicious. Quite creamy."

"The young lady likes it! Would the gentleman care to make her a gift of cheese?"

"Why not? Wrap up a crown's worth."

"I couldn't eat a whole crown's worth of cheese," Anne protested.

"Half crown, then," Henry instructed the cheesemonger.

"That's still too much." Anne laughed.

"You're Mrs. Taylor's lodger, ain't ya? I'm sure she will appreciate a bit o' cheese. I hear you have a fella from Whitstable who delivers you fresh fish 'an oysters every week. Must be nice to have so many gentlemen feeding ya."

"Thank you," Henry said tightly, "but I believe the lady has changed her mind."

"Aww, come now? I've already wrapped it up. You asked for it; now you must pay for it!"

Anne reached up and snatched the parcel from the cheesemonger. "There now, be quiet. You're causing a stir."

Henry glowered at the woman and shoved a coin into her outstretched hand.

"Come back again," she called as they walked away. I'll be here next week. Bring any gentleman you like. It's all the same to me, so long as he has coins in his pocket."

"Silly woman," Anne said, slipping the wrapped cheese into a deep pocket in her skirt.

"Rather uncouth, to say the least," Henry mumbled. The cheesemonger's comment about the fish deliveries irked him. Mr. Trawler irked him. What were the man's intentions? He seemed far too protective over Anne to be a mere friend. But Henry barely knew Anne, and he had no right to question her.

They turned onto Sun Street, which bustled with people and hosted an array of businesses. Henry stopped in front of a toymaker's shop, contemplating the display in its mullioned windows. China dolls with painted faces, meticulously sewn dresses, and lifelike hair sat in various poses.

"I wonder if I can enlist your help in finding a present for my cousin's daughter. I'm embarrassed that I arrived empty-handed at my cousin's house without anything for her little one."

"How old is she?"

Henry frowned, realizing he wasn't certain of the child's exact age. He did a quick calculation of the months since her birth in his mind and came up with the answer. "She's around fifteen months."

Anne laughed. "That's a darling age. My Rupert is only six months, and so much fun."

"Your Rupert?" Henry said, mulling her words over in his mind. He hadn't considered that she might have a child. But why shouldn't she? After all, she'd been married.

"Not mine, exactly. He's Mrs. Taylor's child. But I love him as dearly as if he were my own."

"And what toys delight Rupert?" Henry asked, somewhat relieved to know the child didn't belong to her, although he could not think why. He was certain he'd love anyone Anne loved.

"Everything delights him. A scrap of material fascinates him, and a wooden spoon keeps him occupied for hours."

"I see," Henry said, thinking of Alice's colorful wooden blocks and finely crafted rocking horse.

"Of course, he has toys of his own, too. His mama makes him animals from scraps of fabric, and his papa carved a little wooden ship for him before he sailed out to sea. It's a shame he has to be away from his little boy for so long. Poor Rupert won't even recognize him when he returns."

"When will that be?"

"I'm not sure."

Henry nodded and wondered how that would change Anne's situation in the house. If Mr. Taylor were a decent sort, she'd be fine, but if he wasn't—" Henry shook the thought from his mind.

"When I was a little girl, I liked to play with dolls. Alice is a bit young for a fancy china doll, but it would make a pretty decoration for her room."

"I'd be indebted to you if you'd help me choose the right doll for Alice."

"What color is Alice's hair?" she asked.

"It's flaxen."

"Like yours?"

"Yes, the same as her mama's."

"And her eyes?"

"Chocolate brown, like her papa's."

"That's easy," she said. "Little girls want dolls that look just like them. My sisters—" she stopped as if startled by her own words. "I mean—let's step inside. I daresay the doll maker has at least one flaxen-haired, brown-eyed porcelain beauty in her shop."

"I daresay she does," Henry smiled, still wondering why Anne had censored her words.

It seemed that she, too, harbored secrets from the past that she wished to keep locked away.

SOME FIFTEEN MINUTES later, Annabel and Henry exited the toymakers, he with a package containing a beautifully crafted china doll, and she with a parcel containing a stuffed bear dressed in a sailor's suit for Rupert.

"I can't let you buy that. It's too expensive," she'd protested when he'd suggested the bear for Rupert.

"I can offer you a discount if you buy two items," the toymaker had interjected.

"That settles it," Henry had declared. "Wrap them up."

"Thank you," she'd remarked when he'd handed her the package. "I would not accept such an extravagant present on my own behalf, but it's for Rupert—and well, I can't wait to see the smile it puts on his sweet face."

"I'm pleased that it's put a smile on your face, too."

She met his gaze and saw nothing but kindness in his expression. How could she have let Nate convince her he was a spy for her papa? He was generous and compassionate—everything Lord Craventhorp and her papa were not.

Henry glanced at the afternoon sky. "It's getting late. You still have time for tea, I hope. My stomach will rebel if I don't feed it soon."

"Oh yes, I'm looking forward to it. There's a place across the street that I've been longing to try. It always smells delicious when I walk past, and it's never short on customers."

They crossed the street and made their way to a quaint tea-room, which displayed an array of teapots and porcelain cups in its mullioned windows.

Henry held the door for her, and she stepped inside, inhaling the smell of freshly baked goods.

They sat at a table near the back and enjoyed buttered bread with the cheese Henry had purchased, hot scones laden with jam, an array of cakes, and a freshly brewed pot of fragrant tea.

Oh, how I missed this. Annabel thought as she swallowed her tea.

"I hear it's a marvelous production," A voice trilled. "Better, even, than *Much Ado About Nothing*, performed last summer." Annabel followed the voices to a group of ladies sitting at a table diagonal to theirs.

"Yes, the players have outdone themselves this year."

Henry leaned forward and said, "*Othello* is playing at the Theatre Royal on Guildhall Street. Have you seen it?"

"No," she grinned, recalling he'd wanted to invite her to the theater. "But I hear it is a marvelous production."

"It's a tragedy," Henry said.

"And?"

"And Shakespeare's tragedies are quite"—he pressed his lips together as if searching for the correct word—"well, they're quite violent. *Othello* is particularly disturbing."

"I've seen *Romeo and Juliet* and found it quite moving."

"This one is a little—" he paused again as if searching for the correct word—"harsher."

Annabel put down her teacup. "I've also seen *A Midsummer Night's Dream*, have you?"

"Yes. I thought it quite silly, actually."

"Well, I thought it quite clever. Take, for instance, the character, Bottom. When he and his laboring friends decide to perform the tragedy *Pyramus and Thisbe* for the King's wedding festivities, Bottom thinks the women in his audience are too delicate and feeble-minded to tell the difference between a real lion and a man in a mask. He fears they will die of fright and the king will execute all the players, so he proposes that he only cover half his face. It's so ridiculous that it's funny. But it's also sad because it illustrates how simple-minded some men think the female sex."

"That's not what I was implying," Henry straightened his back. "I only wanted to prepare you. The story is quite powerful."

"Consider me prepared," she said. "I'm quite ready if you are."

"Now? You want to go this evening?"

"If you like," she said, suddenly excited about the prospect.

"Won't your Mrs. Taylor mind?"

"Why should she mind? She's my landlady, not my mama." Annabel laughed to conceal her guilt. Mrs. Taylor would likely need her help with Rupert or want her company as she worked through the evening. While she enjoyed looking after Rupert and helping Mrs. Taylor during the day when customers came into the shop and talked to her, she'd grown tired of spending every evening in a dimly lit room, watching Mrs. Taylor sitting bent over and straining her eyes to sew. The theater would be a treat, but more than that, she didn't want to part from Henry's company yet. And why should she? She was her own woman now, who didn't have to answer to anyone save herself. Another twinge of guilt nudged her insides. She looked at Henry and sighed inwardly. *I'll make it up to Mrs. Taylor tomorrow. But tonight, I'll attend the theater with a handsome gentleman.*

"COME ONE, COME all—the show is about to begin." A top-hatted gentleman, holding a tin money box, ushered ladies and gentlemen into the modest white building that was the Theatre Royal. "The greatest production of Shakespeare's *Othello* you are ever likely to see will commence in a few minutes. Be warned, once these doors close, there'll be no getting inside."

Annabel and Henry rushed forward.

"Do you still have boxes available?" Henry asked, removing a few shillings from his pocket, and handing them to the gentleman.

"Certainly, sir." The gentleman accepted the coins, handed Henry two red tickets, and then gave a slight bow. "Enjoy the show."

They passed through white double doors framed by an arched doorway and entered the foyer, carpeted in red and adorned with a bust of Shakespeare. From there, they climbed the stairs to the upper level. The rowed tiers upstairs were almost full, but they located an empty box with excellent views of the stage and made their way to it. Seconds after sitting down, the gas lights in the theater dimmed, and only the stage remained illuminated.

A short, bearded man in a three-piece suit appeared on stage before the curtain rose and explained that the players were a group of locals who were proud to say that they had been the producers, set designers, and actors of every play since the theater's opening in 1860. And, lest there be newcomers in the audience, he wanted to remind everyone that Charles Dickens himself had "adorned this very stage" and had given a reading of his renowned novel, *David Copperfield*.

The audience broke out into raucous applause.

Annabel giggled. It made no difference to her that she sat in a small theater one street away from Mrs. Taylor's shop or that the players were locals. The last time she'd attended the theater, she'd accompanied her father and stepmother to an opera in London's Music Hall. Her stepmother had thought it important she be seen attending the theater. And while she'd enjoyed the performance, she'd hated being on display all night, sitting up straight in her box seat under the scrutiny of her stepmother's watchful gaze. If she'd dared to slouch an inch or express too much emotion, her stepmother had readily corrected her with a hidden pinch to her back.

She shuddered at the memory. But now, sitting next to Henry in this homespun theater seemed to her the most romantic and exciting experience of her life.

The play was indeed excellent, and the players well-rehearsed. Annabel was captivated by the opening act and immediately sympathized with Desdemona, whose papa turned against her for choosing love. She likened the evil Iago to her nemesis, Lord Craventhorp, and by the end of the third act, her anxiety was so great that she sat with her gloved fingers digging into the bare wrist of the opposite hand.

"If you wish to leave, I will not object," Henry whispered during a brief intermission when the curtain lowered.

"Leave?" She frowned. "Never! I *must* see what happens. I am certain that good will beat evil; it always does, doesn't it?"

"All will be right in the end but not before a costly price is extracted from those involved. It's a tragedy, remember—"

"The curtain's rising. It's starting again!" She edged toward the front of her seat and gripped the railing that bordered the box.

Nausea rose in her throat as Iago's false whispers flamed Othello's doubt, and she shrank back in her seat when, consumed with jealousy, he struck Desdemona across the face for the first time.

Henry shifted in his seat beside her. She straightened her back and forced a smile at him, determined to prove that her emotions remained unaffected. But nothing could have prepared her for Desdemona's murder. Watching the actress struggle for air as her stage husband pinned her under a pillow brought back the helplessness she'd felt when Lord Craventhorp pinned her in place in Lady Dawley's Garden. She recalled his tight grip on her arm and spiteful whisper in her ear and could easily imagine herself under the pillow, pleading for her life. The viscount had trapped her using one hand as easily as a child trapped a butter-fly's wing between two fingers. If he'd wanted to murder her, she'd be as helpless as Desdemona.

She inadvertently sought comfort, reaching for Henry's hand in the darkness.

He took hold of it and clasped it in his.

As soon as the shock wore off, she retracted her hand, grateful for the theater's darkness.

"I'm sorry," she said when they were outside, walking toward her lodgings. "I don't know what came over me. I behaved...I hope you can forgive me."

"Forgive you? There's nothing to forgive," he said. "It's a difficult play to watch. I'm not surprised it scared you."

"You tried to warn me." They stopped outside the seamstress's shop on Orange Street. "But...Well, I can be insufferably opinionated sometimes." Despite the darkness and stillness of the street, she lowered her gaze to hide her embarrassment.

Henry lifted her chin, forcing her to look at him. "Don't apologize for voicing your opinion—not to me, anyway."

They stood so close that she could feel the warmth of his breath on her lips, and her mouth trembled in response.

"Anne," he leaned forward and brushed his lips against hers.

She arched toward him, wanting more of him—more of his fresh scent, more of his touch, and more of his lips against hers.

CHAPTER TWELVE

Sweet, baby, sleep; what ails my dear,
What ails my darling thus to cry?
Be still, my child, and lend thine ear,
To hear me sing thy lullaby.
My pretty lamb, forbear to weep;
Be still, my dear; sweet baby, sleep.

—George Wither, *A Rocking Hymn*

SLIPPING INSIDE MRS. Taylor's dark and silent shop, Annabel closed the door as quietly as she could and then leaned against it to catch her breath and steady her drumming heart. Clutching Rupert's wrapped gift in one hand, she touched her lips with the other, still in awe of the kiss and the tingling sensation that had awakened them to a new purpose. Henry's mouth had become one with hers—so smoothly and effortlessly that she doubted her lips would ever be whole without his again.

She floated, rather than walked into the darkness, grateful that Mrs. Taylor and Rupert had already retired for the night upstairs. It wasn't unusual for Mrs. Taylor to keep a fire burning downstairs while she stayed up late, hunched over her sewing. And Annabel was grateful to see Mrs. Taylor's empty chair and the dying embers in the grate. The darkness would keep her secret and let her relive and relish the kiss in private. She put down Rupert's parcel and hummed to herself as she picked up scraps of material from the floor and deposited them in a small mound on the table.

Mrs. Taylor's shop isn't usually messy. Annabel eyed the mountain of scraps and frowned. Scanning the room, her gaze fell on a half-sewn dress pinned in the sewing machine.

It's not like Mrs. Taylor to leave her work half finished.

She stepped closer to the sewing machine. A basket of needles lay turned over on the floor, and the normally neat pile of clothing waiting to be mended lay scattered nearby. Gooseflesh rose on Annabel's arms.

Something is terribly amiss.

As if in response to her thought, Rupert's cry rang in Annabel's ears, and she jerked her head up. Another shrill cry sounded from above, sending a cold shiver down Annabel's spine. She darted up the stairs, only slowing her gait as she stepped onto the first floor. The door to Mrs. Taylor's and Rupert's bedroom stood ajar. She crept toward it, wondering if she'd imagined the shrill cries she'd heard downstairs. If she could just peep inside and see that all was well with Rupert—that he slept peacefully in his cot next to his mother's bed as was normal then she'd have the confirmation she needed that her imagination had played a trick on her, and all was right in the world.

Annabel stood inches from the door, debating what to do. If she knocked, she might wake Rupert, but if she peeked inside, she'd be violating Mrs. Taylor's privacy. A thought struck her. What if Mr. Taylor had returned home early from his excursion at sea? The idea made her take a step back. The thought of intruding on a husband and wife in their bedchamber horrified her. Yet, she could not rid herself of the worry that stirred inside her. If Mr. Taylor had surprised his family by returning early, surely the atmosphere in the house would be joyous. There'd be a fire in the hearth, a celebratory meal to eat, and chatter and laughter filling the rooms.

She contemplated in the darkness and waited until the cold

silence urged her forward again. Tiptoeing to the door, she bent her head, and listened.

Now she heard muffled sobs coming from within—not Rupert's shrill infant cry—but the quiet sobbing of a woman.

Annabel's heart pulsed as she knocked softly on the bedroom door.

No response came.

"Mrs. Taylor," she called, edging the door open.

A low-burning oil lamp cast a weak light in the room, but it was enough for Annabel to see Mrs. Taylor hunched in her rocking chair, cradling Rupert in the crook of her arm, and pressing a crumpled white handkerchief over her mouth with her free hand to stifle her sobs.

Fear closed Annabel's throat and stole her breath. She crept inside, half faint with dread.

A rasping sound escaped Rupert's throat, and his tiny chest rose and fell as if each breath required enormous effort.

"Mrs. Taylor," her voice quivered, "is Rupert unwell?"

The seamstress glanced up, and Annabel shrank inside at the sight of the woman's red-rimmed eyes and tear-stained cheeks.

"What's the matter with him?" Annabel's stomach churned.

Mrs. Taylor shook her head. "I don't know. It's a fever. He's so hot. I don't know what to do."

"Did you send for the doctor?"

She nodded. "I sent a messenger boy out a few hours ago. Dr. Carter said to keep him cool, and I tried. I bathed him. I did, but his body has only grown warmer."

"What's that?" Annabel glanced at a cloth dipped into a jug of murky water on the table.

"Sugar water. It seems to be the only thing that gives him a little comfort. He's been awake and screaming for hours and only just now fell asleep, poor mite."

"I'm so sorry." Tears spilled down Annabel's cheeks. "I should have been here to help."

"It doesn't matter. You're here now." Mrs. Taylor reached for

Annabel's hand. "And it gives me great comfort to have you." She rested her head against the back of the chair and closed her eyes. "Great comfort, indeed."

"What can I do? Shall I take him so you can rest?"

"No, I want to hold him. It soothes him to be in his mother's arms."

"There must be something I can do. Have you eaten?"

Mrs. Taylor shook her head. "I cannot think of food now. I'm not at all hungry. All I want is to lie down, but Rupert needs me, and I have work to do. Mrs. Whipple needs her skirts readied for her excursion to London, and Mrs. Corby needs her dress for—"

"Don't fret about Mrs. Whipple and Mrs. Corby; I will explain everything to them tomorrow. Stay in your chair and rest. If you stand up, you might wake Rupert. I'll make you some tea and then clean up downstairs. I wish I could help you with the sewing, but I'm afraid my slovenly stitches will only serve to irk your customers."

A weak smile formed on Mrs. Taylor's lips. "Thank you, my dear. I feel a little more at ease now that you're here." She rested her head against the back of the chair and closed her eyes.

Selfish and spoilt, that's what you are. Mrs. Leonard's words echoed in Annabel's mind. Guilt gnawed at her as she stepped into the tiny kitchen to fix tea.

Why didn't I check if Mrs. Taylor required my help with anything before I agreed to go to the theater with Henry? The shop is only a street away, and it would have taken no time at all. Instead, I thought only of myself, and while I enjoyed Shakespeare, little Rupert lay ill, and Mrs. Taylor was left to cope on her own.

She fixed a tray of biscuits and tea for Mrs. Taylor, feeling another stab of guilt for having eaten the cheese with her tea. If only she'd thought of dropping it off at home, then she would have known Rupert had fallen ill. When she returned to the bedchamber with the tray, both mother and babe were asleep in the rocking chair. Annabel set the tray down. Then she tiptoed out of the room and down the stairs where she picked up and folded the clothes that needed mending. All around the room, pieces of material lay scattered on the floor. *Poor Mrs. Taylor must have been frantic in her rush to tend to Rupert.*

A thud followed by a sharp cry sounded above. Annabel raced upstairs and burst into the bedchamber. Rupert lay on the floor, his scrunched face red as a beet and his tiny fists clenched tight.

Annabel covered her mouth to stop her cry.

"I dropped him." Mrs. Taylor shook her head in apparent disbelief. But she didn't move to pick him up. She seemed frozen, unable to do anything but shake her head.

Rupert let out a high-pitched wail as if protesting his mama's inaction.

Annabel raced forward and scooped Rupert up in her arms.

Mrs. Taylor made a feeble effort to stand.

"Don't worry; he'll be fine." Annabel dipped Rupert's rag in the cup of sugar water Mrs. Taylor had at the ready, wrapped it around her finger, and stuck it in the child's mouth. She'd watched Mrs. Taylor do this many times when Rupert needed calming. He sucked greedily on her wrapped finger, extracting what little comfort he could from the sugar. Annabel rocked him and made soothing noises until his exhaustion overcame his pain, and he could no longer keep his eyes open.

"He's asleep." Annabel glanced at Mrs. Taylor. The seamstress lay slumped in her rocking chair with her eyes closed.

The hairs on the back of Annabel's neck stood at attention. She stooped, still cradling Rupert, and took Mrs. Taylor's hand, concerned by the red splotches spreading across the woman's cheeks. Her hand was warm to the touch. She reached up and lightly brushed Mrs. Taylor's cheek, then withdrew it instantly. Mrs. Taylor's skin burned with an obvious fever.

Annabel stepped back and gripped Rupert close to her chest. She looked from Mrs. Taylor to Rupert and then back to the fevered woman.

Heaven help me! What am I to do now?

HENRY OPENED HIS eyes and welcomed the daylight filtering into his bedchamber. He'd slept peacefully for the first time in two years and awoke refreshed. What miraculous transformation had taken place? A smile played on his lips as a picture of Anne Crawford formed in his mind. Spending time with her made him feel alive again. It wasn't simply her lovely green eyes or bright smile that captivated him. She possessed an energy and vitality about her that made his concerns seem small. He admired how she'd taken control of her own life after tragedy—something he'd failed to do. But something dark plagued her too, and when her gloved hand sought his in the darkness of the theater, he'd felt guilt.

He should not have taken her to see such a disturbing play— not because he attributed her reaction to an overactive feminine imagination—he was not so narrow-minded—but because he'd sensed her vulnerability. Her reaction had been visceral rather than overblown, and it made him wonder what her husband had been like. How had he treated her? He hated the thought that something or someone in her past had made her suffer.

With that realization, he threw back his covers and stepped out of bed, stretching once more and embracing the day with his whole body. Then he froze.

He was not alone.

Bastin sat on the tufted red velvet chair in the corner of the room.

"What the devil is happening?" Henry peered at Bastin. "Why are you sitting there like the Red Death?"

"Not a bad analogy," Bastin said, pushing himself out of the chair, "seeing that I have come to warn you of your inevitable demise."

"My demise?" Henry picked up his robe and slipped it on. "Have you adopted the personae of one of your characters?"

"No, I'm afraid I've come as myself." His voice was devoid of playfulness.

"Come for what, exactly?"

"Answers." Bastin slipped his hands into his pockets. "Where were you yesterday? Ottilie was worried sick when you failed to arrive for supper."

"Oh, yes." Henry put a hand to his forehead. "I forgot all about supper. I lost track of time. I'm sorry about keeping your carriage out so late. Did you have need of it?"

"I don't give a damn about the carriage. But I do care when you lie to me. I know *exactly* what you were getting up to last night. I lived that life myself not too long ago."

"I recall only too well," Henry said dryly. "Yet now you see fit to judge me."

"I am not judging you; I'm holding you accountable for upsetting my wife—your cousin—who is with child, remember?"

Henry hung his head. The last person he wanted to hurt was Ottilie. "I wasn't out drinking, gambling, or whoring last night. I promise you. I had a few things to take care of, had a bite to eat, and then went to the theater on a whim—a very fine production of *Othello* at the Theatre Royal." Henry said, keeping silent about Anne and the time he'd spent kissing her after the play. He'd been so elated after they'd parted that he'd taken a long walk before heading back to the old coaching inn where he'd sent Bastin's driver to wait for him earlier that day.

Bastin folded his arms. *Othello*. Well, that ought to have cheered you up," he teased.

"In a way, it did. The actors did a splendid job. I always enjoy a good Shakespearian tragedy."

Bastin strode forward and peered into his friend's face. "It's not your words that convince me; it's your face—there's a sort of refreshed and rested look to your countenance that it previously lacked."

"Thank you," Henry said, vindicated. He picked up his morning tea and gulped it down, grimacing when tasting the now-cold liquid.

"Cold, is it?" Bastin raised his eyebrows, looking amused.

Henry nodded.

"It ought to be. The butler brought it in this morning."

"What time is it now?" Henry reached for his pocket before remembering he was in his dressing gown.

"Past noon. I hope you will join us for tea. Violet said you were helpful in the classroom yesterday, and Ottilie will want to hear all about your first day."

"I enjoyed it. I intend to return for Wednesday's class if she'll have me."

"Don't worry; you'll be employed full-time before the year-end." Bastin strolled to the door but paused before pulling it open. "Although, I'd prefer to see you published," he said.

Henry deflected Bastin's remark and smoothed his hand over his unshaven jawline.

"I'll need a shave before I come down."

Bastin nodded as if understanding Henry wasn't yet ready for that conversation and exited the room.

Henry proceeded with his ablutions, thinking again of Anne. Her terror in the theater continued to disturb him. He could not help but acquaint it with an earlier memory. A young woman, whom he'd held in his arms for mere seconds, her face darkened by the shadows of the night, had aroused a similar feeling inside him. He now knew that young woman to be Annabel Leonard, who had genuine reason to be fearful. But did Anne?

If she did, he'd find out. And he'd send the culprit to an early grave.

He sighed, picked up the parceled doll he'd purchased for Alice, and went downstairs.

"Henry!" Ottilie looked up from the block tower she was building with her little girl. They sat on an ornate pale blue rug, bordered and patterned with gold swirls. Wood blocks, each containing a letter of the alphabet, sat in a tower between mother and child. "I'm so pleased you made it back in time to dine with us. Did you manage to complete your errands in Canterbury?"

"I did, indeed. I had a very special errand to take care of whilst I was there. He crouched next to the child, who sent the blocks toppling to the ground with her chubby hand and then fell into a fit of giggles when Ottilie let out an exaggerated gasp.

"This is for Alice." He handed the package to Ottilie.

"Oh, Henry, how thoughtful of you." Ottilie untied the string and unwrapped the brown paper to reveal a curly-haired, brown-eyed porcelain doll. "Look what Uncle Henry brought you, Alice." She picked up the doll and held it up for her daughter. "She has blond curls, just like you."

"Baba!" Alice's face lit up, and she grabbed the doll's delicate white lace dress.

"Gentle," Ottilie warned, still holding onto the doll.

Alice leaned forward, grabbed a tiny fistful of the doll's hair, and pulled it toward her.

"Careful, darling," her mother warned again.

Henry wondered if his choice had been a mistake but changed his mind when a smile spread on Alice's face as she brought the doll to her chest and hugged it.

"It's perfect for her," Ottilie said. "Did you pick it out yourself?"

"The shopkeeper helped," he said with a shrug. Again, he said nothing about Anne. He wanted to keep that private. He wasn't certain what Ottilie or Violet would think about him spending time with a student—even if she was an adult who'd already been married.

"You seem happier today," Ottilie remarked.

"I feel better. And I had an enjoyable day yesterday. I rather like Canterbury."

"I hope that means you'll be extending your stay with us."

"Yes, I think that very likely." Henry smiled to himself. "Very likely, indeed."

CHAPTER THIRTEEN

Oh, what a plague is love! I cannot bear it.
She will inconstant prove, I greatly fear it;
It so torments my mind, That my heart faileth.

—Thomas Carew, *Phillida Flouts Me*

THREE DAYS PASSED before their fevers broke, but Mrs. Taylor was still too weak to get out of bed, and Rupert still fussed and wailed no matter how much Annabel rocked and soothed him with kisses and gentle words. Even the little stuffed bear in the sailor's suit failed to bring a smile to his face.

The good doctor came to check on them every day, but it fell to Annabel to care for them, and she'd grown weary to the bone. Drops of laudanum helped Mrs. Taylor rest, but it seldom came at the same time as Rupert's. It was one of those rare moments when both were sound asleep that Annabel took the time to wash. While splashing cold water on her face and scrubbing her neck and arms with soap in the kitchen, she thought of the luxurious warm baths she'd taken as the daughter of Bernard Leonard, Bristol's great confectioner. She cleaned her teeth with paste and brushed her hair. Still, she scarcely recognized the woman who stared back at her in the looking glass. Chopped, unkempt hair, sunken eyes, lackluster skin, and a frame so thin it was almost gaunt.

Nate wasn't due to pay his weekly visit until Friday. She didn't think she could wait that long. She crept into Mrs. Taylor's bedchamber and checked on her patients. Both were still sleeping. All she had to do was find a boy willing to take a message to Whitstable. He'd need train fare and want payment for his pains. She dug into her reticule, retrieved the money she'd received from her hair, extracted a few shillings, and then scribbled a note to Nate before creeping downstairs. The shop had remained closed, with customers warned away that fever plagued the house. None came to claim their half-mended clothing, and Annabel was grateful as she did not possess the skill to complete Mrs. Taylor's work. But the neat pile of completed garments, those Mrs. Taylor had spent hours expertly sewing and mending, also went unclaimed, and this terrified Annabel. How would Mrs. Taylor pay her rent, having lost so much income?

She unlocked and cracked open the door to the shop and squinted at the daylight, which now seemed sharp to her eyes. Looking up and down the narrow street, she spotted a ragged boy turning onto Best Lane, where the baker would be baking fresh bread. She stepped onto the street, closing the door behind her, and hastened after the boy. Sure enough, she found him loitering near the baker's shop. It was difficult to determine his age, but she predicted him to be about ten or eleven years.

"Should you like a loaf of bread?" she asked, approaching the child.

He turned to look at her; large, dark eyes dominated his face. "Yes, please, ma'am."

"First, answer me this: Have you ever been to Whitstable?"

"Yes, ma'am. I know it well. There's work to be had there on occasion.

"Last year, a fishmonger learned me how to shuck oysters. But I had to stop working on account of slicing me hand open." He held up his palm to reveal a jagged, raised scar running from the crook of his thumb across the length of his palm.

"Well, I don't need you to shuck any oysters, but I do need

someone to go to Whitstable—to the harbor—and deliver a message for me. I'll buy you a loaf and give you train fare with change to spare for yourself."

A customer exited the bakery, and Annabel caught a whiff of freshly baked bread. Her stomach seized with hunger.

The boy must have smelled it, too. He licked his cracked lips and looked longingly at the bakery.

"Two loaves," he said.

"One and a half," Annabel's stomach twisted with hunger again.

"Done!"

"Wait here." Annabel pulled open the door to the bakery and stepped inside. Almost overcome with hunger, she could barely find her voice to order.

Annabel didn't recognize the sharp-nosed woman behind the counter who eyed her with obvious suspicion.

"Two loaves, please," She opened her reticule, and the woman's face relaxed when she placed a coin on the counter. The shopkeeper snatched the money and put the loaves on the counter. Annabel tucked the bread under her arm and turned to see the hungry-eyed boy standing by the door, waiting for her.

"Get away!" The shopkeeper flew at the child and wielded the broom in the air, striking the lad once on the back before he scrambled away.

"Stop!" Annabel raced outside, but she was too late. The boy had vanished.

The shopkeeper scouted the street, holding her broom like Poscidon's tridcnt.

"Thieving vermin," she mumbled before returning to her place of business.

Sure the lad would follow her, Annabel skirted the corner, broke one of the loaves in half, and bit into the fresh, soft bread. Seconds later, he was at her side.

"What's the gentleman's name I'm to find, ma'am?" He fixed his eyes on the bread. Annabel handed him the other half of her loaf and let him devour it before answering.

"The gentleman's name is Nate. I've written it on this note. Can you read?"

"A little," he said.

She showed him the name written out on the note and touched each letter, sounding it out for him.

"Mr. Nate Trawler," the boy reiterated confidently.

"He's a fishmonger."

"Don't worry, miss. I'll find him."

She handed the boy the second loaf and the coins. "Go directly to the train station," she instructed.

"Yes, miss," he said.

"And mind this, if you make off with that money, Mr. Trawler will be the one looking for you," she warned.

"No, miss. I promise. I'll find Mr. Trawler and bring him to you," he said before scampering off.

Annabel watched until he disappeared from her sight before she made the short walk home, taking small bites of her loaf as she walked, wondering if Mrs. Taylor would have the strength to eat the rest.

She'd subsisted on watery vegetable soup that Annabel had made by boiling vegetables in water as she'd seen Mrs. Taylor do many times before. And although the results weren't the same, Annabel felt reassured by the few weak sips Mrs. Taylor and Rupert had accepted.

Silence greeted Annabel as she reentered the shop. Neither Mrs. Taylor nor Rupert had woken while she'd been out. Her body weakened with relief as if it had been held together by fear alone. She leaned with her back against the door and slid to the floor.

How had life turned dark so quickly? It seemed as if years had passed since that magical day she'd spent with Henry—since he'd kissed her outside this very door. *Will I see him again? Will I feel such happiness again?*

She longed to feel as carefree and weightless as she had that day when life felt exciting and full of possibilities. *But it had all been a lie. Life is cruel, and happiness is nothing more than a magician's illusion. While I kissed Henry, Rupert and Mrs. Taylor lay deathly ill, and now they might die.* Pulling her knees to her chest, she bowed her head and let the tears flow freely down her cheeks.

BY THE TIME Violet strode into the classroom on Wednesday afternoon, Henry was already busy distributing the ink bottles. "How thoughtful of you, Henry." The headmistress dropped her work bag next to her podium. "I've had such a busy day of it today. Did you come early to visit with my brother?"

"Yes," Henry lied. His early arrival had nothing to do with Bastin and everything to do with Anne. He'd thought of nothing but the moment he'd meet with her again in the classroom. The days since he'd last seen her on Saturday had passed as slowly as a march to the gallows.

"We will continue helping the students with their writing again today. I might give them a bit of dictation. Then we will proceed with individual corrections. Some students are more advanced than others, so I'll give them additional writing exercises."

Henry smiled and thought how pleased Violet would be when Anne walked through the door. Violet had been upset when she'd said she wouldn't be returning, but Henry knew that things were very different now.

A bell sounded, breaking into Henry's thoughts. "Is it time to begin?"

"That's the first bell to alert our boarding students that their self-study hours begin in five minutes. They'll start moving to the library or their rooms. Our working ladies should be coming into the classroom now. A second bell will sound next, indicating the start of the class hour."

As she spoke, two ladies entered the class and took their seats.

"Welcome back," the headmistress said.

More students followed, assuming the seats they'd occupied during the first class. Henry's eyes moved to the door as he waited for Anne to enter the classroom. He stood with his hands clasped behind his back, stiffening with disappointment as each student entered. Anne was not amongst them.

The shrill bell sounded a second time.

"Would you be so kind as to close the door, Mr. Hudsyn?"

Henry moved to the door and peered into the empty hallway. His heart lifted when he saw a dark-haired, slim-figured woman in the distance, but plummeted again as she turned and hurried in the opposite direction. He sighed and he closed the door. *He'd been too free with Anne and frightened her away. He should have known better. After all, life had a way of snatching happiness out from under the unsuspecting man.*

"Now, ladies, if you will ready your books and quill pens, I will begin a short dictation, and Mr. Hudsyn will stroll the aisles to assist those in need of help."

Henry forced himself to appear interested as he peered at the composition books, some neatly composed and some so ink-blotted and scrawled they would have earned any schoolboy several lashes. Violet's method of teaching was preferable. No lashing had ever helped him learn better.

Henry sighed. He'd long been free of the master's cane, but he'd gladly feel its sting again if it meant seeing Anne walk into the classroom.

The hour passed slowly, but finally, the class ended, and Henry was free to go. He'd already determined to journey into town and visit Anne at home. He felt certain something had happened to prevent her from attending class. She'd said she was looking forward to it and to seeing him again. He wouldn't be able to rest until he knew all was well with her.

Rushing to pile up the books left behind, Henry nearly made a mess of them before Violet steadied them while adding, "It seems our most promising student didn't return after all. I'm somewhat disappointed. I was hoping she would overcome her fears and change her mind, but perhaps she needs more time. Let's hope we see Mrs. Crawford on Saturday morning. I'll prepare something a little more challenging for her just in case.

"Yes," Henry said, trying to hide his concern.

"Good. Then I shall see you this Saturday. And I hope you will join us for tea this time. The twins haven't seen much of their Uncle Henry since he's been in Canterbury."

"Of course, I'd love to see the twins," Henry promised, trying not to appear to be rushing when he exited the classroom. As he walked, he made a mental note to revisit the toymakers before Saturday. The shops wouldn't be open at this hour, but that was of no concern. He had a far more pressing reason to ride into town than buying toys.

It was a straight path from the college to the town, and Henry, half-fearful and half-hopeful, kept his eyes on the road for the mile-long journey. There was no sign of Anne.

He allowed his carriage to take him through Westgate and down The Friars but instructed him to stop before turning onto Orange Street. He thought it better to approach the seamstress's shop on foot to draw as little attention to his visit as possible. He rounded the corner and then came to an abrupt stop.

Annabel stood outside the small shop, conversing with a gentleman. Though he stood quite a distance away, he could see the man in question was taller and broader built than Nate. A bushel of black hair and an equally thick beard confirmed her companion wasn't Nate, whose build was slighter and whose hair was lighter in color and texture.

Anne's back faced him as she peered up at the brawny stranger, but Henry didn't need to see her expression. He could sense the intensity of their conversation. The man looked down at her, his expression intense. Then he reached into his pocket and withdrew a bag of coins. Anne shook her head as he tried to give it to her. He placed a hand on her shoulder, bent his head close to hers, and spoke again.

Henry sucked in his breath as he saw Anne accept the coins and allow the man into her lodgings—his hand still resting on the small of her back. He turned and hastened back to his carriage, his chest heaving and his mind whirling.

How many gentleman friends does the widow Mrs. Crawford entertain? Am I simply one of many? She claims Nate to be a family friend. How, then, will she explain this gentleman? And how, then, does she explain me to others?

He climbed into his carriage and instructed the driver to turn the carriage around and take him home. "Do not venture down Orange Street!"

The driver took great pains to turn the carriage around in the curved, narrow street. It would have undoubtedly made more sense to traverse down Orange Street, which connected to High Street at its end. But Henry could not chance being seen by Anne. She'd accuse him of spying on her, and he'd look like a jealous fool. After all, he had no claim on her.

Yet, she'd accepted and sought out his hand in the darkness of the theater—under the guise of needing comfort—and she'd let him kiss her goodnight. He'd reacted with genuine concern to her discomfort.

Perhaps Anne used affliction to garner his sympathy and affection. Any decent sort of man would try to comfort a woman in distress, and a widow like Mrs. Crawford would know as much. Surely, it was no coincidence that she'd once again appeared anguished when speaking with her gentleman friend today. She'd even embraced him under the guise of needing comfort and protection. Henry recalled how Anne had lightly protested him purchasing the bear for Rupert, saying she'd never accept such an expensive present on her own behalf. He remembered how she'd led him to the tearoom on Sun Street with confidence and afterward insisted he take her to the theater, even though he made his reluctance about the play clear. He recalled how she'd snatched the cheese from the cheesemonger's hand, even after Henry refused it on her behalf. And then there were the cheesemonger's words as they left the market, *"Bring any gentleman you like; it's all the same to me so long as he has coins in his pocket,"* she'd said.

Henry gritted his teeth until his jaw felt tight. Anne Crawford had played him for a fool.

CHAPTER FOURTEEN

Love bade me welcome;
yet my soul drew back,
Guilty of dust and sin.

—George Herbert, *Love*

"Letters for you, my lord." Henry's valet, Jamison, lowered a silver tray in front of him.

"Letters?" Henry frowned at the tray. "I had no idea anyone knew I was here." He put down his egg-filled spoon and reached for the envelope.

"It came from your estate in Sevenoaks," Jamison said.

"Ahh," Henry nodded, taking the letter opener, and slitting the envelope open. "That makes sense."

Jamison nodded and left the room.

"Who sent it?" Ottilie asked as Henry scanned the note.

"My friend, Hobsworth. He wants me to visit him at Stoke-ford Manor. He says he's going to perish of boredom if he spends one day longer holed up with my mother and his uncle." Henry groaned. "Poor sod."

"Why don't you ask him to join us in Kent? We have plenty of room," Bastin offered.

"He'd be most welcome." Ottilie wiped the remnants of Alice's breakfast from her mouth.

"Let's see what my mother has to say first." Henry slit open the second envelope and unfolded the letter from his mother.

Dearest Henry,

I trust you are spending your time wisely and have given serious thought to our last conversation. For my sake, Lord Stokeford has decided to give you yet another chance in allowing Hobsworth to invite you for a visit. I expect you will accept the invitation and take the opportunity to show your stepfather that you are remorseful and have reformed your ways.

Your loving mother,
Lady Stokeford

"Oh dear, your face tells me Hobsworth won't be permitted to visit us here." Ottilie picked up Alice and kissed her on the cheek before handing her to Bastin, who kissed the child's face until the little girl shrieked with laughter.

Ottilie pushed back her chair and stood up. "I'd be sorry for you to leave us. Perhaps a short visit will satisfy your mother."

"I don't have to go at all," Henry said. "I am my own man. Lady Stokeford has no hold on me."

"But she's still your mother, Henry, and the only one you will ever have." Ottilie caressed her stomach. "Trust me, until you have your children, you won't understand how much she loves you."

Henry sighed. An image of Anne embracing the burly stranger flashed in his mind, and escaping Canterbury suddenly seemed very desirable.

"Very well. I'll go. You'll give my apologies to Violet?" He raised his eyebrows in question.

"Of course; when will you leave?"

"Today." Henry pushed back his chair and stood up. "If I wait, I'll likely change my mind." He walked over to his cousin. "But not to worry, I'll be back within a week—two at the most." He kissed Ottilie on the cheek, and Bastin brought the baby forward so he could kiss her.

"Goodbye, Alice. I'll have another present for you next time I see you." He bent to kiss the little girl's rosy cheek.

"Baba!" she said.

"All right, I'll bring you another one of those."

"You'll spoil her," Ottilie said.

"That's what uncles are supposed to do, isn't it?" He shook Bastin's hand. "Perhaps seeing Hobsworth will lift your spirits."

"Jack's right. You seem a bit down lately. Did something happen?"

"No, I'm perfectly fine." Henry worked to keep his voice light. He hadn't realized his gloomy mood had been noticeable to others.

The three of them left the room, and Henry returned to his breakfast, thrusting his spoon into the white flesh of his boiled egg. He held the spoon to his mouth and then plopped it down again.

He had no appetite for food. All he wanted to do was forget the image of Anne in that stranger's arms.

"I'M SO SORRY we have to leave you," Mrs. Taylor sat next to her husband on the couch with an orange and brown blanket spread across her lap and spoke in a breathy whisper, "You've been such a help to me. And Rupert simply adores you."

"I wish I'd been more helpful. If only I hadn't stayed out—"

Annabel swallowed the guilt that sat like bitter medicine in her throat. Mrs. Taylor's illness had left her too weak to continue her work and care for Rupert, who'd made a remarkable, full recovery. The doctor said it was likely the strain of continuing to work and care for a sick child while feverish herself that had caused Mrs. Taylor's body to weaken permanently. But by a stroke of luck, Mr. Taylor had arrived home unexpectedly from the sea and was so shocked to discover that his wife and son had been near death that he decided to close her little shop and move them to live with his sister in Cornwell. The good woman, who now worked diligently to complete Mrs. Taylor's unfinished sewing, had rushed to Canterbury to help her brother and was forced to share a room with Annabel until Nate found alternative lodging for her. He seemed to think it a good idea to move her out of town and farther into the countryside.

"Don't blame yourself for anything," Mrs. Taylor continued and then paused to catch her breath. "If it weren't for you—" she rasped—"I fear the outcome would h-have been quite different." The sentiment seemed to have exhausted her, and she leaned against her husband's strapping frame and closed her eyes.

"Hush now, my love," Mr. Taylor said. "You mustn't speak. You need your rest."

Annabel pulled Rupert onto her lap, and he grinned. She reached for the wooden horses his father had carved for him, and he clutched one in each fist, chewing first on one and then the other.

Mrs. Taylor's eyes fluttered open. She gave her husband a faint smile before her eyes closed again. Mr. Taylor put his arms around his wife's shoulders and gently maneuvered her body into a lying position on the couch as he stood up. Annabel watched as he lovingly placed a cushion under her head and rearranged the blanket to cover her body. Mr. and Mrs. Taylor's marriage was very different from Papa's and Mrs. Leonard's, who'd always behaved like stiff soldiers and never displayed the tender care she witnessed here.

"You know we appreciate all you've done for us, don't you?" he said, turning to Annabel. "I don't know what would have happened to them if you'd not been here." He wiped an emerging tear from the corner of his eye, and Annabel lowered her gaze. She'd never seen a man cry before—certainly not her Papa—and it shocked her to see a rugged sailor succumb to tears. She was glad to see it. Mrs. Taylor was the kindest person she'd ever encountered—aside from Stella—and she deserved a river of tears.

"I'm sorry," he said, shaking his head. "It's selfish of me, considering what you've been through, being a widow."

Annabel pressed her lips together. Now, she felt ashamed that she'd taken on the identity of a widow. How foolish of her to have been excited about the freedoms it afforded her. She hadn't thought about how experiencing the death of a spouse would have been horrible—at least if the marriage was a love match like the Taylors.

But she'd done what was necessary. She'd done right to run from that dangerous arrangement Papa had made for her. *When I marry, it will be to a man who loves me as much as Mr. Taylor loves his wife.*

Rupert dropped his wooden ponies and clutched Annabel's dress.

"Why don't you go outside and get some fresh air?" Mr. Taylor reached for his child and scooped him off Annabel's lap.

Rupert gurgled and buried his head in his papa's neck. He was a sweet-natured baby who went smiling and trustingly into everyone's arms. Annabel supposed a baby who'd only known love and never had to fear adults would do so. She'd seen some sad sights on the street of Canterbury—starving children, carrying their infant siblings, forced to beg. It tore at her heart every time, knowing she didn't have enough coins to help them all.

"I can take Rupert out for a walk," she offered.

"No, you need some time to yourself, and little Rupert, here, needs to spend some time with his papa." He kissed the child's cheek.

"I suppose I could go to the ladies' college. If I hurry, I can still make the morning class."

"School?" Mr. Taylor shook his head. "You're a funny lass, you are."

Annabel would have preferred to take a hansom cab than walk the mile-long stretch outside the city to the school, but she didn't think it prudent to waste money when her future was uncertain. Mr. Taylor had insisted on repaying the advance she'd given them on the rent, and she felt too guilty to spend money on luxuries, knowing how his family suffered from having to close their shop, something for which she felt partially responsible.

As soon as she entered the iron gates that surrounded the college grounds, Annabel's thoughts turned to Henry. They hadn't seen each other since the night Mrs. Taylor and Rupert had fallen ill two weeks before. She'd missed three classes and was too beset with work and worry to send a message to Henry.

Now she realized he hadn't even come looking for her. She vaguely remembered him saying he would like to take her to tea again, but she couldn't be sure. It all seemed so long ago. She wondered how he would react to seeing her again. Did he think she'd been avoiding him? Perhaps Henry had inquired after her and learned about the illness that plagued the family where she lodged. She couldn't blame him if he thought it best to keep his distance.

Annabel sighed as she entered the main building, quite possibly for the last time. What did it matter what Henry thought now that she was moving away? She hoped they would part as friends, but she'd likely never see him again.

The college's interior, like its exterior, was all stone, which gave it the appearance of a dungeon—or at least what Annabel imagined a dungeon would look like. But an effort had been made to warm the area with navy blue velvet curtains, yellow armchairs, and fresh flowers in the lobby. Two busts—one of Shakespeare and one of Canterbury's very own Kit Marlow—sat at the foot of the stairs. Annabel walked down the long stretch of hallway that housed several rooms. She'd never ventured upstairs but heard that the science laboratory and library were on the first floor. *If only I could...*she bit her lip. *What use is it to wish?*

She wished her mama had not died during childbirth, she wished her papa loved her better, she wished her stepmother hadn't allowed her ambitions to rule her heart, she wished Stella did not have to hide away in Italy, she wished Mrs. Taylor had made a full recovery, and she wished she could go back in time and change the events of that night—but she could not.

The free class had already begun, and Annabel faced a closed door. She knocked softly and waited. The prospect of seeing Henry again aroused a nervous excitement within her. Perhaps it was time to stop wishing and look forward to a better future.

"Mrs. Crawford. How wonderful to see you again." Headmistress Thomas greeted her with a warm smile.

Annabel stepped inside and scanned the room. The students sat with their heads bent over their notebooks, some paused in thought, and others made slow movements with their quills as they wrote in their composition books.

Annabel's heart sank. Henry was nowhere to be seen.

CHAPTER FIFTEEN

Stokeford Manor, Dorset

Body fished from Thames, suspected to be Daughter of Confectionary Giant, Bernard Leonard

"Have you seen this?" Hobsworth thrust a newspaper at Henry as he entered the lavish dining room.

He took the newspaper from Hobsworth and frowned. "I thought she ran off to Scotland with her lover. Isn't that what they reported a few weeks ago?"

"Yes, it is. And can you imagine what that did to Craventhorp's pride—being jilted by a commoner?"

"You think he murdered her?"

"I never thought him capable of murder, but—"

"Of course, he is capable. He's an animal. You saw what he did to that poor girl's wrist at Madame Katrina's. It made me sick to my stomach. And you and Burdington just sat there and laughed at his revolting jokes."

"Don't take your anger out on me because I had the good sense not to engage in fisticuffs with a viscount over a courtesan. Do you know how many peers frequent that place and witnessed your behavior?"

"My behavior?" Henry shook the newspaper. "Doesn't it strike you as odd that my behavior came under scrutiny and not that of the man who brutalized a woman in front of a roomful of people?"

"He acted like a brute, to be sure, but he didn't break the harlot's wrist. He grabbed it and left a bruise—unacceptable, yes—but he was drunk, as were you. And, you know you tend to overreact when you drink too much."

Henry's jaw tightened. "I know what I saw, and the only thing I am starting to regret is this friendship of ours."

"What are you two whispering so furiously about?" Lady Stokeford swept into the room.

"This terrible business in the newspaper," Hobsworth said.

A footman appeared from one of the corners of the lavish room and pulled out Lady Stokeford's chair.

"Tea, my lady?"

"Yes, and a newspaper."

The footman left and reappeared minutes later to place a newspaper in front of his mistress.

Runaway Heiress's Drowned Body Discovered in Thames! Lady Stokeford picked up the newspaper and scoffed at the title. "It's that Leonard girl again. She's been in the paper for weeks. One would think she was the queen's daughter, the way they go on about her disappearance."

"Well, they appear to have found her now," Henry said dryly.

"Good, perhaps it will bring an end to the story. I am tired of reading about it every day."

The footman placed Lady Stokeford's tea in front of her, and she pushed the newspaper toward him, indicating that she wanted it taken from her sight.

Henry shook his head. Marrying an earl hadn't done his mother any good. He spun on his heels and marched toward the room's exit with the newspaper in hand.

"Where are you going? Your father will return from his

morning ride soon and will want to see you at the breakfast table."

Henry stopped. His body bristled. He hated it when she insisted on referring to the earl as "his father". It was both ludicrous and embarrassing. Hobsworth was Lord Stokeford's heir presumptive, but it seems his mother harbored some fantasy that the earldom would be passed onto him as though she could rewrite the ancient inheritance laws simply by wishful thinking.

"Did you hear me, Henry? I said, your father—"

"Which father are you referring to, Mother?" He snapped. "I seem to have lost count."

"I see you are determined to be disagreeable today, so I shall spare you my company." Lady Stokeford raised her chin and assumed the look of a person deeply wronged.

Hobsworth frowned in apparent confusion at Henry's needless cruelty. *If he knew the truth about Lady Stokeford, he wouldn't have an ounce of sympathy for her,* Henry thought before striding out of the room.

Once alone, he turned his full attention to the newspaper.

The body, having deteriorated in the water, cannot be identified.

However, the clue to the victim's identity comes from a piece of jewelry around her neck, which Mr. Leonard identified as belonging to his daughter.

Again, no picture of Leonard's daughter accompanied the article, which would have been in bad taste. Still, Henry would have liked to have seen one. He'd tried many times to remember her face but the only image that ever came to his mind was the terror in her eyes. He could not even recall their color—only the panic emblazoned within them. Their encounter had only lasted seconds, and as Hobsworth pointed out, he'd been rather drunk that night. And it had been dark in the garden. But he hadn't imagined her terror. It had been real. He'd seen the same expression in the harlot's eyes at Madame Katrina's earlier that evening.

As always, when he thought back to that night, Craventhorp's arrogant face came to mind. Once again, Henry recalled how Craventhorp stepped out of the shadows and watched the young lady with bemused interest from afar, like a hunter lying in wait.

A suitable analogy, Henry thought, for one who'd spent his free time at school pulling the wings off flies and watching insects burn after he'd dropped a match on them. Boarding schools were the perfect place for the sadistic. It was as Darwin suggested—survival of the fittest. Unfortunately, the fittest were often the cruelest.

There was no doubt in his mind that Lord Craventhorp was sadistic, but was he capable of murder?

Henry tossed the newspaper aside and rang for his valet. The urge to leave Stokeford Manor and return to Canterbury swelled inside him. He couldn't abide staying in a house with his mother or Hobsworth, for that matter, a second longer.

A knock sounded at his door. "Come in, Jamison. No need to knock; I rang for you."

The door opened, and Hobsworth stepped into Henry's bedchamber.

"What is it?" Henry snapped.

"I've come to apologize." Hobsworth's plump cheeks reddened, and Henry's heart softened. He'd always liked Hobsworth for his humility. He was the unintended heir to an earldom and lacked the hubris Henry despised.

"You rang for me, sir?" Jamison appeared in the doorway.

"Yes, I'll need you to pack my trunk. I intend to return home today."

"Today, sir?"

"Yes, as soon as possible." He glanced at Hobsworth.

"You don't have to leave, Henry."

Henry slipped his hands into his pockets. "My sudden departure is not to escape you, but my mother."

"I don't mean to judge you or take Craventhorp's side over yours," Hobsworth said, apparently not believing Henry's declaration. "Heaven knows I don't even like the man, but I worry when you speak so freely about him."

"Why are you afraid of him, Hobs? He's a bankrupt viscount with nothing but a run-down estate to inherit. Whereas you are an earl-in-waiting, with a fortune to inherit."

"I'm not afraid of him but would not make him my enemy as you have done. And if you accuse him of murder—" he shook his head—"well, you cannot do so without solid proof." Hobsworth folded his arms. "Go back to Canterbury and forget this business. I fear, if you do not, it will not bode well for you."

THE ROOM EMPTIED around Annabel, yet she could not force herself up from her desk. Sadness overwhelmed her as she closed her composition book. It was likely the last time she'd sit in this classroom or be asked, as she had today, to write down her impressions of a book she'd read. Annabel had so many thoughts about the books she loved that it had been difficult to choose just one. She could hardly believe that anyone was excited to know she loved reading or cared about her ideas.

"Mrs. Crawford?" The headmistress stood next to her desk. "It seems as though you had a lot to write about today. Did you enjoy the exercise?"

"Very much," Annabel said.

"What book did you choose to write about?"

Annabel pressed her lips together. What if the headmistress didn't approve of her choice or thought her remarks ridiculous?

Headmistress Thomas grabbed hold of a chair, placed it next to Annabel's desk, and sat down. "You were free to choose any book you liked. I shan't judge your choice."

"It's not a new book." She glanced at the headmistress.

"Some of the best books are old books. You need only think of Shakespeare."

"This book isn't as well-known as Shakespeare's plays, I'm afraid."

"May I?" The headmistress asked, reaching for Annabel's composition book.

Annabel nodded; her throat too dry to answer with words.

"Aah, *The Female Quixote* by Charlotte Lennox—one of my favorite novels."

"Truly?" Annabel straightened.

"Absolutely! But let's not talk about what I think, just yet. Tell me why you chose to write about it."

Annabel wet her lips. "You've heard of Don Quixote, I suppose."

The headmistress nodded again.

Annabel swallowed. "Well, my papa always encouraged learning, but he didn't approve of novel reading. He believed novels could be dangerous for a young woman."

The headmistress nodded. "Yes, I'm aware that some people still believe that falsity."

"He wasn't opposed to all novels, only those I read in secret. But he thought so highly of *The Female Quixote* that he purchased it and instructed me to read it." The tale she told as Anne wasn't entirely fictional. *The Female Quixote* and *Clarissa* were the only two novels that had survived the burning and both had been given to her by Mrs. Leonard.

"Did he?" A smile pulled at the corners of the headmistress's lips. "And what did you think of the novel?"

"I adored it, but not for the same reasons as Papa." Annabel shifted in her seat to face the headmistress. "He said it would teach me a good lesson on the dangers of reading novels. But as I read, I saw that wasn't the case, and I felt as though the author, Miss Lennox, and I shared a private joke."

The headmistress's face brightened. "Go on."

"Arabella—that's the heroine's name—foolishly confuses real

life with the French romance novels she loves to read, and her behavior is so outlandish that it is comical. I knew immediately that the author intended to mock the notion that women cannot tell the difference between stories and real life."

Headmistress Thomas clapped her hands. "I couldn't agree more, and I look forward to reading your essay on the subject." She reached for the composition book again.

"I'm afraid I can't let you have it."

The headmistress retracted her hand. "I expect you noticed that Mr. Hudsyn isn't here today. Do you still fear—"

"It isn't him," Annabel interjected. "I—I'm sorry, but I might not be able to attend these classes in the future. You see, the woman with whom I lived fell ill and has moved to be with her family. Because of this, I need to find a new place to stay. It may be far away from here. I don't have any skills or talents, and I have little money of my own to spend, so I think I must go to a farm and earn my keep or something. I don't know."

"No skills or talents? Is that what you believe?"

Annabel dropped her gaze. *If the headmistress knew the truth— that I've only ever known wealth, luxury, and idleness—she'd surely despise me.* "Babies seem to like me. Perhaps I will find a job as a mother's helper."

"That sounds like an excellent idea. Tell me, how would you like to become a student at this college?"

"I should love it," Annabel said, "but as I said, I don't have the funds."

"We have scholarships available. I could arrange for you to attend free of charge."

"On charity?" Annabel stiffened.

Do you wish to bring shame to your family by choosing spinsterhood and living off your papa's charity? Her stepmother's voice resounded in her mind. *That your papa has immense wealth does not entitle you to his charity. A woman must fulfill her obligation to society by becoming a wife and a mother. That is a woman's sole purpose. Those who refuse to do their part and rely on charity are an albatross around society's neck.*

It was easy for Annabel to envision the stares and disdain she would incur from the students and masters as a charity pupil. They would think her lazy and idle. She shivered. "I cannot accept charity."

"It wouldn't be charity. You said you'd like to find work as a mother's helper. Well, it so happens that one of our school mistresses requires such help."

"And you think she would approve of me?" Annabel said, unable to believe her luck.

"I know she would. In fact, why don't you come with me now? I'm expected at her home for tea. My husband and children are already there and no doubt wondering what has delayed me."

"I don't want to impose," Annabel said. "They are not expecting me."

"Oh, we are not so serious in our lives as to worry about such trivialities. You will be most welcome."

⇛⇛❯❮⇚⇚

ANNABEL'S NERVES SANG as she sat in the carriage beside the headmistress. If all went well, she would finally be one of those students she'd watched from afar. The thought of reading, studying, and discussing books without censure made her dizzy with glee.

"You have nothing to fear," Headmistress Thomas reassured as if she could sense Annabel's anxiety. "This won't be an interview, only a casual introduction over tea."

The carriage turned onto the grounds of a palatial home built of red brick and stone, surrounded by greenery and fountains adorned with statues of Greek gods and goddesses.

"What do you think?" Headmistress Thomas said.

"It's a lovely country house," Annabel said, and then, reminding herself that a girl in need of charity would be awed by such opulence, she quickly added, "I mean, it's beautiful, just like a palace."

The front door opened before Annabel alighted from the carriage. Two children raced down the steps, shouting, 'Mama!" The headmistress opened her arms to receive the children, who showered her with kisses. A little girl in a yellow dress toddled outside behind them and attempted to climb down the stairs on wobbly legs. Annabel raced forward to intercept her dismount.

"There you are, little rabbit! You were supposed to wait for Mama, remember?" A beautiful flaxen-haired woman with bright blue eyes and rosy, dimpled cheeks came toward them and looked questioningly at the stranger holding her child.

"Allow me to introduce my new protégée"—Headmistress Thomas stepped forward—"and, I hope, your new nanny."

Annabel stood up so the headmistress could make the proper introductions, and the little girl pulled at her dress and shouted, "Up."

She scooped the giggling child in her arms.

"This is Mrs. Anne Crawford, who just saved your daughter from tumbling down the stairs. I think that is reason enough to hire her." She turned to Annabel. "Anne, meet my sister-in-law Mrs. Bastin."

"Pleased to meet you, ma'am," Annabel said.

"And this little one is called Alice." The headmistress reached over and tickled the child in Annabel's arms.

The little girl shrieked with laughter.

Annabel studied her blond curls and chocolate-brown eyes. Then she turned to look at the child's mother—the woman looked distinctly like Henry.

One of our school mistresses requires help, the headmistress had said.

Annabel froze. The child in her arms was Henry's Alice.

CHAPTER SIXTEEN

Ay, truly, for the power of beauty will sooner transform honesty
from what it is to a bawd than the force of honesty can translate
beauty into his likeness.
This was sometime a paradox, but now the time gives it proof.
I did love you once.

—Shakespeare, *Hamlet*

Henry was so eager to escape Stokeford Manor that he departed for Kent without sending word to Ottilie or Jack, and he smiled at the idea of surprising his cousin with his arrival. She was always delighted to see him, and he missed her home's warmth and lively atmosphere. Stokeford Manor was like a mausoleum in comparison and returning to his cousin felt very much like returning home—or at least, what he'd always wanted home to feel like.

A footman greeted him at the front door, and Jamison promptly ordered him to "see to Lord Hudsyn's luggage."

"Hang on." Henry stopped the man. "Is my cousin home?"

"Yes, my lord. I believe she's in her chambers, and Mr. Bastin is in his study. Shall I inform them of your arrival?"

"No, leave them to their business. Where's the little one?"

"In the drawing room with her nanny."

"Excellent." Henry turned to Jamison and asked him to retrieve the present he'd purchased for Alice from his luggage. When his valet returned with the parcel, Henry took it and went to the drawing room.

"Does a little girl live here?" He stepped into the room, placing his hand over his brows as if searching a vast landscape and deliberately avoiding "seeing" the child who sat on the floor with her building blocks. "I have an important package for a brown-eyed girl named Alice."

The child clapped her hands and giggled. Then she pushed herself up and ran to tug on the hem of his coat.

"Where can she be?" he muttered, looking everywhere but the spot where the little girl stood.

"Up!" Alice shrieked, tugging harder.

He dropped his eyes to look at the little girl, bouncing with excitement. "Is that a mouse, tugging at my coat!" He pretended to dance on his tiptoes.

The child clapped her hands and stomped her feet, attempting to copy him.

"Oh? You look just like Alice. Let me see for sure. You could be a mouse pretending to be Alice…" He lifted her into his arms, the present still in his hand, pulled her close, and hugged her. "Oh yes. *This* is my Alice."

Then he saw Anne. His body went rigid.

Anne sat on Alice's blanket, wooden blocks heaped before her, and smiled at him.

He set the toddler down and straightened.

What are you doing here? He asked a voiceless question, staring at her as though she were an apparition who would disappear at any moment.

"Up!" Alice tugged at his coat, but he could not tear his eyes off Anne.

"You look surprised," Anne said, getting to her feet. "Didn't they tell you? I'm the new nanny—actually, I'm more of a nanny's helper, to be exact—Alice is getting a little too rambunctious for Mrs. Teal to manage on her own."

He narrowed his eyes. *What is she talking about? Is my mind playing tricks on me?*

"Your cousin hired me on Mrs. Thomas's recommendation," she continued as if that would help clarify things.

Alice wandered from Henry's side as if sensing the game was over and plopped down next to her blocks.

"I don't understand," he finally managed to speak. Did *Violet send her here? Why?*

"I'm to attend regular classes at the college, too." She came toward him, her face glowing with excitement.

"You returned to college, then? I thought you'd lost interest."

"No, never. I—"

He raised his eyebrows. "You had to tend to someone else's needs?"

"Yes." She lowered her gaze.

Henry squared his shoulders, his suspicions confirmed. "Well, it seems you have since been freed or jilted."

"What?" Anne looked up, her eyes wide.

"I saw you," Henry said bitterly. "On Orange Street, outside the shop. With him."

"Who?"

"That man. That sailor. He gave you a bag of coins."

"Do you mean, Mr. Taylor?"

"I don't know. How many men do you hold a private meeting with each week?"

Her face paled. "Is *that* what you think of me?" She stepped back, increasing the distance between them.

"Am I wrong? Should I disbelieve my own eyes?" He despised the coldness in his voice but felt powerless to control it.

"No," she said, "your eyes didn't fail you, but your heart and mind did. You aren't the person I thought you were."

"And, it seems, neither are you."

She shook her head and stepped away from him.

"Answer me." Henry caught her arm. "If you are going to be a nanny to my cousin's daughter, then I need to know what sort of person you truly are."

"Henry?" Bastin's voice sounded behind him, and he dropped Anne's arm.

"Is something the matter?" Bastin came up beside them.

"Not at all," Henry forced a casual tone. "I was just talking to Alice's new nanny."

"Papa! Alice shrieked and ran to him.

Bastin glanced at Anne before turning to his daughter. "Hello, sweetheart." He picked up the child and kissed her.

She leaned forward and reached for the package tucked under Henry's arm. "Baba!" she said.

"What's that?" Bastin asked.

"She's right. It's a present for her." He handed Bastin the package.

Jack took it and tucked it under his free arm. "A present!" he said, turning to his daughter. "Shall we open it?"

Alice tried to grab the package, and her father set her down on the blanket and placed the present before her.

"Excuse me, sir. If you don't mind, I need to tend to something." Anne said, looking close to tears. "It'll only take a few minutes."

"Of course, take as long as you need." Bastin settled on the blanket next to his daughter. "I've been waiting all day to spend time with my favorite princess." He smiled at Alice, who banged on the package with both hands.

Anne exited the room.

"What was that all about?" Bastin turned to Henry.

"I don't know what you mean."

Henry tried his best to appear nonchalant.

"Have you met Anne before?"

"Once at the college."

"Only once?" Bastin frowned, indicating that he suspected his friend wasn't forthcoming with the facts.

Wanting to avoid Bastin's scrutiny, Henry strolled to the window. "I recall Mrs. Crawford saying something about working in a seamstress shop. How did she come to be your nanny?"

"She's one of my sister's protégées. Violet thinks she has tremendous potential. But the young lady is too proud to attend school on charity, and when the seamstress she worked for fell dangerously ill, she lost both her job and her lodgings. I suppose she would have had to move and leave the college had Violet not intervened."

"What?" Henry turned from the window, genuinely shocked.

"She demonstrated good character, caring for the seamstress and her sick baby while the husband was at sea."

My God! Of course, little Rupert's father was a sailor. He recalled how Anne had chosen a stuffed bear clad in a sailor's suit for the boy.

"Did you say, sick baby? How awful. Did Rup—I mean— what happened?" Trepidation crept into his throat.

"I believe they recovered. Then the husband came home and decided to take his family to his sister's residence in Cornwell. I'm not certain, but I think Violet said he was good enough to return Mrs. Crawford's rent for the month. And that is how Violet discovered that the young lady needed a place to stay. It suits us perfectly." He stroked his daughter's hair. "This little tiger is getting too energetic for Mrs. Teal. And Mrs. Crawford has an abundance of energy. Alice worships her."

"Are you talking about our wonderful Anne?" Ottilie entered the room, and Henry went to greet her. "She displayed such bravery, nursing that sick woman and her child. We are lucky to have her." Ottilie kissed both his cheeks.

"Mama!" Alice patted the half-unwrapped package.

Ottilie went to her daughter, and Henry turned to look out the window again.

I'm a fool. Of course, the man outside the shop had been the seam-stress's husband—Mr. Taylor. That explained everything—their distress, his hand on her shoulder, and the bag of coins.

"It's another beautiful doll," Ottilie's voice sounded behind Henry, and he turned to see her pulling the dark-haired, green-eyed porcelain doll from the package. "Thank you, Uncle Henry."

"Ba Ba." Alice clapped her chubby hands.

"She's lovely," Ottilie said, holding the doll in front of Alice. "She looks just like your new nanny, doesn't she?"

"Ba Ba." Alice pulled the doll to her chest and squeezed it.

Bastin's eyes flicked to Henry, but he couldn't meet his friend's gaze. *He'd behaved dreadfully to Anne. Would she ever forgive him?*

⟫⟫⟫⟪⟪⟪

OF ALL THE times she'd thought about Henry returning and finding her living at Greyson Manor, Annabel never imagined him being cross or cold toward her—but accusing her of being loose with her morals and assuming Mr. Taylor was her lover—*that* was beyond her comprehension. But she only had herself to blame. It had been foolhardy to believe he loved her. Perhaps she was a Female Quixote, after all. *Maybe Papa had done right burning my books. I proved his point, behaving like a silly girl, foolishly hoping—*

Mrs. Teal snorted; Annabel jumped in fright as though her private thoughts had been spoken aloud and her shame lay displayed before the world. She peered at the elderly nanny, who snored in her rocking chair. Annabel sighed her relief. The woman slept as soundly as Alice did in her cot. She reached into her skirt pocket and retrieved her collection of folded newspaper articles. Peeling open the first article, she held her breath as she revisited it:

Body fished from Thames Suspected to be Daughter of Confectionary Giant, Bernard Leonard

The last time Mr. Leonard saw his daughter was 27 July. She was in excellent spirits, preparing for her wedding and her future as the Viscountess Craventhorp. The day morning, she'd vanished from her home, with only a note to say she'd eloped to

Scotland with a mysterious lover left in her wake. The young lady's father immediately suspected foul play, but wary of scandal, he was reluctant to go to the police and so hired a team of investigators to trace his daughter's whereabouts. Months of intense searching yielded nothing. Still, Mr. Leonard vowed to continue searching and refused to believe his daughter had left the house willingly. Unfortunately, he was correct.

A breakthrough in the case emerged last Thursday when detectives fished a bloated and decaying body from the Thames. They suspect the corpse became trapped under a barge after being dumped into the Thames weeks earlier. Nonetheless, they were able to determine that the victim was a young female in her early twenties, petite in stature, with dark hair. These features match the description of Miss Leonard. But the most conclusive evidence comes from an emerald pendant found around the victim's neck, which Mr. Leonard has identified as belonging to his daughter. The exquisite and costly piece of jewelry, detectives say, will also help to identify the killer and his motive. Whoever murdered Annabel Leonard had no interest in robbing her—it would take a wealthy man to leave such a fine piece of jewelry floating in the Thames. This begs the question—did Annabel Leonard leave home willingly with a man she thought loved her, or was she abducted by one who burned with jealousy and desire as he admired her from afar?

Annabel's hand went to her throat as she tried again to remember what had happened to the pendant her papa had given her the night before Lady Dawley's ball. She'd worn it to match the green dress her stepmother had picked out for her, but what had happened to it? Had it come home with her? Or had she lost it? She'd been so frazzled; she could not remember. Nor did she recollect seeing the pendant in the turbulent days that followed the ball.

Thinking back to that dreadful night, she recalled the pressure of Lord Craventhorp's hand on her arm and heard the hateful whisper of his voice in her ear. Fear and anger flooded her, and she drew back, just as she had then. She'd run from him, and he'd tried to grab her—hadn't he? Had the pendant come unclasped and slipped from her neck? She couldn't remember. But the more she thought about it, the more convinced she became that the pendant had indeed slipped from her neck and that Lord Craventhorp had used it to save face by faking her death. He would never stand to be labeled a jilted lover and have his reputation besmirched. No, he would have murdered her if he'd found her, but since he did not, he settled for a young lady who looked like her.

Annabel shuddered.

"My, how peaceful it is here." Henry's voice brought Annabel back to the present. Still shaking inside, she was relieved to see him standing casually in the doorway with his hands in the pockets of his black trousers. He flicked his eyes to the slumbering Mrs. Teal.

She lowered her gaze, pleased to see him but still too angry to forget how he'd treated her.

"May I sit?" he asked, gesturing to the empty chair beside her.

"Of course." She tucked the newspaper articles into her skirt pocket. "I'm not exactly in a position to refuse you," she said as Henry sat down.

He hung his head and clasped his hands together as if taking the time to absorb the sting of her words.

Annabel turned her eyes from him and wished she could silence her pounding heart.

Henry cleared his throat. "I came to apologize."

"I'm sure there's no need." Annabel avoided looking at him.

"There is. I acted like a fool. I had no idea Mrs. Taylor fell ill—and Rupert—I'm so sorry. It must have been dreadful for you."

"It was." Annabel stared straight ahead. "That's hardly the point. The fact is you thought—you—that I..." A lump rose in her throat.

"I was mad with jealousy," he said.

His honesty caught her by surprise; she inhaled sharply.

"It's true." He glanced at the slumbering Mrs. Teal before angling his body toward her. "When I saw you with Mr. Taylor, I didn't think—I merely reacted. It made me so angry."

"But you thought I was capable of taking money from a man who wanted my company?" Annabel shook her head. "How could you?"

"My misjudgment is not a reflection of you but of me, and my own…selfishness." He swallowed. "I despise myself for it; you must believe me."

Annabel's heart softened. She didn't want to remain cross with Henry, but—

"Master Hudsyn!" Mrs. Teal's shrill exclamation broke into Annabel's thoughts. The portly woman jumped out of her rocking chair and straightened her bonnet, which had fallen askew during her nap. "Good afternoon, sir. I didn't realize you'd slipped into the room." Her face flushed pink as she tucked several stray hairs under her bonnet. "I'm afraid little Alice is still fast asleep. She's an excellent sleeper, you know—has been since she was a babe," the woman said proudly, as though she were solely responsible for the child's sleeping habits.

"Not to worry, Mrs. Teal. I just came in to have a word with Mrs. Crawford."

Mrs. Teal glanced at Annabel and flushed an even brighter pink as though she'd just realized her presence.

"Would you mind if I borrowed her for a minute?"

Annabel felt her face heat. What would Mrs. Teal make of this situation? Would she tell Mrs. Bastin? And what if she did? Mrs. Bastin was a very liberal-minded woman. Even the servants in her household seemed to operate on their own rules.

"I…of course not, my Lord," she said and gave an odd little curtsy. "Take her. I shall remain here in the event the little miss wakes up from her nap."

"Thank you, Mrs. Teal."

"Of course, my lord." She gave a little bow.

Annabel turned to Henry and frowned.

My Lord? What did she mean by that? Was Henry a peer? And if so, why did he call himself Mr. Hudsyn? What truth was he trying to hide?

CHAPTER SEVENTEEN

She half enclosed me with her arms,
She pressed me with a meek embrace;
And bending back her head, looked up,
And gazed upon my face.

—Samuel Taylor Coleridge, *Love*

ANNE LOOKED PENSIVE as they strolled side-by-side in the garden, and Henry had felt her mood shift when Mrs. Teal addressed him in the formal. So he imagined she was wondering why he'd kept his title from her. He didn't want her to think he was trying to fool or trick her, so he would have to try and explain. But her question came before he had a chance to speak.

"Why did Mrs. Teal address you as *my lord* when everyone else calls you *Henry* or *Mr. Hudsyn?*"

"Not everyone," he said. "My valet always addresses me as my lord."

Anne's forehead creased, and Henry imagined she was visualizing Jamison, whom she had not realized worked for Henry rather than his cousin. She shook her head as if to clear her thoughts.

"I'm a baron by birthright, but I asked Headmistress Thomas to introduce me as Mr. Hudsyn to the young ladies because I didn't want to intimidate anyone. I wanted the students to feel open about approaching me. Do you think that incorrect?"

"That was thoughtful of you, but why keep up the charade outside school? Why not tell me the truth?"

Henry shoved his hands into his jacket pocket and worried a pebble with the tip of his boot. *How can I possibly explain the whole sordid truth to her? What can I say that will make her understand?*

He glanced up at her. She was still looking intently at him, waiting for an answer.

"I suppose I was trying to escape myself. There are things in my past—my family's past—that I don't wish to face." He shook his head, thinking of a better way to explain. "Have you ever wished you could take on a new identity—become someone else entirely—start fresh?" He shook his head again. "Of course, you haven't. Why would you?"

"I understand," she said.

"Do you?" he asked, surprised. He couldn't fathom how such perfection could ever wish to be someone else.

"I do. We all have things in our past that hurt—things we'd rather not remember or from which we wish to disassociate ourselves. Sometimes it's easier to play a part and forget."

He searched her face, looking deep into her lovely green eyes and thinking she was most likely referring to her husband and the hurt she suffered at losing him. "He's a lucky man," Henry heard the desire in his voice and wondered if she recognized it too.

"Who?" she said, her eyes still locked on his face.

"Your husband—Mr. Crawford. I thought you were referring to him when you said—"

"You're right. I mean—that is whom I was referring to." She turned her face from his and looked out onto the garden.

"He was lucky to have had you. I hope he realized that."

She shifted her stance and continued to gaze out into the garden.

Henry cursed himself inwardly. He'd made her uncomfortable with his free talk.

"Shall we continue walking?" he asked, wishing to change the subject.

"Yes, but first tell me, how shall I address you now?"

"As you did before. Call me Henry."

She shook her head. "I'm Alice's nanny. I cannot address you—a baron—by his first name."

"You can. Haven't you noticed that my cousin doesn't run a traditional household?" He smiled. "Her servants seem to make up the rules as they go along. And I like the way my name sounds when you speak it."

Her cheeks colored. "Regardless, the other servants will talk, and I don't want—I mean, like—to draw attention to myself."

"Then call me whatever you like in public, but don't deny me the pleasure of hearing my name on your lips in private."

The color in her cheeks deepened, and she lowered her head. Henry sensed her discomfort. He'd gone too far—been too forward. They proceeded along a path of clipped hedges. "I enjoy your company," he said, trying to downplay his true feelings. "I like talking to you and taking walks with you. We are friends, and I don't wish that to change."

"Speaking of friends," Anne pulled a crumpled piece of newspaper from her pocket. "Did you know this Lord Craventhorp, who was betrothed to Miss Leonard? I mean, I imagine you ran into him once or twice since you're both peers."

Henry ran a hand through his hair.

Did he imagine the accusation in her voice, or was it real? He decided that he best tell the truth. He'd withheld it from her long enough.

"We were at Eton and Cambridge together, but I never liked him. He's the cruel, bully type. I'm not at all surprised Miss Leonard tried to escape him. He treats women with utter disdain."

"Do you think he murdered her?"

Nausea swam in Henry's chest. He wondered if the guilt he felt was evident on his face. "It doesn't matter what I think. No one will believe Craventhorp is guilty. He's a viscount."

"But you grew up alongside him and have spent time in his company, so you *must* have an opinion."

Henry frowned. "Why are you so taken with this case? One would think you have a personal interest in Miss Leonard."

"I do. As does every woman, I imagine. If someone of Miss Leonard's stature and wealth isn't safe, then how can any woman be safe? I think all women ought to take notice of this case."

Her words settled on Henry's chest with the weight of an albatross. "I should have done something to help—if I hadn't been—" He stopped.

"Help? How could you have helped?"

Henry swallowed. No doubt she would abhor him for his cowardice, but he had to speak. If she despised him, it was no doubt what he deserved.

"I saw her—or rather—she ran into me one evening. It was at a ball in Mayfair. I'd stepped into the garden for some fresh air. That's when a young lady flew into my arms out of nowhere. I had no idea what was happening, but I could sense her fear. I asked her if she needed help, but she ran off. That's when I saw Craventhorp watching her with that same look—the one he used to get when he'd cornered one of the younger boys. He liked to see them cower in fear."

The color drained from Anne's face. "You saw her? You know—"

"It all happened so fast. And I was—well, in an unfit state. So, I have no memory of her face. If I hadn't been..." Shame prevented him from continuing.

"Go on," she urged.

"I could have done something to help her. Instead, I did nothing."

"What could you have done? You could not have stopped the marriage."

"I don't know, but I should have done something. Now, she is dead, and Craventhorp will never be held accountable for his actions."

"Do you believe him capable of murder?"

Henry nodded. "I believe him guilty of hubris greater than Zeus's, and one only needs to think how cruelly the king of gods took his revenge."

ANNABEL'S THROAT CLOSED. She tugged at the neck of her white blouse. Everything Henry had told her about Craventhorp confirmed her fears. He was evil; he liked to torture those weaker than himself, and he treated women with contempt. It all added up in her mind. Craventhorp murdered that young woman, which meant someone died because of her. An uncomfortable warmth spread throughout Annabel's body, and the ground beneath her spun. She closed her eyes trying to stop the ground from moving.

"Anne?"

Henry's voice sounded distant. He was calling her name, but where was he? Why was he so far away?

"Anne."

This time she felt his arm encircle her waist, propping her up. She opened her eyes and blinked to clear the blur away. Henry's anxious blue eyes examined her face. Her legs felt insecure beneath her, and she doubted her ability to stand if he let her go. But he didn't let go, and, as if sensing her need, tightened his grip around her waist.

"I'm sorry if I frightened you. That wasn't my intention. I let my anger at Craventhorp get the better of me."

She nodded, too weary to speak or stand on her own two feet. Liking Henry's strength, she let him hold her up. His arms made her feel safe. She no longer cared that they were outside in the garden and that anyone might see them; she never wanted him to let go. She'd kept the fear at bay and held onto the lies she needed to protect herself for so long. So very long. And now, she was weary. Annabel rested her head against Henry's chest and breathed in his fresh, clean scent.

He caressed her cheek with the back of his hand. Her heart raced as he leaned toward her and brushed his lips against hers.

A horse whinnied in the distance, and her eyelids flew open. Someone rode toward the house. Annabel stiffened and stepped away from Henry.

"Who is that?" Henry peered at the rider.

The horse trotted up the driveway, and Nate came into view.

"Afternoon." He dismounted and doffed his cap at Henry.

"Afternoon," Henry said curtly, indicating that he resented the interruption.

"I need a moment of your time," Nate said to Annabel, his voice as curt as Henry's.

"I'll be inside if you need anything," Henry said before turning toward the house.

Annabel watched until he was safely out of earshot before turning to Nate. "I thought we agreed to meet outside the college."

"And I thought you were employed as a nanny by a Mrs. Bastin."

"I am," she said.

"So, what's he doing here?" Nate loosened his hold on the reins, and his horse lowered his head and nibbled on the manicured lawn.

"He's Mrs. Bastin's cousin." Annabel frowned at the horse, who stretched his neck in an attempt to chew on one of the manicured bushes. "Let's walk to the stables. The groom will take care of your horse."

"You sound like the lady of the house already."

"Mr. and Mrs. Bastin have radical ideas. They don't run their household the way most do."

NATE SNORTED. "I'VE been making some inquiries about your Mr. Hudsyn. It turns out he is Lord Hudsyn, the eighth Baron Hudsyn, to be precise."

Annabel folded her arms. "I know," she said.

Nate stopped walking and turned to face her. His expression hardened. "I trusted Stella when she told me you weren't a foolish girl who would get us killed."

"I'm not—I wouldn't put you or Stella in danger. Henry— Lord Hudsyn—is trustworthy. He told me everything. He knows Lord Craventhorp, but the two despise each other. They always have."

"What?" Nate's dark eyes flashed angrily. "He *knows* Craventhorp?"

"I told you, he—"

"Does he know who you are?"

Annabel shook her head. "No," she said firmly. "I didn't tell him. I haven't told anyone."

"But you will, won't you? You trust him." He narrowed his eyes. "Are you in love with him?"

"He's a good person. I told you, he despises Craventhorp."

"Don't be foolish. These types always stick together in the end. Preserving their precious titles and wealth is all they care about. Do you truly believe Lord Hudsyn cares about you? He either thinks of you as a servant girl, or he knows you're a rich man's daughter who has ruined her reputation for life. Either way, he is in an excellent position to take advantage of you."

"You're wrong," Annabel said, stepping back.

"I'm not wrong. You know nothing of this world and all its cruelties."

Nate reached into his saddle and pulled out a newspaper. "Have you seen this?"

Annabel pressed her lips together and nodded.

"This is how far his lot will go to safeguard their reputations. Your foolishness has put my life, and possibly Stella's, in danger."

"What do you mean? I haven't—I wouldn't."

"I mean, your growing friendship with one of Craventhorp's lot doesn't sit well with me. I believed Stella when she told me you were trustworthy."

"What do you want me to do? He'll be more suspicious if I suddenly stop talking to him."

"You must disappear from this place, maybe even from England, before it's too late."

"I can't keep running away. I'm happy here. No one knows the truth. I won't tell anyone; you have my word."

"What if I arranged for you to go to Stella," he said.

"In Italy?"

"Perhaps."

"Have you heard from her?" Hope filled Annabel's chest.

"Maybe, but I can't trust you with such delicate information when you've shown me your loyalties lie elsewhere." He mounted his horse.

"Nate, please! Wait." She put her hand on the reins. "You mustn't think I don't appreciate all you've done for me."

He bent toward her. "If that's true, you'll do what's necessary to keep all of us safe."

"Let's continue our discussion and walk to the stables. Your horse needs water. Don't leave like this."

"There is nothing more to discuss. I told you what needs to happen. If you decide you care more for Stella than Lord Hudsyn, you know where to find me." He jerked the reins, forcing her to release her grip. "Don't worry about my horse. The river will do him fine." He spurred the horse into a gallop.

Annabel dropped her head in her hands. Then she took a few deep breaths, attempting to compose herself before turning toward the house.

Henry stood in the doorway, watching her.

As she stepped forward, he turned and strode inside the house.

CHAPTER EIGHTEEN

In Venice they do let heaven see the pranks
They dare not show their husbands. Their best conscience
Is not to leave undone, but keep unknown.

—Shakespeare, *Othello*

HENRY DISAPPEARED INTO the house before Anne reached the front door. He did not want to make assumptions about what he'd just witnessed—as he had done once before—but he would not ask her for an explanation either. Asking would only lead to more untruths. Anne had not been honest about Nate and the role he played in her life—and one thing was certain—he was far more to her than a friend of her late husband.

Making his escape to the library, he extracted a book from the shelves and ensconced himself on a chair in a far corner of the room. He opened the book, *A Discourse on the American Civil War*, and used it as a prop while he brooded over the day's events. He remained deep in thought until the time arrived for tea, which the family enjoyed every Sunday at five o'clock, in lieu of their usual six o'clock dinner. Like everything in the Bastin household, it was a casual affair and a time for family togetherness. Under normal circumstances, he would have looked forward to it, but knowing that Anne would be at the table with little Alice, who on weekdays ate her supper an hour before her parents, Henry entered the dining room with a sense of apprehension.

As usual, he stooped to kiss first Ottilie and then Alice's cheeks whilst trying not to look at Anne, who sat beside the child. Despite the hours he'd spent contemplating things in the library, he hadn't resolved anything in his mind. He wanted to remain impartial, but he found he could not. He cared too much. He could not look at or think about Anne without seeing her grasp the reins of Nate's horse and plead with him to wait. Nor could he look at her without hearing the desperation in her voice as she called out to the man, as if heartbroken he was leaving her.

He took his seat next to Bastin and found himself sitting directly opposite Anne. The table stood laden with an assortment of meat pies, cakes, scones, triangled sandwiches, and pedestals filled with fruit. Henry pulled one of the tall silver fruit bowls toward him, using it to obscure his view of Anne. Then he lifted a bunch of grapes from it and placed them on his plate, after which, he busied himself by pouring a cup of tea.

"Where were you all afternoon?" Ottilie asked.

"The library. I had some reading to catch up on."

"Really? Does that mean you've rekindled your interest in poetry?"

"No," Henry said flatly and reached for the honey pot. As a boy, Jack had been indentured to an American who owned a ranch and a sugar plantation in Texas. The horrors he'd witnessed on the plantation turned him from using sugar forever. It wasn't in protest—slavery had long since ended—but looking at sugar triggered disturbing memories; consequently, sugar had been banned from the Bastin household.

"Good girl," Ottilie praised her daughter as she grasped a piece of cucumber from her plate and took a bite. "Is it delicious?"

The child smacked her lips and took another bite. "Mum mum."

Henry smiled. He enjoyed having the toddler at the table.

Radical thinkers like Ottilie and Jack did not believe in enforcing a bland diet on their little girl. They exposed their child to all the colors and tastes of the rainbow, and she enjoyed excellent health and sported rosy cheeks because of it.

Ottilie stirred a teaspoon of honey into her tea and turned to Henry. "I've always hoped you'd reignite your interest in writing poetry. It seems a horrible waste to squander such talent."

"I don't have talent," Henry said, aware of Anne's eyes on him. "I had to labor over my writing. It didn't simply flow from my quill onto the page."

"Oh, come now," Bastin said. "You know very well I labor good and long to get the words right. The talent lies in the writer's ability to understand human nature and connect with his readers."

"Or *her* readers," Ottilie said.

"Or hers." Bastin smiled.

"Well, I suppose that's my failure, then. I fail to connect with people both in person and on paper." A trace of bitterness rose in Henry's chest. He could sense his mood turning dark but felt powerless to stop it from happening.

"Don't talk rubbish, Henry. You are the most compassionate and kind man I know—aside from Jack, of course." Ottilie gave her cousin a dimpled smile.

"As my cousin, you are obliged to say so." Henry helped himself to a piece of pre-sliced meat pie and hoped Ottilie would change the subject.

But she did not.

"In that case, we shall consult with a neutral party." She turned to Anne. "What do you think? Is Henry not a kind and compassionate individual?"

"You don't have to answer that." Henry glanced at Anne and then lowered his eyes back to his plate. He wished there was some way to put an end to this conversation.

"I quite agree," Anne's voice floated across the table in a sweet bubble, enticing Henry to look at her, but he willed his eyes to stay on his plate, forking a piece of meat pie into his mouth and chewing slowly.

"Did Henry tell you he was a poet, Anne?" Bastin asked.

"I believe he said he dabbled in writing it," she said.

Hearing the implied admonition in her voice, Henry tightened his grip on his fork. "I haven't written anything in two years. So I think it's safe to say I am no longer a poet."

"I disagree, and so does Jack's publisher," Ottilie said. Why did they both continue to act as though he wanted to be published? They wouldn't let the matter rest. It had been two years since Bastin's London Publisher had offered to publish his poetry. Wasn't it obvious it wasn't something he wished to pursue?

Henry gave no answer. He'd given up writing poetry after learning that the deceased Lord Hudsyn was likely not his father, and his true father was the same man who fathered Ottilie—a poet and an amoral rake. He'd refused publication of his poetry and asked Bastin to destroy the manuscript. So, thinking about it now was pointless.

"I kept it, you know," Ottilie said as if she had full access to his thoughts.

He put down his fork and turned to Bastin. "I thought I told you to burn it."

"I'd never let him do that," Ottilie said. "It means too much to me."

Henry sighed. "If it brings you joy, dear cousin, then it has met its purpose."

Ottilie's smile appeared tinged with sadness.

"Do you enjoy poetry, Mrs. Crawford?" Bastin said.

"I prefer novels." Her cheeks pinked. "I am in the process of reading one of yours—Mrs. Bastin was very kind to provide me with a copy of *The Renegade*. It's wonderful."

"I'm pleased you're enjoying it. A writer never tires of validation from his audience."

"Perhaps you can write an essay on it when you're finished," Ottilie suggested. "What does Mrs. Thomas have you working on at the moment—*The Female Quixote*, is it?"

"I completed my essay on that novel, and now I have moved to Shakespeare."

"Tragedy or a comedy?"

"Tragedy." Anne paused. "Othello."

Henry's heart drummed to a mix of emotions his mind couldn't make sense of, and he forced himself to focus on his food, slicing a piece of lamb and forking it into his mouth.

"That's a difficult play," Ottilie said. "Did you select it, or did the headmistress suggest it for you?"

"I saw a production of Othello recently—" Anne's voice faltered—"and I wanted to read it for a more in-depth study."

"Are you speaking of the production at the Theatre Royal in Canterbury?" Bastin addressed Anne but shifted his eyes to Henry.

"Yes," Anne said. "It's a local production, but very well done."

"You saw that, too, didn't you, Henry?" Bastin said.

Henry cleared his throat. "Yes, I went on a whim. It's a wonderful production indeed. You and Ottilie might think of going." He forced a casual tone. The last thing he wanted was to give rise to Bastin's suspicions and learn what a fool he'd made of himself.

"More," Alice banged her spoon against her empty plate, providing a welcome distraction. Henry felt a flood of affection for Anne as he watched her slice a piece of meat and potato pie into little pieces for Alice.

"What are your thoughts on the play itself?" Ottilie asked as Anne chopped a slice of meat and potato pie into small pieces for Alice. "Have they changed with a closer reading?"

"When I saw the play, Desdemona's murder shocked and frightened me. Now, it gives rise to feelings of anger rather than fear."

"Because?" Ottilie prompted.

"The injustice of it all—not just the murder of an innocent— but the injustices that women in our society face."

"You mean, society's prejudices against women?" Ottilie said.

"Exactly. As a woman, particularly a young woman, you feel pressure to be perfect in every way. You must relinquish your ideas, interests, and desires, lest society frowns upon you for behaving as 'less than'. There's no room for mistakes. And should you make a mistake, or go against society in any way, the consequences are dire. It's as though women are not allowed to be human." She shook her head. "Desdemona was near perfect, but even that wasn't enough. Society always judges women so harshly."

Henry shifted in his seat. Was she talking about *Othello* or him?

"Hang on," Bastin said. "Othello's the flawed one—unable to control his jealousy and so easily manipulated. That doesn't put men in a very flattering light, does it?"

"Othello is every man, is he not? Though he loves Desdemona, and though she is loyal and honest, he doubts her because society teaches us that women are not trustworthy. That is why we must be passed from father to husband, chaperoned, and censored. It's assumed we cannot think or do for ourselves. And in the case of the play, Othello ultimately uses Desdemona's love for him against her. She betrays her papa out of love for him, and instead of that making her loyal in his eyes, it serves as proof of her deceitfulness. In society's view—like Othello's—women are guilty because it's assumed they are deceitful and disloyal from birth. It's been my experience, and I feel sure, the experience of many women that a man will condemn a woman first, and only ask questions to determine the truth later."

Henry's stomach knotted with guilt, knowing that Anne directed her words at him. He shifted his eyes from his plate to Anne, expecting to meet her scorn. Instead, he saw hurt in her lovely green eyes. A wave of shame engulfed him. Once again, he'd allowed jealousy to rule his emotions, and once again, he'd behaved like a cad. How could he expect Anne to trust him if he kept doubting her?

>»»«««

ANNABEL HEARD HENRY'S footsteps before he sank into a chair next to her writing desk. She'd gone directly to the library after handing Alice over to Mrs. Teal so she could continue working on her essay for Headmistress Thomas. But she'd found it hard to concentrate. Nate's words of warning still troubled her. Had she put too much faith in Henry? He'd doubted her once already, and his silence this evening confirmed her fears that he doubted her yet again. Now he sat staring at her.

It wasn't to be borne. She lifted her head to glare at him. "If you've come to reprimand me—"

"I haven't," he said, cutting off her words. "On the contrary, I believe I owe you another apology."

An apology? That was unexpected. She put down her quill and waited.

"I shouldn't have watched you and Nate. I should have gone inside. I told myself that I remained to ensure you were safe, but I wasn't being entirely honest. In truth, I'm curious about your relationship. I can't help but wonder what hold the man has over you. Even if it's none of my business. It feels off to me, and I'm concerned."

She pressed her lips together. What could she say? She couldn't tell him the truth. The secret wasn't only hers. Others were involved.

Henry continued, "There's another reason I didn't mention my title to you. I didn't want it to scare you away—spoil my chance to know you. I didn't—*don't* want you to think I wish to take advantage of you. My feelings for you are genuine. All that I have expressed to you is true."

Her heart thundered at his words. She longed to reciprocate and tell him how his touch made her weak with happiness and how she longed to feel his lips against hers again.

But she could not.

Poor Henry thought she was upset because he'd withheld the truth about himself from her; if only he knew her own dishonesty was the thing that was crushing her.

What would he do if he discovered she was the daughter of Bernard Leonard, the same young woman whose life and death they'd frequently discussed? Even if he forgave her for lying, she couldn't expect him to lie on her behalf. He would have to tell Headmistress Thomas and Mrs. Bastin the truth about her. And what would they do, knowing her secret jeopardized the ladies' college? They'd send her home, and her papa would never let her out of his sight again—not until she'd been delivered to the sacrificial altar. She'd never be allowed to pick up a book again, let alone write essays and discuss her thoughts with a learned woman like Mrs. Thomas. And that was *if* Craventhorp let her live! More than likely, she'd end up floating in the Thames. And what about Stella? She would never stay in hiding. Stella would come to her rescue. Then Craventhorp would…she couldn't bear the thought of Stella coming to harm.

I cannot maintain my freedom and the safety it provides me and Stella, and my friendship with Henry.

It's simply impossible. I have to let him go. But how to tell him gently? An idea occurred to her.

"You don't have to say anything," Henry said. "I don't blame you for being angry. I've behaved abominably."

"I'm the one who should be apologizing. I've misled you— not by my feelings—those, like yours, are indeed genuine. But I am not free."

Henry straightened, and the pained look on his face tore at Annabel's heart. *This is the gentler way.* If she kept telling herself that, then she could persevere. It was imperative. Her life—and Stella's!—depended on it. "You are promised to Mr. Trawler, then?"

"What? No, of course not."

Henry blinked, and his body relaxed once again. "I don't understand."

Annabel steeled herself. She hated this, hated lying to Henry, but she saw no alternative. "My husband only died a little over a year ago, and—well—my heart is not ready."

Henry leaned forward in his chair, clasping his hands together on his lap and looking at her intently. "I beg to differ. You have opened your heart to me. Perhaps the affection you've shown me has made you feel guilty as if you are betraying your husband, but if he loved you as much as—well, as much as I imagine he did— then he would want you to be happy."

Anne swallowed. How she wished she truly was an impoverished widow and not the daughter of a confectionary-making tyrant.

"What you said tonight at the table—about your reading of *Othello*—that struck me. I've always thought of myself as a radical thinker. With a cousin like Ottilie, it would be hard not to be. But what you said made me realize that certain events in my life have colored my thinking." He met her eyes with his own in a gaze as intimate as a touch. "There is something I wish to confess."

"Confess?" A bubble of nervous laughter escaped her throat. "That's a rather strong word."

He ran a hand through his hair. "I haven't been entirely honest with you about who I am."

Annabel's heart stilled. *Was Nate correct? Is Henry going to confess to being a spy for my father? Or worse—Craventhorp himself?*

"Do you remember when I told you my mother lived in Germany?"

Annabel nodded.

"She didn't go voluntarily. My grandfather sent her there because—" he closed his eyes as if trying to absorb the pain of what he was about to reveal and then opened them again— "because she cuckolded my father before I was born. The timing of that event put a question mark on my lineage. My father never knew about the affair, so he accepted me as his own. He died shortly after my birth, and I inherited his title, but I will never know if it truly belongs to me."

Annabel nodded. She could understand his pain and admired his desire to admit the truth to her. It couldn't have been easy for him. "I don't think that changes who you are, Henry."

"The man in question was of very ill repute"—he bit his lip and frowned as if suppressing something painful. Annabel's heart ached for him.

"When I discovered these events—three years ago—it changed me. I've been bitterly angry at my mother for showing no remorse and denying any wrongdoing. But that is not why I'm telling you this. My anger at her has come to dominate my life. Now I wonder if it has clouded my judgment and made me unnecessarily suspicious and distrustful, particularly to those I care about."

"That does explain a great deal," Annabel said. "I am relieved to learn that your distrust in me has other roots."

"I never realized it until your comments tonight. But I wish to apologize now for making assumptions." He shook his head as if internally admonishing himself. "I had no right to burden you with my mother's faults. I was wrong not to trust you—not to believe in your inherent goodness and honesty."

His words struck Annabel like a forceful gale and toppled her resolve. How could she continue to be in this house or at the ladies' college and lie? How could she deceive Henry that way after what he'd just told her? She couldn't bear it. Either she'd have to tell the truth or disappear and become someone else, yet again.

CHAPTER NINETEEN

Farewell to thee! but not farewell
To all my fondest thoughts of thee:
Within my heart they still shall dwell;
And they shall cheer and comfort me.

—Anne Brontë, *Farewell*

ALTHOUGH ANNE ACCEPTED Henry's apology with grace and kindness, he knew it was too late—the damage had been done—and he wasn't able to untangle the knots he'd made in their relationship. She'd remained guarded throughout their conversation, and despite his confession as to how he felt about her, he could not recapture the intimacy they'd shared earlier that afternoon.

He could not lay the blame at her feet. She had no reason to trust he would not hurt her again. He'd lived in limbo for two years, thrown off balance by the question of his paternity and the lies his mother had enforced on him. He'd gone from carefree and confident to a trespasser in his own life. But worst of all, he'd become suspicious of others and mistrustful of love. She was better off without him.

And then, there was Nate. Perhaps he felt it his duty to ensure that his deceased friend's wife stayed loyal. They'd appeared to have quarreled—at least, that is how it'd looked to him. Had Nate made her feel guilty? Had he accused her of being disloyal to her husband's memory and not letting enough time pass? She no longer wore mourning attire, so at least two years must have passed since her husband's death. Yet, she said her heart was not ready. But was it her heart, or Nate's judgment?

Yet, she allowed me to kiss her, and she kissed me back.

But her heart is not ready.

The confusion and doubt that played on Anne's face ate at him.

She isn't ready, and neither am I. And I won't force either of us. We both have things to work through.

"I've made a decision," he said.

She blinked as if pulled from her thoughts.

"I'll be returning to my estate in Sevenoaks tomorrow."

"You mustn't leave on my behalf! This is your cousin's home. I shall leave—"

"I'm not leaving because of you," he said gently. "I must see to a few things on my estate, and then I have business to attend to in London."

She lowered her gaze but said nothing.

He stood. "I need to ask that you not repeat the information I told you tonight."

"You needn't ask. I shall never breathe a word of it, I promise."

"Thank you." Henry gazed down at her, and sadness washed over him. "Well, it's likely I shall return at Christmas. Until then." He gave a slight bow, turned, and strode out of the room.

Henry went to the drawing room and found his cousin sitting in an easy chair beside the fire. She sat with her feet elevated by an ottoman and an open book in her hands. Henry sank into a chair beside her.

She lowered her book and smiled at him.

"I've decided to return to Sevenoaks tomorrow, but I will be back at Christmas."

Ottilie straightened in her chair. "You're not upset with me, are you?"

"Upset?"

"For making Jack give me your manuscript instead of letting him destroy it? You seemed aggravated when we brought it up at dinner."

Henry smiled. "How could I be upset when I know you acted out of love for me? In fact, I wanted to ask if you'd return it to me."

"So you can destroy it?" His cousin's forehead creased with apparent disappointment.

He took a deep breath, then admitted, "I want to read it again and perhaps make a few improvements."

Ottilie's face brightened. "You mean to publish it?"

Henry shrugged. "I'm willing to reconsider publishing—if they're still interested."

"If who is still interested?" Bastin entered the drawing room and strode toward his wife.

"Chilton & Hancock. Henry wants to reconsider their offer."

Bastin kissed his wife's forehead before pouring himself a whiskey. "What brought this on?"

"You did. Wasn't that part of your master plan? Inviting me to stay and volunteering my services at the college?" He shrugged. "It's as you said, helping others has a way of healing one."

Bastin carried his whisky to his seat and sank into his easy chair. "Does this sudden change of heart have anything to do with Alice's new nanny?"

Henry shifted in his chair, discomforted by the notion that Bastin suspected he'd been courting Alice's nanny. "I can't think why you'd say that."

"Come now, Hudsyn, I'm a writer, same as you. We observe things in others."

"I've observed it too," Ottilie said.

"Well, you are both wrong," he said abruptly. "We're friends, nothing more." Henry pretended not to notice the look his cousin exchanged with her husband. He gazed at the dancing flames in the hearth, thinking of his walk with Anne that had ended everything that day. His chest tightened. He hadn't even left, yet he missed her already.

⁂

LEANING BACK IN his leather chair, Henry put his clasped hands behind his head and grinned. He'd been in Sevenoaks four days, and the peace had done him good. He'd revised his manuscript, and it had provided some distraction from his constant thoughts about Anne. Now he was ready to hand it over to Chilton & Hancock. It was time to go to London.

"Sir," Bales interrupted Henry's thoughts. He glanced up to see that concerned lines creased his butler's forehead.

"What is it?" Henry asked.

"Mr. Hobsworth is here to see you, my lord."

"Hobsworth? Are you sure? I'm not expecting anyone."

"He says he needs to speak with you urgently."

Henry's first thought was for his mother. *Has something happened to her?*

"You'd better show him in, right away."

"Yes, my lord." Bales retreated.

Seconds later, Hobsworth swept into the dining room, his burgundy morning coat billowing up behind him and his walking stick puncturing rather than tapping the floor. Despite the chilly weather, beads of sweat glistened on his forehead under his top hat.

Henry stood up. "What's going on, Hobs? Is it my mother?"

Hobsworth removed his hat and hung it absentmindedly on a chair. "Lady Stokeford is fine," he said, reaching into his pocket and fishing out his handkerchief to mop his forehead.

Henry eyed his friend. He'd never seen the usually jovial Hobsworth in such a state.

"It's…it's *uhm…*" Hobsworth seemed to choke on his words.

He wetted his lips and massaged his throat.

"Sit down. I'll pour you a drink." Henry stood and approached the sturdy walnut cabinet that housed the crystal decanter of whiskey and matching glasses. He poured the drink and set it down on the table.

"It's whiskey, not brandy."

His friend didn't seem to care and drained the glass in one long swallow. "Thank you," he said, putting his hand on his chest and breathing as if he'd drunk an elixir.

"Now," Henry clapped his hands, "tell me what is so urgent."

Hobsworth ran a hand over his mouth as if he wanted to stave off the words a few seconds longer. "You've been identified as a suspect in the murder of Annabel Leonard."

He spoke so fast that Henry had to pause to digest his words; they were ridiculous. He threw back his head and laughed. "You're hilarious, Hobs. Is Stokeford Manor so boring that you came all this way for entertainment?"

Hobsworth stared blankly at Henry. Beads of sweat reappeared on his forehead, and Henry could see his fear was genuine. Hobsworth had never been a good trickster. He was hopeless at telling lies—so it didn't make sense that he would come all the way to Sevenoaks with such an outlandish tale if it wasn't true. Henry let the smile fall from his face.

"Someone's playing a trick on you, Hobs. Is it the earl? Is he trying to scare you into keeping your distance from me?"

"This isn't a joke." Hobsworth leaned forward and grasped Henry's arm.

Henry forced a smile despite the lump of fear that formed in his stomach. "Come on now, Hobs. Have you gone mad? What reason would anyone have to accuse me?"

"I told you not to make an enemy of Craventhorp."

"I don't understand. Craventhorp cannot simply point a finger and accuse me of murder without proof—witnesses—that sort of thing."

"They have witnesses."

"What?" The air left Henry's lungs, and his question came out in a whisper.

"Craventhorp and Leonard have built a case against you." He tugged at his collar. "They have three witnesses who claim they saw you with the Leonard woman and many more who saw you attack Craventhorp twice the night of Lady Dawley's ball."

Henry shrank back into his seat. "Three witnesses say they saw me with Annabel Leonard? This is ludicrous. It's impossible. I don't know her—unless they saw her run into me in the garden."

"Immediately before you lunged at Craventhorp in a drunken state and attempted to strangle him?"

"I agree it looks bad, and I suppose people could've wrongly assumed that we were fighting over the young lady—that I was jealous."

"Exactly," Hobsworth said.

"Well, then I'll have to explain it to the police."

"Yes, that's why I'm here." Hobsworth nodded and lowered his gaze. His pale face had become a blotch of red.

"What do you mean?"

"They came to Stokeford Manor out of courtesy to the earl. He's made some important connections at the Yard over the years, and whoever is in charge there decided to give him fair warning of the accusations against his stepson. They wanted to give him the chance to convince you to turn yourself in for questioning." Hobsworth shook his head. "When they arrived your mother nearly fainted."

Henry paled. "They can't arrest me, can they? I'm a peer."

"I think they can, Henry." Hobsworth said flatly. "But I'm sure they won't after they speak with you. In either case, they can't try you for a felony. That would take place in the House of Lords."

"Oh, God!" Henry felt as though he might be sick.

Hobsworth scrambled to his feet and poured Henry a drink. "I'm sure it won't come to that. You'll go in, answer a few questions, and then it'll all be over. You're innocent. They'll see as much."

Henry accepted the whiskey from Hobsworth and drained his glass. "So why are you here then, instead of the earl?" he asked, putting his glass down.

"I begged him to let me come."

"And he agreed?"

"Yes, but only because I promised to deliver you to the Yard by day's end tomorrow."

The nausea returned to Henry's throat, but he pushed it back down. There was no sense in panicking. He'd go and answer their questions, and they'd see he was innocent. If not, it would be his word against Craventhorp's in the House of Lords.

"I'm sorry, I was trying to help. I hope you don't think I betrayed you."

"No, I don't" Henry placed a hand on his friend's shoulder. "Thank you, Hobs. You did the right thing." He forced a smile. "I was planning a trip back to London anyway, and now I have company. We'll get this mess cleared up, and then go out to celebrate." Henry said with false cheer.

Hobsworth breathed a sigh of relief. "Yes, all will be well again tomorrow."

Henry rang for his valet and got up to pour himself another drink. How many glasses of whiskey would it take to quiet the feeling of dread that had settled in his stomach?

CHAPTER TWENTY

What a fool Honesty is! and Trust, his sworn brother, a very simple gentleman!

—Shakespeare, *A Winter's Tale*

FIVE SLEEPLESS NIGHTS after Henry's departure from Greyson Manor, Annabel made up her mind. She'd do as Nate advised and disappear—take a new name and become someone else entirely. Nate was right; she was too close to Henry. But he was wrong about the rest of it because she trusted Henry with all her heart. She believed him when he said he despised Craventhorp. He was a loyal person—that much was obvious to anyone who'd witnessed how much he cared for his cousin and her family.

But that's also how she knew he'd despise her if he ever found out her true identity. He'd been lied to by his mother all his life, and she would not do the same.

The day ahead was bittersweet. She both wished for and dreaded its end, savoring her lessons while dreading having to tell the headmistress and the Bastins that she would not be returning.

"I've had a letter," she explained when all three had convened in the headmistress's office at her request. "It's from my uncle— my mother's brother. He's been searching for me and only just discovered my whereabouts."

The headmistress tilted her head, either in interest or in question. Annabel couldn't tell. She cleared her throat.

"He wants me to go and stay with him—and his family—that is to say, he has a wife and five children." As she spoke, Annabel almost started to believe the pleasant lie, forgetting her harsh reality.

"My goodness," Mrs. Bastin said. "Then, I am certain your help will be appreciated. Though, we will be sorry to lose you. Alice has grown attached."

A lump rose in Annabel's throat, and tears threatened, but she stayed them and forced a smile. "I shall be heartbroken to leave her, but I…"

"Say no more," the headmistress interjected. "No one can replace family."

"Where does your uncle reside?" Mr. Bastin asked.

"York," Annabel replied without hesitation. She'd thought about this question and knew she had to choose a place far enough from Canterbury that visiting would be difficult.

"That's a wonderful city," the headmistress said. "And do you know, I have a former student who opened her ladies' college there last year? I shall write to her."

A jolt of panic skittered through Annabel. Thinking quickly, she added, "Oh, I don't know if my uncle will—"

The headmistress held up her hand. "I shall write, and you will see her whenever you are ready."

"Thank you," Annabel said but all she could think of were the lines of poetry from Sir Walter Scott, about the webs we weave when we deceive. They seemed particularly apt.

On the way home from the college at the end of the day, Mr. and Mrs. Bastin talked about how wonderful it would be for her in York, surrounded by such a big family, and promised to bring Alice to visit her should they ever find themselves in that part of the country. Their kindness almost brought tears to her eyes again, and she had to work even harder to stave them off when her mind wandered to Henry. He'd left for Sevenoaks days ago, and she'd likely never see him again. She felt his loss even more keenly when they arrived at the Bastin's red-brick mansion. Then, she was glad of her decision. She'd rather leave Henry behind than wait for him to return.

THE FOLLOWING MORNING, Annabel said her final farewell to the family before they left for the ladies' college. She almost broke down in tears when she hugged little Alice goodbye, but she steeled herself, not wanting to upset the child. She lingered in her room awhile after they'd gone and then some in Alice's room. It broke her heart to leave this house where she'd been so happy. Had she doomed herself to a life of loneliness and goodbyes by running away?

One of the Bastin's coachmen drove her to the train station. They, like her family, were wealthy enough to keep more than one coach. Even with train travel and hansom cabs readily available, the rich still enjoyed the privacy and convenience of riding in and owning their carriages, especially in the countryside where train stations might be a long walk from their grand estates.

Annabel's father never kept a country home. He was too busy working. During the Season, they rented in Park Lane. And they spent the remainder of the year at their sprawling mansion in Bristol. But she'd never been happier than she had been at the Bastin's country estate. It was such a beautiful and relaxing place, and she'd miss the security and peace that came from being in a nonjudgmental space where reading and expressing one's ideas was encouraged. Now her life was in total upheaval again. And she couldn't even think about Henry without wanting to cry. Her only consolation was that Nate had promised to reunite her with Stella. If not for that, she couldn't bear to go on.

The journey to Whitstable took less than an hour and thirty minutes by train, and Annabel soon found herself standing on a long stretch of pebbly beach gazing out at the ocean, dotted with sailboats. Seagulls swarmed and fished the waters and soared in the air squawking and pecking. November's autumnal breeze brought the salty ocean air to her nostrils, and she breathed in deeply. This was the season when the fishmongers would be out harvesting the cold waters for oysters, and that meant Nate might be gone for hours. Her only recourse was to wait outside his fishmonger's hut. Perhaps, he had the day off—unlikely, but she could try.

Turning, she trudged forward, keeping her eyes on the colorful pebbles and shells crunching beneath her boots as she walked. Pretty as it was, she couldn't stay in Whitstable with Nate, and she wasn't about to live with strangers again—she'd insist that he send her to Stella right away. Her spirits rose at the possibility of seeing Stella soon. Leaving England for Italy would help her forget Henry, and she couldn't imagine a life without the woman who'd been like a mother to her since birth.

She'd saved the rent money returned to her by Mr. Taylor, and now she wondered if it was enough for passage to Italy. Nate would know, she thought, as she came upon his wood-slatted hut. She knew that it stood at the very end of a long row of identical fishmonger'shuts, which made it easier for her to identify.

But as expected, her knock yielded no answer, so she sat on a grassy knoll at the edge of the beach and watched the boats that came with their first catch onto the pebbly shore. Fishmongers dressed in yellow raincoats and Wellington boots carried baskets of oysters ashore. It wasn't long before she spotted Nate climbing out of a boat and sloshing through the water, hauling his own large basket of oysters to the sand. That is when he looked up and saw her. She waved. He nodded in response before turning to the young men who worked with him. After speaking briefly to them, he strode up the beach toward her, leaving his catch behind for them to take to market.

"Come with me," he said, walking past her and not stopping

to greet her. When she didn't move, he turned and hissed, "Now!"

It was the urgency in his voice that made her comply. She would have resisted had it been a command, but now she followed him out of concern.

"Why the urgency?" she asked.

"I told you to come in three days; it's been almost a week."

"I needed time to think," she said. "I'm here now. Isn't that what matters?"

He pushed open the door and held it open for her. "I have to get back to work. We'll talk this evening. There's some bread, marmalade, and tea if you're hungry presently." He gestured to the counter. "We can dine on oysters tonight."

"Thank you. That sounds nice. I'll have some tea and then go for a walk. I quite like watching the fishmongers. Perhaps, you can teach me how to shuck the oysters so I can be useful."

"No." Nate's abruptness surprised her. "You need to stay here and keep quiet. No one is to know you're here."

"What?" She protested.

"Trust me. You want to be with Stella, don't you?"

She nodded. "Of course, that's why I came here."

"Then do as I ask, and you shall."

And with that, he shut the door and locked it—from the outside.

HENRY SAT ON the plank that served as his bed in his Newgate cell and stared at the filthy peeling wall. Had Hobsworth betrayed him? Had he lured him to the police, knowing they would arrest him for a murder he did not commit? And where were his mother and her powerful husband now?

The sound of footsteps turned his head. A guard appeared at his cell door accompanied by a grey-haired, bearded gentleman dressed in a pristine, three-piece black suit.

The guard jangled his keys, turned the lock, and pushed open the door.

The suited man stepped into Henry's cell.

"Twenty minutes," the guard said.

"Thirty," the gentleman barked. "And bring us a table and two chairs."

To Henry's astonishment, the guard bowed his head and answered, "Yes sir," before backing out of the cell and locking the door again.

"Charles Upwey, barrister," the man extended his hand, and Henry sprang to his feet.

"Thank goodness, I've been waiting for you," he said, shaking the man's hand.

The jangle of keys again drew Henry's attention toward the prison door as the guard reopened the cell, and three men marched inside. Two carried a square table, and one hauled a chair in each hand. They set the furniture down and promptly left.

"Thirty minutes starting now," Mr. Upwey said, checking his pocket watch as the cell door closed with a bang.

The guard nodded.

"Right," said Mr. Upwey, tucking his watch back into his vest before taking a seat on one end of the small table, "let's discuss your case."

"My case?" Henry sat down. "Don't they realize they have the wrong man yet? I've been in this bloody cell since yesterday, and you're the first person I have seen who isn't a policeman, or a prison guard."

"I'm sorry about that. I've arranged for these imbeciles to transfer you to the Tower after your indictment later today."

"My indictment? But I'm innocent!"

"That may be, but there's still enough evidence against you to warrant an indictment. You'll be tried by your peers, of course. The Lord Chancellor will issue a writ of certiorari to remove the indictment from the inferior court and have it transferred to the superior court.

"And when will that be?" Henry asked exasperated. "Parliament isn't even in session. Am I to rot in jail for months?"

"The public interest in this young lady's murder is high, so they likely won't want to wait until parliament goes back into session. In that case, you will be tried in the Lord High Steward's Court. He will act as judge and your jury will consist of those peers who are available to attend."

"Well, that's a bit of good news, I suppose," Henry said, "I don't relish the idea of being maligned in front of the entire House of Lords."

"Oh, I imagine every peer in the realm will race back to London to participate in this case. A nobleman hasn't been tried in the House of Lords since 1841.

Henry sprang out of his chair and paced the small cell. "This is outrageous! I do not even *know* Miss Leonard. I told the police her murderer is no doubt Lord Craventhorp."

Regardless, the only way out of this mess is for you to plead 'not guilty' and for me to prove your innocence."

Mr. Upwey opened his work bag and withdrew a stack of papers. Then he fished a pair of spectacles from a pocket inside of his jacket, put them on, and consulted the documents. "According to the police, on the night of 23 July, two witnesses saw you harass Miss Annabel Leonard at the Mayfair home of Lady Dawley. According to their witness statements—" he lifted the papers and peered at them—"the young lady freed herself from Lord Hudsyn and fled inside the house, passing the witnesses who saw a look of fear inscribed on the victim's face." He put the papers back onto the table.

"She ran into my arms." Henry sat down and looked his lawyer in the eye. "But she was fleeing Craventhorp. I tried to help her, but she was so frightened that she ran off."

"Is that why you attacked Lord Craventhorp—" he peered again at the document—" '*in a murderous, drunken rage for the second time that night'?"*

"No!" Henry shook his head. "I mean, I was enraged, and I did lunge at him on a separate occasion that night, but only to stop him from badly injuring another young woman."

"Are you referring to Miss Smith in the employ of Madame Katrina?"

"I am. Lord Craventhorp snapped her wrist in front of me, Hobsworth, Burdington, and a roomful of others."

"Police interviewed the young lady in question. I shall read you her statement." Mr. Upwey cleared his throat. *"After serving Lord Craventhorp and his friends their drinks, I slipped—the floor being wet from a spill—and Lord Craventhorp reached out and grabbed my wrist. Thereby saving me from falling to the ground and cracking open my skull."*

The barrister lowered the paper and peered at Henry. "No one has come forward to contradict this statement."

"Have you asked Hobsworth?"

"The police have taken statements from all witnesses. Mr. Hobsworth claims to be an unreliable witness because he was concentrating on the cards and didn't see precisely what unfolded. He does, however, remember holding you at bay after you"—again, he referred to his notes—"leapt to your feet and took a swing at Lord Craventhorp. The viscount then clipped your jaw with his fist in self-defense."

Henry gritted his teeth. "That's Hobsworth's statement?"

"Corroborated by your friend Burdington, I'm afraid."

Henry shook his head and rested his forehead on the palm of his hand. "They've all been paid off by Leonard and his deep pockets."

"That may be so, and I've thought of using it as part of your defense, provided we can find the evidence. I have a man gathering information as we speak." He paused and cleared his throat before saying, "But I'm afraid there is more bad news."

"Another witness?" Henry recalled Hobsworth telling him there were three witnesses.

"An eyewitness who saw you and the victim together in the early hours of the morning when she disappeared from her home."

"That's impossible! I never saw Miss Leonard again after Lady Dawley's ball. Even then, I didn't actually see her. It was so dark, and things happened so quickly that I—"

"The police refuse to release his name to me—for his own protection—they say. But I have seen his statement, and he claims to have seen a young woman exit the Leonard residence and enter a brougham carriage bearing the Hudsyn family crest during the early hours of 28 July."

"That's simply not true," Henry said. "Craventhorp must be paying this witness."

"Yet, you told the police that at 3:00 am on the morning of 28 July, you climbed into your carriage and instructed your driver to take you to your estate in Sevenoaks."

"That's correct."

"The police claim you made a stop at Park Lane first."

"But Miss Leonard ended up dead in the Thames, not in Sevenoaks with me. Their theory makes no sense."

"Well, that's what I hope to prove. On the other hand, the Attorney General will work equally as hard to convince your peers that you strangled Miss Leonard in your carriage and disposed of her body in the Thames."

Henry ran a hand across the back of his neck. "Their theory is full of holes; it shouldn't be too difficult to prove my innocence."

"It shouldn't, but the press has sensationalized the story, and the public is out for blood. Your stepfather has managed to keep things quiet until now, but when your arrest and indictment headlines tomorrow's newspapers, I'm afraid the pitchforks will come out."

CHAPTER TWENTY-ONE

*"Five paces by four and a half, five paces by four and a half,
five paces by four and a half." The prisoner walked
to and fro in his cell, counting its measurement.*

—Charles Dickens, *A Tale of Two Cities*

ANNABEL LAY AWAKE in the darkness, listening. She heard Nate stoke the fire in the grate and move around in the outer room as he boiled water for his morning tea. The sun had not yet risen, and the wind rattled the thin windowpanes. Despite this, all she could think about was getting outside.

As soon as she heard the front door open and then shut, she strained to listen for the sound of the key turning, locking her inside. She couldn't hear it, but she knew it had happened all the same, and she gritted her teeth. *Three days! Three days he'd kept her locked in this fishmonger's cage. How dare he keep her prisoner and tell her it was for her own protection? He was lying. She no longer trusted him. There was something out there he didn't want her to know—or someone he didn't want her to see.*

She threw off her bedcover and got out of bed. Shivering, she washed with the water she'd set below the small washbasin the evening before. Then, she quickly dressed in multiple layers to stave off the cold. The kitchen fire was a welcome sight, and she sat beside it after making herself a cup of tea. A stream of daylight filtered in through the small windows high above—too high to look through and too small to squeeze through. Those were the only windows in the hut, and the hefty green door that Nate bolted every day was the only way out. She'd searched for something heavy, something she could use to break it open, but there was nothing. A chair would only splinter and fall apart if she swung it at the door, and it was the heaviest object she could find within these walls.

Annabel sipped her tea and gazed into the fire. Nate gave her everything she needed to survive—food, fire, tea, and plenty of fresh oysters for dinner, but that didn't justify his taking away her freedom. How could he say it was for her own good that he locked her up like a caged animal?

The heat of injustice rose in her chest. She stood up, strode to the door, and pushed against it with both hands. It didn't budge, of course, but it made her feel better—for a moment. Then the anger returned, and she lunged forward again, pushing the hateful door with both hands.

To her surprise, it swung open, and she almost fell onto Nate.

She steadied herself. He stood in the doorway, and they stared at each other for a minute.

"What are you doing back?" She folded her arms. "Why aren't you out harvesting?"

"The wind is too rough. I thought you might want to go for a walk along the beach before I—"

"Before you lock me up again for the day?"

"I told you, it's to keep—"

"Keep me safe?" She glared at him.

He shook his head, sighed, and reached for the door handle.

"No, wait," she said.

He paused.

"Let me get my coat." The thought of being locked in again for seven hours or more gripped her by the throat. She snatched her wrap from the hook on the wall and followed Nate outside.

THEY WALKED IN silence along the beach. Nate, bundled in an overcoat, hat, and scarf, strode with his hands in his pockets and his head bent against the cold, but Annabel faced it head-on, relishing the feel of the icy wind against her skin. She let her eyes roam and embrace the ordinary sights. Part of her wanted to sprint across the sand the way she did when she was a little girl picking up seashells with Stella, but she dared not.

Anger still burned in her chest. The ocean's roar seemed to echo the scream trapped in her throat. She took a deep breath, waiting for calm. When she felt a touch calmer, she spoke. "I miss being outside, Nate. You promised you'd take me to Stella, and instead, you've kept me prisoner."

"You're not a prisoner," Nate said. "I'm being cautious, that is all."

They were already on their way back to the cottage, and Annabel needed to make him see reason before he could justify locking her up again. "I know you're trying to keep me safe, but I don't understand the need. My father either thinks I'm dead, or he told the world that I am—either way, he will have no reason to come looking for me."

"The police might still be investigating, so you must be careful. The less you are seen now, the better. Everything will be over by the end of the week, and then I'll be able to get you out of the country so you can join Stella."

She folded her arms and said nothing. It didn't feel right. *Something was amiss, and she felt sure Nate was keeping something from her.*

As if reading the doubt on her face, he said, "You want to keep Stella safe, don't you?"

"Stella? Why would my being outdoors affect Stella's safety?"

"Because if the police are investigating and discover you're alive, they'll find out she helped you escape, and Stella will end up in prison—perhaps even at the end of a rope."

"Don't say that!" Fear constricted her chest. "You promised she was safe in Italy."

"She is—but you know your father—we can never be too careful about all this, can we?" He paused as they approached his hut. "And what about me?" His face distorted with rage. "Have you thought of *my* neck?"

Ordinarily, those words would have elicited a strong reaction from Annabel, but she was too busy looking at the newspaper that lay in front of Nate's green door.

Lord Hudsyn To Stand Trial for Murder of Confectionary Merchant's Daughter

The blood in her veins froze. She reread the large, printed letters before her but couldn't comprehend their meaning, so she reached for the newspaper. But someone shoved her hard from behind. A silent scream escaped her mouth as she flew forward. And then the world went black.

ON THE DAY of his trial, the Lieutenant Governor of the Tower and the Yeoman Goaler, carrying a tall ceremonial axe, escorted Henry from his cell in the Tower of London to the Palace at Westminster. A bowl of warm water and soap had been brought to his cell for his ablutions, after which he'd dressed in a clean suit, chosen by his valet, and delivered by his barrister earlier. A mob, staved off by police, jeered at him as he exited the carriage and entered the Houses of Parliament. Once inside, Henry's escorts ushered him to the magnificent Royal Gallery, which had been turned into a temporary courtroom for his trial.

They waited until the Serjeant at Arms called for Henry to be brought forward and then took him to the bar. The rows of chairs that had been put in place on both sides of the room were filled. It seemed that every peer in the realm had indeed flocked back to London for the trial just as Mr. Upwey had predicted. Henry kept his head high as he walked past his peers, despite wishing the floor would open and swallow him whole. This walk of shame down the Royal Gallery, one of the most exquisite rooms in the Palace of Westminster, which was most often used for ceremonies and pomp, struck Henry as particularly ironic. And he was relieved when it came to an end in front of the Lord High Steward who sat as judge of the court. The Garter King at Arms and the Gentleman Usher of the Black Rod who kept the Lord High Steward's white staff, were seated to his right. Henry knelt before His Grace, and after being given permission to rise, he turned toward his peers and bowed. He took this opportunity to scan the room for Ottilie in the rows behind the robed noblemen, terrified she might have been called as a witness. But before he could see anything, the Lieutenant Governor of the Tower took him by the arm and directed him to sit on a stool in the bar. Both he and the axe-bearing Goaler then loomed behind Henry, standing guard, and making Henry feel as though he'd already been condemned and now waited for the axe to fall upon his neck.

"Oyez, Oyez, Oyez. My Lord High Steward of England, His Grace, calls for silence," the Serjeant at Arms proclaimed.

The Right Honorable Lord Henry Arthur Hudsyn, you stand before this court accused of the murder of one Annabel Bianca Leonard," the Lord High Steward said.

Then the Clerk of the Court stepped forward and said, "How plead you to this felony, my lord, guilty or not guilty?"

Henry stood up and cleared his throat. "Not guilty, my lords."

"Oyez, Oyez, Oyez," the Serjeant at Arms proclaimed again.

The Lord High Steward signaled to the Clerk of the Crown, who then announced, "My Lord High Steward, His Grace, calls for the prosecution to open for the Crown."

The Attorney General stood. "My lords, prosecution for the

Crown will show that during the early hours of 28 July 1869, the accused, Lord Henry Arthur Hudsyn, motivated by an ongoing rivalry with Lord Renwick Silas Craventhorp, lured Miss Annabel Bianca Leonard into his coach under false pretenses, strangled her, and later disposed of her body in the Thames." He paused as if to let the lords in the room digest this information. "The Crown now calls James Arnold Hobsworth as its first witness."

Hobsworth proceeded to the witness stand, and the Clerk of the Crown swore him in. After which the Attorney General started his questioning.

"Mr. Hobsworth, on the evening of 23 July, did you accompany Lord Hudsyn to an establishment called Madame Katrina's in St. James's Street?

"I did."

"Did Mr. Burdington and Lord Craventhorp join you at this establishment?"

"Yes. We met to play cards."

"And at some point during the evening, did the conversation between Lord Hudsyn and Lord Craventhorp become heated?"

"Yes," Hobsworth said.

"Do you recall Lord Hudsyn insulting Lord Craventhorp," he paused to consult his notes, "calling him 'a bankrupted viscount who believes himself a duke'?"

A low murmur rippled through the court.

"Yes," Hobsworth said, "however, before that, Lord Craventhorp—"

"A yes or no answer will suffice, sir," the Lord High Steward silenced Hobsworth.

"And did the argument then escalate to a physical altercation?"

"It did," Hobsworth said.

"And, according to your statement to police, Lord Hudsyn lashed out at Lord Craventhorp, and you were forced to restrain him."

"Correct, but Lord Craventhorp goaded him. He stood up,

took off his dinner jacket, and said, 'You are a baron in need of a good thrashing.'"

"Well, one can hardly blame him," the Attorney General said, "A man must defend his reputation, after all."

Laughter rippled through the courtroom.

Henry's heart sank. While he had been languishing in Canterbury, Craventhorp had been spreading the seeds of discord against him.

"Mr. Hobsworth, you have spent a great deal of time in the accused's company, have you not?"

Hobsworth nodded. "Yes."

"Both you and Lord Hudsyn have resided at Albany for the past two years, correct?"

"Yes, sir."

"During that time, how often have you seen Lord Hudsyn sober?

"I don't quite recall," Hobsworth said, and Henry could see the sweat collect on his friend's forehead.

"You don't quite recall ever seeing the accused sober?"

"Well, no, of course, I've seen him sober. I just—" he sighed.

"Would you say then that you are more accustomed to seeing him in a drunk and disorderly state than sober and orderly?"

"Not disorderly. He keeps to himself most of the time, drunk or sober."

"Not on this occasion it seems." The corners of the Attorney General's lips curled into a smile, and he turned briefly to face the lords before asking his next question. "Mr. Hobsworth, at any time during that evening, did Lord Craventhorp mention his plans to attend Lady Dawley's ball?"

"Yes, to meet his new betrothed, Miss Annabel Leonard."

"And did you recognize the name, 'Leonard'?"

"Of course," Hobsworth said.

"Were you surprised to hear that Lord Craventhorp was engaged to be married?"

"Extremely, and especially to a woman with such a sizable

settlement on her."

"Did he mention that settlement amount?"

"Eighty thousand pounds."

A murmur rumbled through the courtroom.

"And is it true that Lord Hudsyn became agitated after hearing this and instigated the fight?"

"I don't know that he instigated a fight…"

The Attorney General strolled to his bench and picked up a paper. "According to your earlier statement, he became agitated and accused Lord Craventhorp of having 'no decency,' correct?"

"Well, he…yes, but—"

"Yes, will suffice. Thank you. Nothing further, sir." The Attorney General sat down.

Henry clenched his jaw. This was outrageous.

The Clerk of the Crown called for Mr. Upwey to cross-examine the witness, and the barrister stood and stepped forward. "Mr. Hobsworth, how long have you known the accused?"

"Twelve years. We attended Eton and Cambridge together."

"And do you think this man," he gestured to Henry, "whom you've known since boyhood, capable of murder?"

"Definitely not, sir,"

"Thank you, Mr. Hobsworth. That will be all."

That will be all? Henry gritted his teeth. *Is my barrister incompetent, or is he trying to get me hanged?*

CHAPTER TWENTY-TWO

Ashes denote that Fire was—
Revere the Grayest Pile
For the Departed Creature's sake
That hovered there awhile—

—Emily Dickenson, *Ashes denote that Fire was*

November 16, 1869
Whitstable, Kent

THE BACK OF Annabel's head ached. She frowned into the darkness, trying to remember what had happened. They were walking on the beach—her and Nate. She'd recalled the delicious salty air and icy wind on her face. Had it all been a dream that she'd just awoken from? Was it, in fact, only morning now? And was she, then, to face another day locked indoors?

She listened for Nate stoking the fire and making his morning tea and smelled smoke. Her heart sank. She'd been right, it had all been a dream. Struggling out of bed, her head throbbing, she got to her feet and staggered to the door.

The smell of smoke grew thicker; she coughed and reached for the doorknob. It seared her palm. She jerked her hand away. Smoke filled her lungs. She coughed again, staggering away from the door. She fell to her knees, now coughing so hard that it made her retch. Only she had nothing in her stomach to bring up. She coughed until her throat was raw. Her head whirled and she collapsed to the floor.

A great uproar sounded in her ears. People shouted, and someone banged on her door. She tried to crawl toward it, but her eyes burned, her throat ached, and her head spun.

Then a thunderous crashing sound filled her ears, followed by the sound of footsteps, voices, and men running. Suddenly, someone pulled her up to a sitting position.

The room swayed.

"Where's Nate?" One of the men shouted.

Annabel shook her head. *Where's Nate?* The words reverberated in her mind.

She didn't know.

The man clutched her by the shoulders and gave her a sharp shake. "Is Nate inside his hut?"

I don't know. I don't know!

"What are you doing?" Someone pulled the man away from her. "We have to get out of here, all of us. This hut is about to blow."

Then there were two of them, dragging her out of the hut, out into the bright night.

Orange. The sky was bright orange.

Annabel was back on the sand, gulping for air.

"I'm going back inside to look for Nate," a man's voice sounded nearby.

Annabel blinked the man into focus. He was a fishmonger—one of Nate's friends.

"It's too late for Nate," a second fishmonger yelled, and Annabel turned to see the hut collapse in a heap of flames. "But there are others to save; let's go."

The men sprinted away, and Annabel sat alone in a world of chaos. People ran in different directions, screaming instructions, screaming for help, screaming, screaming.

Annabel staggered to her feet and stumbled toward Main

Street.

Great billows of black smoke poured from buildings, and people filled the street, huddled together, watching their homes and shops destroyed.

The fight to end the flames carried on all night. Horse-drawn fire pumps lined the street, and muscled men churned the handles, pumping water high into the air to douse the flames. They must have come from nearby towns to join the Whitstable Fire Brigade. Firefighters were still fighting the flames when Annabel stumbled down the road to Canterbury at the earliest light.

She'd spent hours trying to work out what had happened before the fire. At first, she had no memory beyond her walk on the beach with Nate. The men had dragged her out of the hut well past eleven o'clock at night, but she'd walked with Nate on the beach early in the morning. The back of her head ached and felt tender to the touch. Had Nate hit her? Why? And how had she lost so many hours? She'd sat on the sand with the fire roaring on the Main Street behind her—thinking, trying to remember. Then it came to her—the newspaper headline: **Lord Hudsyn To Stand Trial for Murder of Confectionary Merchant's Daughter**

Someone had hit her from behind then—Nate. But why?

After, she remembered someone—him?—putting a bottle to her lips and a dark, bitter liquid that had pooled in her mouth. *Laudanum.* She knew the taste. But she'd never swallowed that much. Nate must have wanted her to sleep for a very long time. He'd drugged her, and then he'd left. What time, she did not know. Yet she felt certain it had something to do with Henry.

That's when she knew she had to take the chance to escape. Wherever Nate had gone, he'd be back once he heard about the fire that ravaged Whitstable, burnt his fishmonger's hut to the ground, and taken all his possessions. It had taken Annabel's carpetbag too. She was left with nothing but the sooty besmirched dress she now wore. Yet, she had to save Henry. She had to see Ottilie.

"I'm Annabel Leonard," she whispered over and over as she stumbled through her trek through the countryside. *I'm Annabel Leonard.* If she dropped down, unable to walk a step farther, she wanted whoever found her to hear those words so they could save Henry.

When Greyson Manor finally came into view, Annabel's legs almost gave way, but she forced herself to keep going as she stumbled in a daze toward the house. She grabbed the knocker, slammed it once against the door, and then collapsed.

I'm Annabel Leonard... Annabel Leonard.

ON THE SECOND day of his trial, Henry sat wearily on his stool at the bar. The proceedings from the day before had left him deflated. After Hobsworth, the Attorney General had called Burdington and repeated the same line of questioning. He'd also called Madame Katrina and the young harlot as witnesses, both of whom had clearly been either paid or frightened into keeping silent. Unfortunately, Mr. Upwey had failed in his quest to secure proof of such. The only thing Henry had to be thankful for was that neither his cousin, mother, nor Anne had been called to testify against him—yet. He dreaded the thought of them being forced to hear, or worse, give testimony that maligned his character. He only hoped they'd stayed away from the newspapers as well but that was wishful thinking.

The first witness of the day was a regal-looking woman wearing a fashionable green dress, who sashayed across the courtroom to the witness box as though she were promenading in Hyde Park.

She identified herself as Lady Boothe and testified for the prosecution that she had witnessed a frightened Miss Leonard run from Lord Hudsyn in the garden at Lady Dawley's residence on the night of 23 July.

"Lady Boothe," Mr. Upwey approached the witness box after the Attorney General finished questioning the witness, "did you actually see the accused attack or detain Miss Leonard?"

"It was too dark, and they were too far away. But the young lady ran past me and my companion, and she looked terrified. Both Lady Collins and I saw fear on her face."

"The witness will direct her answers about what she alone witnessed, and no one else," The Lord High Steward said.

Lady Boothe pursed her lips and nodded.

"To clarify, then, Lady Boothe, you didn't actually witness any attack on Miss Leonard's person by Lord Hudsyn, correct?"

"Yes, that is correct."

"Did you say anything to the victim as she ran past you? Offer to help her, perhaps?"

"No, we—I was distracted by a commotion in the garden."

"Please tell the court what commotion you're referring to, Lady Boothe."

"Shouting, scuffling. I saw two men engaging in fisticuffs."

"Lady Boothe, you said it was dark. Were you able to identify either of the men at the time of the incident?"

"Not during the actual scuffle, no, but we saw both men's faces when they passed us on the terrace to reenter the house.

"Yes, but you weren't able to see which of the men attacked Miss Leonard or each other first?"

"Well, I—" She frowned. "I don't remember seeing it so much as hearing about it later. And that is when I realized what I'd witnessed."

"Let me reframe the question, Lady Boothe. You cannot positively identify Lord Hudsyn as either Miss Leonard's or Mr. Craventhorp's attacker, correct?" Mr. Upwey said.

"Well, I know it was because—"

"Because the newspapers told you so?" Mr. Upwey interjected.

"Well, I..." she faltered.

"No further questions. Thank you, Lady Boothe."

Henry cheered inwardly. Finally, his barrister was showing a measure of skill.

After this, the Attorney General called another witness for the Crown. To Henry's surprise, he declined to call Lady Collins, who'd accompanied Lady Boothe on the terrace that night and instead opted to recall Hobsworth.

Henry's heart drummed as he faced his friend across the courtroom. The Attorney General had been able to unnerve Hobsworth during his last testimony, and he undoubtedly hoped to do so again.

"Mr. Hobsworth," the Attorney General said, "did you witness Lord Hudsyn and Lord Craventhorp engage in fisticuffs at 16 Audley Street, Mayfair on the evening of 23 July?"

"I did."

"And did you intervene or do anything to stop the scuffle?"

"I did."

"Can you describe their positions when you intervened? Were the two gentlemen in question standing or on the ground?"

"On the ground. Lord Hudsyn was sitting on top of Lord Craventhorp."

"And where were Lord Hudsyn's hands, sir?"

"Around Lord Craventhorp's neck."

A gasp rippled through the room.

Henry grimaced inwardly but kept his face stony.

"And how did you prevent Lord Hudsyn from choking the viscount to death?"

"I don't think that was his intention."

"Answer the question, sir," the Attorney General said. "What did you do to prevent Lord Hudsyn from choking Lord Craventhorp?"

"I pulled Lord Hudsyn off the viscount and dragged him away, at which point Lord Craventhorp got to his feet and returned indoors."

Henry frowned. His scuffle with Craventhorp that night was a blur in his mind. But he must have been severely provoked and intoxicated to have done something so stupid as to attempt to strangle the man.

"Thank you, nothing further." The Attorney General turned to the lords. "My lords, I'll ask you to note that Lord Hudsyn's attempt to choke Lord Craventhorp, matches the coroner's description of Miss Leonard's demise. She'd been choked before her body was discarded in the Thames."

A murmur rustled through the courtroom.

Then the Attorney General returned to his seat, and the Lord High Steward turned questioning over to Henry's barrister.

"Did you see Lord Hudsyn strike Lord Craventhorp first?" Mr. Upwey stood and strode to the witness box.

"No, sir. I was inside and stepped onto the terrace for some air when I saw the two gentlemen fighting."

"Yet, before, you testified that Lord Hudsyn lunged at Lord Craventhorp."

"I testified that he'd lunged at him earlier that evening at Madame Katrina's…" he paused, apparently searching for the best word. "Club. I didn't see who started the fight in Lady Dawley's Garden, so I cannot testify to that with certainty."

Henry thought back to the night in question. He couldn't remember how the scuffle had started either. But he remembered Hobsworth dragging him away as Craventhorp pointed an accusing finger and shouted, "That lunatic attacked me. Someone lock him up!"

Mr. Upwey continued, "Tell me, Mr. Hobsworth, doesn't it seem odd that Lord Hudsyn gained access to Miss Leonard's person while she was under Lord Craventhorp's protection?"

"Yes, it does."

Mr. Upwey turned to address the lords. "My lords, Lady Boothe stated that she saw a young woman struggling with a young man, but they're unsure of who that young man was. I ask you, where was Lord Craventhorp at the time? Isn't it more likely that young Miss Leonard was trying to escape Lord Craventhorp, and Lord Hudsyn was trying to help her?"

"Outrageous!" Lord Craventhorp shot out of his seat. "That villain lurked in the shadows and dragged Miss Leonard off when I had my back turned."

"Oyez, Oyez, Oyez. My Lord High Steward, His Grace, commands silence in the court on pain of imprisonment," the Serjeant at Arms proclaimed and Craventhorp sat down.

"Mr. Upwey, do you have further questions for the witness?" the Lord High Steward asked.

"Yes." Upwey turned back to Hobsworth. "Did the accused tell you that he was trying to *help* Miss Leonard because she was frightened of Lord Craventhorp?"

"He did, sir."

"And did you—or rather—*do you* believe that is the truth?"

Henry watched his friend; Hobsworth's eyes met his before he responded. "I do," he answered with certainty.

A buzz rippled through the courtroom, but it died instantly when the Serjeant at Arms called for silence.

Hobsworth was excused and the Attorney General stood. "My Lord, we call Sebastian John Greyson to the witness stand," he said, using Bastin's legal name rather than the one he'd adopted as an author.

Henry's breath caught in his throat. *Will they call Ottilie too?* He prayed she was in good health, but he knew she must be suffering greatly.

A murmur rippled through the crowd as Bastin stepped into the witness box. His fame as an author had no doubt brought even more attention to the case.

"Mr. Bastin, you are married to the accused's cousin—one Ottilie Alison Hamilton, correct?"

"Correct."

"And is it true that the accused was a guest at your home in Kent during September and October of this year?"

"Yes."

"Why is that, sir? It is my understanding that Lord Hudsyn has an estate in Sevenoaks."

"Lord Hudsyn has a close relationship with my wife, his cousin, and enjoys spending time with our daughter."

"Before September, when had you last seen Lord Hudsyn?"

Bastin shifted in his seat. "It had been several months. The visit was overdue."

"So you didn't have to coerce him into staying with you?"

"Of course not. Why would I?"

"Because you were concerned that his behavior had become self-destructive. Isn't that why you traveled to his estate on the tenth of September and brought him back to your estate that same day?"

"I told him my wife wanted to see him, but she wasn't able to travel due to health concerns if that is what you mean."

"Did you or your wife have any concerns about Lord Hudsyn's health—or more specifically—his drinking and anger?"

Bastin hesitated.

"May I remind you that you are under oath, sir," the Lord High Steward said.

He nodded. "Yes, we had a letter from Mr. Hobsworth, telling us Henry had gone to Sevenoaks and asking if we'd heard from him. We had not, so I went to check on him."

"In fact, Lord Hudsyn had been in Sevenoaks for six weeks, yet he had not yet contacted you or his cousin with whom you profess he has such a close relationship. True?"

Henry bit the inside of his lip. *God forgive me. I behaved like such a fool.*

Bastin cleared his throat. "Yes."

"And when you arrived at Sevenoaks, did you feel your concerns were well-founded?"

"It was clear that he'd been drinking heavily, and he seemed depressed."

"Did he tell you why he was depressed, sir?"

"No," Bastin said decisively.

Henry exhaled, thankful that Bastin had omitted the truth to protect Ottilie.

"During his stay at your estate, did you have any conversations with the accused about Lord Craventhorp or Miss Leonard?"

"Only concerning what we'd seen reported in the papers. He said that Craventhorp treated women poorly and he was not surprised that the young lady in question ran off with someone else."

Whispers erupted amongst the spectators, and the Serjeant at Arms called for silence.

"I think His Grace and my lords will see that Lord Hudsyn had an ongoing rivalry with Lord Craventhorp and that his jealousy turned deadly when he learned of his nemesis making such a good match," the Attorney General turned to the lords.

"That isn't what I said," Bastin exclaimed. "You're twisting my words!"

"You will remain silent unless asked a question, or face imprisonment, sir," the Lord High Steward ordered.

"I have nothing further, Your Grace." The Attorney General said.

The Lord High Steward invited Mr. Upwey to cross-examine.

Upwey stood and approached the witness box. "Mr. Bastin, during the six weeks that Lord Hudsyn stayed at Greyson Manor, how did he occupy his time?"

"He took plenty of walks, went into town, attended the theater, spent time with my wife and daughter, and volunteered twice at my sister's ladies' college where he taught English to working women who wanted to improve their reading and writing skills."

"So, this supposed predator spent his time doing charity work and helping young women improve their lives?"

"That's correct."

Henry swallowed, thinking guiltily of Anne and hoping the Attorney General didn't know about her.

"Thank you. Nothing further, Mr. Bastin."

Jack stepped down from the witness box and returned to his seat.

"Does the Crown rest its case?" The Lord High Steward looked at the Attorney General.

"No, Your Grace. We have one more witness."

Henry's throat constricted, and his heart froze. *The mystery witness his barrister had told him about. Who could it be?*

The Crown calls Mr. Nathaniel Trawler," the Attorney General said.

Henry sucked in his breath. *Nate!*

CHAPTER TWENTY-THREE

But hark, what sounds have struck his ear;
Voices of men they seem;
And two have entered now his cell;
Can this too be a dream?

—Anne Brontë, *A Prisoner in a Dungeon Deep*

ANNABEL'S EARS BUZZED. Someone was talking to her, but she couldn't make sense of the words. Her eyelids fluttered. She blinked several times and then forced them open. A blurred face bent toward hers. *Where am I?*

"Mrs. Crawford, can you hear me?"

She blinked again, and slowly the face came into focus. She recognized the fresh, round face and ruddy cheeks. It was Lena—one of the younger housemaids at Greyson manner. Annabel tried to speak, but her throat felt as though it was scorched.

"Can you sit up? And take a sip of tea?"

Yes, please. Tea. Give me tea. My throat. She attempted to push herself to a sitting position, but her arms seemed to have lost all their strength.

"Here, let me help you. Don't tire yourself, now." Lena stepped behind Annabel, clasped her under her arms, and pulled her to a sitting position. Then she arranged the pillows, and when she'd finished, Annabel felt more comfortable and relatively stable.

She tried again to speak.

"Don't try to talk before taking some nourishment." The doctor was here and left strict instructions for you to rest. He said he's seen a lot of folks like you these past few days on account of the fire in Whitstable. They all have scorched throats, blackened faces, and weak and shocked bodies, just like yours. Horrible it is. They say it started late at night when folks were already in their beds, and the winds kept it going until morning." Lena held the teacup to Annabel's lips.

She took a tiny sip and let the warm liquid trickle down her throat. Feeling bolder, she took a longer sip. That one hurt. It stung her raw throat, but once it was down, she felt better.

"But I told the doctor you couldn't have been near the fire because Yorkshire is a long way from Whitstable. And he said, 'No matter, I'm telling you that this young lady's lungs have been injured by smoke, and she needs rest. She is not to exert herself. Those are my strict orders.' That's what he said."

Annabel smiled weakly. "The doctor is right, Lena. I was in Whitstable—" she paused to rest her aching throat and chest— "and I was caught in the town when it burned."

"Oh my!" Lena's hand flew to her mouth.

"The aftermath was chaotic, and all my possessions burned," Annabel wheezed, "that's why I came here for help. I walked all the way."

"You poor dear." Lena put down the teacup and picked up a bowl of broth. "You're safe now. But you must take some broth before you rest so as to build your strength." She spooned some into Annabel's mouth.

Annabel ignored the pain it took to swallow. She had to get well and quickly so that she could help Henry.

"How long have I been here?" She asked between spoonfuls of soup.

"Three days and two nights." Lena put down the near-empty bowl of broth. "But you're not strong enough yet. The doctor said you require a lot of rest."

"No," Annabel caught Lena's arm. "I need to speak with Mrs. Bastin," she rasped. "It's urgent."

"She's not here. None of the family are. They're in London on account of Lord Hudsyn's trial."

Annabel felt her eyes widen.

"You must have read about it in the newspapers." Lena's face crumpled, and her eyes welled up with tears. "It's been awful. Poor Mrs. Bastin. Her cousin is so dear to her."

"He's not guilty," Annabel pushed herself up higher on the pillows.

"Of course, he isn't! None of us believe he's guilty." The maid burst into tears. "I just don't know what Mrs. Bastin is going to do. The stress will certainly kill her unborn babe, and it might even kill her too."

"It's okay, Lena. Lord Hudsyn is innocent. I am living proof that he didn't murder anyone," Annabel asserted.

"You can't. No one can. It's too late." Lena took a handkerchief from her pocket and dabbed her eyes.

"What do you mean, too late?"

"He's been found guilty and is sentenced to hang any day now."

A heavy weight landed on Annabel's chest and squeezed the air from her lungs. "How? What proof do they have?"

"An eyewitness who saw Miss Leonard climb inside his carriage during the early hours of 28 July."

"What? Who?"

"A fishmonger who'd lost his way while in London."

"A fishmonger?" The hair on Annabel's neck stood on end. "Was it a Mr. Trawler? Tall man, thick shoulders, tanned, with a healthy head of brown curls?"

"I dunno." Lena shook her head. "All I know is it's too late." Fresh tears ran down her cheeks. "Poor Mrs. Bastin and little Alice," Lena said. "A dark cloud has settled over this house, and it will never be the same again."

The room grew unbearably cold. Annabel's body trembled.

It can't be. That must be what Nate was keeping me from. How treacherous! But I won't let Henry die. I've got to get to London today.

"Lena!" Annabel grabbed the maid's hand. "Listen to me. I know a way to save Lord Hudsyn from the gallows, but I'll need your help."

"What can I do?" The maidservant drew back.

"I'll need you to give me Mr. and Mrs. Bastin's address in London."

"You can't! The doctor—"

"Never mind the doctor, Lena! A man's life is at stake here."

Lena wrung her hands and blinked as if doing so helped to clear her mind. Then she nodded.

"Good. Now, draw me a bath and find me something decent to wear. Then, I'll need you to pin my hair up, so I look presentable. We don't have much time, and I'll need to be ready within the hour. I want to get to London while it's still light."

Lena nodded.

"One more thing. I'll need money—enough for train and cab fare at least. I've lost all my belongings."

"I have a small bit saved, but it's all I have in the world." The maid frowned.

"I promise you'll get it back. Every penny. And I'll tell Mrs. Bastin how you helped me to try and free Lord Hudsyn. She'll be eternally grateful. I promise."

Lena nodded and smiled through her tears. "I'd like to make Mrs. Bastin happy. She's been ever so kind to me."

"You will make her happy if you help me, Lena. But you must make haste."

The maid nodded and scurried out of the room.

Annabel closed her eyes and breathed deeply to calm herself. But an image of Henry at the gallows plagued her mind and continued to haunt her as she bathed and began to get ready.

A knock came at the door; Lena was back to help her get dressed. "Come in," she called, getting out of bed.

Lena entered, followed by the doctor. He immediately began to issue orders.

"Now, Mrs. Crawford, when I arrived to check on you, Lena told me you were awake and are a bit agitated. I can see she is right, so I've brought you a little something to help calm you down."

"I don't want laudanum," Annabel said. "I must get to London."

The doctor squared his shoulders. "Now, now. There's no reason to refuse. Lena told me you didn't eat very much, and your body has been through a great struggle. I insist that you take in a full bowl of broth before you venture out of bed. If you ever want to make it to London, you must keep your strength up."

"I had some broth an hour ago."

"To be fair, Mrs. Crawford, you only took a few mouthfuls," Lena said.

Annabel threw her as scathing a look as she could manage; it occurred to her it was one learned from her stepmother, and she wasn't surprised to see the maid shrink away. "Very well, Lena. Fetch me another bowl, and I will drink it all."

The doctor nodded at Lena, and she left the room to fetch the broth. Then he put down his bag and retrieved his stethoscope. "May I?" he asked.

She nodded and he came forward to listen to her lungs, making sounds of encouragement as if she were a child. Annabel frowned at him.

But then Lena returned.

"Help our patient into a comfortable position for eating first," the doctor said, taking the cup of broth from the maid.

Lena helped Annabel back into the bed and fluffed her pillows.

Then she fetched the cup of broth from the doctor and handed it to Annabel with an apologetic smile. "We've all been so worried about you these past few days. We just want to make sure you're all right."

"Thank you, Lena." She accepted the broth and drank it down under the doctor's watchful eye. She'd do anything to get him out of her room so she could dress and leave for London. If Lena tried to stop her from leaving after that, she'd have to think of a way to outwit her. She'd outwitted others to gain her freedom before, and she could do it again.

She had to. Henry's death was as imminent as she'd been afraid her own had been.

"Wonderful," the doctor said when Lena took the empty bowl from Annabel. "You'll feel much better now, I expect."

Annabel rubbed her eyes. The doctor's face seemed to be fading. She blinked. No! She'd been drugged!

"What did you put in that broth?" She turned to Lena who now appeared to have three heads.

"Just a little something to help you rest." The doctor's voice sounded distorted, and Annabel's head grew heavy.

I must get to London. I must save Henry. Dear God, let it not be too late.

She fought against the overwhelming urge to close her eyes and rest her head on the soft pillows but in the end, she sank to her knees and the room darkened as she began to fall.

⭲⭲⭲⭲⭰⭰⭰⭰

"THERE MUST BE something we can do. I'm not going to let you hang for a murder you didn't commit." Bastin paced Henry's cell. "Why are people so willing to believe this damned fishmonger from Whitstable over you? Why does he seem to have more influence than the Earl of bloody Stokeford?"

"You know why. The public wants an eye for an eye, and Mr. Leonard's a powerful man. A beautiful, innocent young lady, who also happened to belong to one of the richest families in England and who was engaged to a viscount, has been murdered, and the people want answers. Unfortunately, I am the only person who has been tried and convicted of the crime."

"We must prove that this man has personal reasons for pointing the finger at you."

"It's too late." Henry slumped against the stone wall of his cell. "The trial is over. A verdict from the Lord High Steward's Court cannot be appealed."

"Not by another court, no. But Upwey says the Lord High Steward can overturn his own court's verdict if new evidence comes to light, so we must try. If I could only find Anne. I've sent a man to York to search. She said she was going to her uncle's home. But I don't know the family's surname, so it won't be easy."

"None of it makes sense," Henry said. "Why would Trawler go to all this trouble after Mrs. Crawford left to go to her family? It just doesn't make any sense." Suddenly a thought seized him by the throat. "Do you think he might have hurt her?"

"What do you mean? How?"

"If he could blame me for another—" Henry couldn't say the words. "He might have—"

"Do you mean…murder?" Bastin stopped pacing to stare at him.

"God, I hope not." Nausea rose in Henry's throat at the thought of Anne suffering at the hands of Nate. He wrapped his arms around his stomach. "Whatever happens to me, promise you will find Anne and make sure she is safe. If that bastard has done something to her—" he swallowed the bitterness in his throat—"make him pay. I cannot go to the gallows with her death on my conscience."

"You're not going to die." There was a fierceness in Bastin's voice that Henry recognized, and he knew it meant his friend would stop at nothing. "There's a solution out there," Bastin continued, "and I'm going to find it—all I need is a few minutes alone with that rat." He clenched his fist.

"It won't help Ottilie or Alice if you do something criminal."

"I know that. Do you think I want to put my family at risk?" Bastin sank into the chair by the table. "But if I cannot solve this puzzle, then I'm afraid the risk to Ottilie and our babe's health will be even greater."

"Then take your family and get out of England until my execution is over." Henry went to sit next to Bastin at the table. "Keep your family safe. That's all that matters."

"I'd never abandon you, and neither would Ottilie." His friend reached to grab Henry's arm.

"No contact with the prisoner!" the warder stationed by the barred door snapped, and Bastin made a face before he let go of Henry's arm and leaned back in his chair.

"Ottilie…She wants to see you, and I—it's not in my power to deny her."

"But it is in mine. Tell her I will not have her come to the Tower—it'll be too upsetting for her. Keep her as far away from me as possible, Jack. Do it for the health of your unborn babe."

Bastin nodded.

"I asked the same of Lord Stokeford—to keep my mother away. He's arranged for me to have ink and paper brought to my cell tonight, so I can write to her and to Ottilie. That way, they'll have something that can bring them comfort after—"

"Enough!" Bastin stood abruptly. "I won't hear any more talk of death." He stood and swiped his hat off the table. "There's work to do, and you can rest assured I won't stop until I find Anne, or I get hold of the fishmonger and force the truth out of him." Bastin strode to the cell door. "Let me out!" he called.

To Henry's surprise, two more warders appeared at the cell door as the first warder withdrew his heavy set of keys, unlocked the door, and pushed it open. But instead of letting Bastin out, the other two warders marched inside and stopped at either side of Henry.

"You are to come with us at once."

Henry's heart spiraled and as he tried to stand, he discovered his knees had weakened from the sudden shock flooding his system. The yeomen grabbed him by the elbows and held on tightly. They'd moved up his execution. He'd heard of such ploys before.

"Where are you taking him?" Jack strode forward.

"Don't worry, Bastin. I'm ready." Henry slumped against his friend. "Tell Ottilie I love her and to remember—"

"Stand back!" One of the warders withdrew his baton and used it to push Bastin away from Henry.

"I'll get Mr. Upwey. Don't worry; he'll sort this out." Bastin made for the cell door.

"You'll stand back." The guard waved his baton. "The prisoner is to come with us immediately."

They proceeded to drag Henry from the cell.

"Goddammit, I demand to know where you're taking him!" Jack flew at the guard.

"Get back!" The warder with the baton struck Bastin's arm. He winced and staggered back.

Terror engulfed Henry as Bastin lunged at the guards a second time and the warder sent his baton crashing against Jack's skull. His friend dropped to the floor.

"He needs a doctor!" Henry struggled to free himself, but the other guards tightened their grip and dragged him from the cell. Then the third guard stepped forward and locked the cell door, leaving Bastin lying on the filthy stone floor, a pool of blood surrounding his head and matting his dark hair.

Henry's knees weakened beneath him again, and he stumbled forward. *Dear God, Ottilie is going to lose me and her husband on the same day.*

CHAPTER TWENTY-FOUR

Orlando, hear our joyful news:
Revenge and liberty!
Your foes are dead, and we are come
At last to set you free.

—Anne Brontë, *A Prisoner in a Dungeon Deep*

WHAT IS HAPPENING? Henry thought as the warders escorted him through the stone passages of the Tower. *Are they taking me to the gallows?* Public executions had been outlawed a year earlier, but perhaps Her Majesty was making an exception because of the public's anger about his case. Or maybe, she thought his immediate execution, be it public or private, was an appropriate way to satisfy the people's thirst for bloody justice.

He'd never watched an execution, but he'd heard they were gruesome. He knew what he'd suffer at the gallows—if he were lucky, his neck would break, and death would come quickly, but sometimes the incompetence of the executioner left prisoners choking slowly. His face would turn blue, his tongue would swell, and he'd suffer the indecency of soiling himself.

In the courtyard, the warders thrust Henry into an awaiting carriage where the Lieutenant Governor of the Tower and the Yeoman Goaler with his ceremonial axe sat waiting for him.

They're here to escort me to the gallows, Henry thought. But what did that matter when Bastin lay dying in his cell? He had to get help!

"Wait!" he appealed to the Lieutenant Governor of the Tower as one of the warders was about to shut the carriage door. "Those two warders injured my friend badly with a blow to the head and locked him in my cell. He will die if he doesn't get help."

The Lieutenant Governor frowned. "Is this true?" He looked to the warder.

"The gentleman in question was interfering with our orders to deliver the prisoner from his cell, sir."

"Fetch the Tower doctor and take him to the injured man immediately," the Lieutenant Governor barked.

"Yes, sir," the warder said and shut the carriage door.

"Thank you." Henry breathed a sigh of relief. Then he steeled himself for what was to come.

To his surprise, the carriage rolled to a stop outside the Palace of Westminster, and he was escorted inside and back to the Royal Gallery where the courtroom had been resurrected.

What in the world is going on? He could not make sense of anything.

Relief flooded him when he saw Mr. Upwey hurrying toward him. As soon as he reached Henry's side, Upwey began to talk. Henry found it hard to focus. He was about to die, and he didn't know how Bastin would fare. He took a deep breath and resigned himself to his fate. The tension drained from Henry's body, and he turned his mind to what his barrister was telling him.

"A new witness has come forward with compelling evidence," Upwey said. "She arrived at the police station yesterday and gave a statement. I managed to secure an audience with the Lord High Steward, and upon reading her statement, he agreed for the lords to hear the new witness's testimony today. He will then decide if it is strong enough to overturn the verdict made by his court." Upwey clutched Henry by the shoulders. "If he does, you'll be spared the gallows at least for the meantime."

Henry couldn't believe what he was hearing. It all sounded too impossible. Perhaps he was dreaming.

"Oyez, Oyez, Oyez. My Lord High Steward of England, His Grace, calls for silence," the Serjeant at Arms proclaimed.

"I must go," Upwey said and hurried back to the bar.

The Clerk of the Crown stepped forward. "My Lord High Steward of England, His Grace, requests that the accused be brought to the bar."

The Lieutenant Governor of the Tower and the Yeoman Goaler ushered Henry forward, and once again, he found himself seated on a stool at the bar.

The Lord High Steward spoke, "My lords, I have summoned you back to court today because a witness previously not heard has come forward with claims that put doubt on this court's verdict. We shall hear the witness's testimony. After which, I shall determine whether it is compelling enough to overturn the guilty verdict."

A tumult erupted in the courtroom.

"Oyez, Oyez, Oyez. My Lord High Steward of England, His Grace, calls for silence," the Serjeant at Arms proclaimed.

Henry focused his eyes on the short, plump, middle-aged woman who stepped up to the witness box and was sworn in by the Clerk of the Crown. *Who is this woman who comes to save my life?*

Upwey stood and approached the witness. "Are you Mrs. Stella Rosa Bruno who was employed by Mr. Leonard first as a nanny and then as a lady's maid for Miss Annabel Leonard?"

"I am. I have served Miss Leonard since her birth."

"When was the last time you saw Miss Leonard?"

"On the evening of 28 July 1869, in Canterbury, Kent, where she'd taken up lodgings with one Mrs. Taylor, a seamstress."

Henry drew in a breath and a sharp pain shot through his chest. He doubled over, almost collapsing in the dock. *Anne Crawford and Annabel Leonard are one and the same?*

A warder rushed forward and helped him back to his feet.

"Are you fit to continue, Lord Hudsyn?" the Lord High Steward asked.

Henry nodded. "Yes, Your Grace," he said, still thinking of Anne. How could he have missed the clues? They'd all been there. The chopped hair, connection with a fishmonger, and lodgings at a seamstress's shop that didn't match her education and upper-class mannerisms. And then, there was her deep interest in Miss Leonard's murder—her endless questions about his friendship with Craventhorp—and of course, her suspicions against him.

"Who was driving the carriage that carried you and Miss Leonard to Canterbury?" Mr. Upwey asked, and Henry forced his mind back to the trial.

"Mr. Nathaniel Trawler, a Whitstable fishmonger by trade."

A rumbling sounded from the lords who shook their heads and looked from one to the other.

"Can you please explain to the lords why Miss Leonard changed her name and took up residence with a seamstress in Canterbury?" Mr. Upwey continued.

Mrs. Bruno extracted a handkerchief from her pocket and dabbed her eyes. "She was terrified of Lord Craventhorp and wanted to escape the marriage arranged by her father."

"That's a lie!" Lord Craventhorp sprang out of his seat.

"Oyez, Oyez, Oyez," the Serjeant at Arms proclaimed. "My Lord High Steward, His Grace, commands silence in the court on pain of imprisonment."

Craventhorp sat down and drew his lips into a tight line.

"Do you mean to say that Mr. Leonard attempted to force his daughter into a marriage she'd not agreed to?"

"Yes. Miss Leonard was vehemently opposed to the marriage, but her father intended to drag her to the alter against her will."

"To what end?" Mr. Upwey asked.

"He intended for his daughter to marry a title and paid Lord Craventhorp handsomely for the privilege."

"Against her will?" Mr. Upwey said again as if to emphasize

his shock that a respectable man would behave in such a distasteful manner.

"Yes."

"Mrs. Bruno, why have you only come forward now?"

"I have been on the continent, sir. And when I learned that an innocent man is being tried for a crime he did not commit, I couldn't have it on my conscience, so I set sail to England. And also, because I fear for Miss Leonard's life."

"Her life? Do you mean she is alive?"

"I do."

A gasp could be heard rippling throughout the room.

"I don't know who killed that poor woman found floating in the Thames wearing Miss Leonard's pendant, but I *do* know that whoever did probably wants Annabel dead."

"Do you know where Miss Leonard is now?"

The woman shook her head. "No. But we must find her!"

"Thank you, Mrs. Bruno. Nothing further."

The lords looked at each other in astonishment; some of them shook their heads in apparent disbelief.

The Lord High Steward invited the Attorney General to cross-examine the witness, but he declined.

"My Grace," Mr. Upwey said, "the defense would like to call Mr. Bernard Leonard to the stand.

"Granted." The Lord High Steward said.

Henry watched in awe as a short but powerfully built man with black hair and bushy eyebrows stepped up to the stand.

"Mr. Leonard," Mr. Upwey addressed the confectioner after he'd been sworn in by the Clerk of the Crown. "Are you acquainted with this Mrs. Stella Bruno who testified before this court minutes ago?"

"I am. She was, as she says, my daughter's nanny for many years before becoming her lady's maid."

"Mr. Leonard, did you, as Mrs. Bruno claims, arrange a marriage between your daughter and Lord Craventhorp?"

"I did."

"And was the dowry you offered to Lord Craventhorp eighty-thousand pounds?"

"It was, yes."

"And did your daughter object to this union?"

Mr. Leonard hung his head.

"The witness will answer the question," the Lord High Steward said.

Mr. Leonard looked up and cleared his throat. "Yes."

"Do you believe Mrs. Bruno has any reason to lie at this point in time?"

"No, if she thinks my Annabel is alive, then it must be true." He pulled out a handkerchief and dabbed his eyes.

"Thank you, Mr. Leonard, nothing further."

The Attorney General declined to question the witness, and Mr. Leonard stepped down.

The Lord High Steward then turned to address the lords. "My lords, in light of this new testimony, I suspend the accused's sentence to allow for further investigation into this matter. The prisoner will remain in the Tower until more is known."

A great uproar sounded.

"The story will be in every paper tomorrow," Mr. Upwey said. "If Miss Leonard is alive, she'll either come forward or she's fled from England."

Henry only blinked in response. He was too stunned to answer. Anne was Annabel Leonard, but she'd have to give up her freedom to save him, and he did not want that.

❯❯❯❯❮❮❮❮

"*Mia cara*. I'm here; it's your Stella. Wake up."

Annabel opened her eyes, and Stella's blurry face hovered over her. It was a lovely dream. The same one she'd had every night. Reaching up, she touched Stella's face. *How lovely and lifelike this dream is.*

"Oh, thank the blessed Lord." Stella took Annabel's hand

from her cheek and clutched it in hers. "You're alive."

Annabel blinked Stella's face into focus. "Stella? Am I dreaming? Have you truly come for me?" She struggled to sit up, and Stella bent to help her.

"I'm here, my darling. All your troubles are over."

The room came into focus, and Annabel saw the doctor, Mr. and Mrs. Bastin, and a stranger all standing together, watching her.

Where is Henry? Fear seized hold of her chest. *Why are they all here? Have they come to tell me that it's too late?*

"Henry?" she managed to whisper. Her throat felt incredibly dry.

"Spared the gallows, thanks to Stella." Mrs. Bastin came forward and placed a newspaper on Annabel's lap.

Is Annabel Leonard Alive? the headline read, and then, *"The Lord High Steward suspends gallows for Lord Hudsyn in light of lady's maid's claims,"* appeared in the subtitle.

Relief flooded Annabel. "How? When did you come from Italy?"

"I was never in Italy, my dear. I went to my cousin's in Portugal. I was heartbroken when I read Nate's testimony in the newspapers, but I knew he was only acting in the best way he could to protect all three of us. Still, I couldn't leave an innocent man's death on my conscience, so I boarded a ship the very next day."

"Nate kept me prisoner in his hut at Whitstable, and I almost died in the fire." Annabel shook her head. "I cannot believe he almost sent Henry to his death. I trusted him."

"I could wring his neck for that," Stella said. "But I try to remember that he acted out of fear. He's not a bad man, but he deeply distrusts the upper class. I imagine he saw Henry as a threat—someone who wanted to take advantage of a young, trusting girl without a family—and saw him as a member of the class who would be more loyal to Lord Craventhorp than you."

"Where is he now?" Anne asked. "Have the police arrested

him?"

"It appears he's fled the country." Stella retrieved her handkerchief and pressed it to her eyes. "And to tell you the truth, I'm glad. I don't want to see any harm come to him."

Annabel sighed. "Yes, terrible though his actions were, I agree that he probably thought he was doing what was necessary to protect himself and me. Still, if Henry had hanged—" The thought made Annabel choke on her words.

"But he didn't hang. He's alive and well. And now that we have found you, he'll be released from prison."

"Do you think anyone will believe me? Will Papa care to recognize me as his daughter? I think he'd prefer it if people thought I was dead rather than ruined."

"That's why I'm here." The stranger, a tall man with dark brown bushy mutton chops and piercing dark eyes, stepped forward. "Detective Regis." He gave a slight bow. "I'm in charge of investigating this case. What I witnessed today just now proves that you are Annabel Leonard. You recognized your lady's maid immediately, and the bond between you two is plainly evident to all in this room. It is genuine, I am certain. As for your papa, he has expressed remorse for trying to force you into a marriage with Craventhorp. The press has maligned him for his actions—calling them mercenary, ancient, and even barbaric."

Annabel bit her lip. *She was sorry for her papa. Angry as she had been, she never wanted him to be publicly shamed.*

"I spoke with him, and he is desperate to see you and welcome you back home again.

Annabel gasped. "But he was furious with me—burnt all my books. She shook her head. "He didn't believe me."

"According to him, your stepmother told him that you refused to marry until you found your Heathcliff so you concocted a wild story about Lord Craventhorp attacking you at Lady Dawley's ball. That is what led him to burn your books. She convinced him that obsessive novel reading had made you irrational."

"It's my fault for trusting Mrs. Leonard," Stella said. "I thought that, as a woman, she would want to protect you from marrying a man who enjoyed hurting women, but I was wrong."

"Only because you have a kind heart yourself." Annabel leaned forward and embraced Stella.

"And now we must get you in front of the Lord High Steward as soon as possible so we can release Henry from that horrible prison." Mrs. Bastin said. "The doctor is here to examine you, and he'll let us know if you're well enough to make the journey. Stella can remain here with you, and we'll be outside."

They started to leave when a thought occurred to Annabel. "Wait! Who was the unfortunate young lady they found in the Thames? I am afraid someone—a woman—may have died in my stead," Anne told the detective as her stomach clenched. It was a horrifying thought.

"We believe she was a lady of the night. Craventhorp is known to frequent brothels, and we have accounts of him injuring some of the women during his—encounters with them."

"So you think Lord Craventhorp murdered her? But how did he get my pendant? I wonder if it fell from my neck in Lady Dawley's garden and he picked it up there.

"Not quite. Your sister Florence confessed to taking the necklace from your room the day after the ball."

Shock engulfed Annabel. "What? My sister—but she's only twelve…" Annabel thought back to the night her papa gave her the pendant. Florence and Flora had been brought to the drawing room to share in the 'good news.' And Florence had turned purple with jealousy when she'd seen the pendant.

"She claims she only wanted to try it on but forgot to remove it from her neck. Her mama caught her wearing it and took it from her. Mrs. Leonard claims to have returned it to your room. She never told you about the incident because she saw no reason to. No harm had come to the necklace, and you didn't notice its disappearance. Later, she assumed you took the necklace with you when you fled your home."

"But I did not," Annabel whispered, scarcely able to breathe. Was her stepmother capable of murder?

"Which begs the question," the inspector said, "did your stepmother keep the pendant, and for what purpose?

Annabel gasped. *Oh, poor Papa! Poor Florence and Flora. Let it not be true.*

But then, she discovered it was…

CHAPTER TWENTY-FIVE

O Italy, how beautiful thou art!

—Samuel Rogers, *Italy: a Poem*

July 1870

"THEY LOOK HAPPY," Annabel sat beside Henry on the balcony of her father's house in Portofino, Italy, and peered through her binoculars at her papa, two sisters, and Stella as they romped on the beach. All four had taken off their shoes and let the water lap over their feet. Her sisters had followed Stella in hitching the sides of their cotton summer dresses as they stepped into the water—something their mama would never have allowed them to do.

"I can hardly believe the change in my sisters. They are so full of love and life these days—especially after all they've endured these past months." Annabel shivered, remembering her stepmother's arrest and trial. She'd been in league with Lord Craventhorp and given him the necklace. Together, they'd planned the murder of the unfortunate woman, specially chosen for her build and coloring which was similar to Annabel's. Mrs. Leonard had given Craventhorp the pendant with the express purpose of using it to falsify Annabel's death. He had engaged the victim's services, strangled her, and put the pendant around the woman's neck before dumping her body in the Thames. For both, preserving their reputations was far more important than the young woman's life. Mrs. Leonard would not see her daughters' futures destroyed because her stepdaughter chose to ruin herself by running away with a man unknown to the family. And Craventhorp wouldn't tolerate the stain of rejection. Both were found guilty of homicide. Mrs. Leonard pleaded insanity and was sent to an asylum. Lord Craventhorp was given the death sentence, which was subsequently pardoned by the queen. Instead, he was to spend his life in prison.

Annabel shuddered.

"What is it?" Henry asked. "Did you see something disturbing through those spy glasses of yours?"

"No," Annabel lowered the binoculars. "I was just thinking how different things could have been had they not gone our way."

"But they did, so why dwell upon it? You'll only upset yourself, my darling. And I would rather you enjoyed this spectacular scenery. In fact, I have to ask—why have I never visited Italy before?" Henry leaned back in his chair.

Annabel adjusted her large hat, shading her face from the sun, and leaned back in her chair too.

"Well, now that my papa has decided to sell his business and move my sisters here permanently, I think we will be spending a lot more time in this country."

"That sounds marvelous." Henry closed his eyes and reached for her hand. She twined her fingers with his as he sighed, "I find I have a fondness for all things Italian."

Annabel smiled as she lay in her deck chair beside her husband, eyes closed and hands linked, basking in the sun's warmth, and inhaling the fresh, salty sea air. Henry was right. There was no need to dwell on what could have been when everything had turned out so well.

Their winter wedding on Greyson Estate was magical. They'd kept the guest list to family and a few close friends. Still,

Papa had filled the Bastin's home with flowers and cakes. Flora and Florence were bridesmaids, and Stella was her maid of honor. But the best surprise of all had been her mama's dress, which Stella had kept especially for Annabel's wedding day. Made from exquisite white tulle, it fit perfectly, with a cinched waist and a full-bodied, ruffled skirt. She'd paired it with a diamond tiara, white gloves, a bouquet of pink and white winter roses, and a gauzy veil.

When Papa had seen her, tears had glistened in his eyes. She could not believe the change in him. His notorious temper seemed to vanish overnight as though the dark cloud that had been hovering over him since her mama's death had finally cleared away.

Henry had looked dashing in his blue morning suit, paired with a white, buttoned waistcoat, and a white silk cravat. He wore a white Christmas rose in the lapel of his coat, taken from Annabel's bouquet. When Henry lifted her veil and kissed her, surrounded by all the people who loved them, Annabel thought her heart would burst from happiness.

All in all, she decided, she couldn't have asked for a better ending for her story; she was certain that she and Henry would live happily ever after, no matter where they traveled, as long as they were together.

Author's Note

Canterbury, Kent.

Last year, I visited Canterbury and fell in love with its narrow streets, historic buildings, and the breathtaking cathedral. And I knew right away that this historic town made famous by Chaucer, Christopher Marlowe (who was born there), and Dickens (who featured the town in *David Copperfield*) was the perfect setting for *Love and Liberty*. If you haven't had a chance to visit Canterbury, take a trip to Orange Street via Google Maps to see where Annabel lived. Then wander past the old Theatre Royal on Guildhall Street, go up to Sun Street and see the Sun Hotel where Dickens stayed, and then visit Buttermarket Square where Annabel and Henry bought their cheese. While you're there, be sure to visit the magnificent Canterbury Cathedral.

The Great Fire of Whitstable, 1869

North of Canterbury lies Whitstable, a gorgeous fishing town famous for its oysters. As depicted in *Love and Liberty*, late one windy night (November 16, 1869), a fire started in a shop and quickly spread through Whitstable. Firefighters from the Whitstable Fire Brigade and those from nearby towns fought valiantly until morning to extinguish the flames, but the destruction was immense. This fire became known as the Great Fire of Whitstable.

Incapacitated by the Whitstable fire, Annabel cannot get to London in time to save Henry, whose peers have sentenced him to death for her murder. Until 1948, peers of the realm accused of a felony were tried in the House of Lords. If Parliament wasn't in session (as in Henry's case), the Lord High Steward's Court would try the case. These trials were rare and difficult to research. For a measure of historical accuracy, I mimicked some of the official language found in records of past peer trials, particularly the language used by the Serjeant at Arms, and I followed the general procedures of these trials (leaving much out, of course, in the interest of brevity). That said, this is a work of fiction, and the story took precedence. The last peer of the realm to be tried in the House of Lords was Edward Russel, 26th Baron de Clifford. He was accused of manslaughter and tried in the Royal Gallery in 1936.

About the Author

Aviva holds a master's degree in English and has a keen interest in British literature. She is an anglophile and Brontë enthusiast who is happiest when traveling to or writing about England. Inspiration for her first book, The Mist on Brontë Moor, came after she visited the Brontë Parsonage in Haworth.

Born and raised in Cape Town, South Africa, Aviva now lives in Southern California with her husband, two daughters, and rambunctious Yorkshire terrier—named for the oft-forgotten Brontë brother Branwell.

Website: www.avivaorrauthor.com
Twitter: twitter.com/aviva_orr
Facebook: facebook.com/AuthorAvivaOrr/
Goodreads: goodreads.com/author/show/6464067.Aviva_Orr
Bookbub: bookbub.com/profile/aviva-orr

www.ingramcontent.com/pod-product-compliance
Lightning Source LLC
Chambersburg PA
CBHW070339200726
48294CB00003B/715